W9-BMI-973
02/2020

BACKTRAIL

A RIDGE PARKMAN WESTERN

BACKTRAIL

GREG HUNT

FIVE STAR
A part of Gale, a Cengage Company

Farmington Hills, Mich • San Francisco • New York • Waterville, Maine
Meriden, Conn • Mason, Ohio • Chicago

LIBRARY OF CONGRESS CATALOGING-IN-PUBLICATION DATA

Names: Hunt, Greg, 1947- author.
Title: Backtrail / Greg Hunt.
Description: First edition. | Farmington Hills, Mich. : Five Star, 2020. | Series: A Ridge Parkman western
Identifiers: LCCN 2019023208 | ISBN 9781432861049 (hardcover)
Subjects: GSAFD: Western stories.
Classification: LCC PS3558.U46768 B33 2020 | DDC 813/.54—dc23
LC record available at https://lccn.loc.gov/2019023208

First Edition. First Printing: January 2020
Find us on Facebook—https://www.facebook.com/FiveStarCengage
Visit our website—http://www.gale.cengage.com/fivestar
Contact Five Star Publishing at FiveStar@cengage.com

Printed in Mexico
1 2 3 4 5 6 7 24 23 22 21 20

BACKTRAIL

★ ★ ★ ★ ★

Part One

★ ★ ★ ★ ★

CHAPTER ONE

A frigid wind blew up the steep mountainside of the western Rocky Mountain slope, bearing an on-and-off mixture of mist, fine-grained sleet, and chilling rain. The moon had risen early, allowing the two lone riders to press on a little bit further, but now its light came and went, making their progress up the narrow trail more dangerous.

Their intent had been to top the ridge ahead, then descend far enough that when they stopped for the night, they wouldn't wake in the morning freezing under a blanket of fresh snow. Even now in mid-April that was a common occurrence here in the higher elevations.

Without discussion, they were both coming to the same conclusion. Snow or not, they were going to have to stop before long. The clouds blowing in from the west would soon block out the moon entirely, and the perilous trail they were following would be impossible to see. There would be no way they could ride under such risky conditions. They had hoped there was even a chance that they might happen across some hospitable fellow travelers with a fire built and coffee boiling. But that seemed unlikely at this point.

On the right-hand side of the trail the mountainside rose almost straight up, impenetrable in most places because of the scrub brush and the dauntless, stunted trees that somehow found sustenance in the jumbled slabs of rock. On the left, the land fell away just as steeply, as dark and forbidding as the road to hell.

"So much for taking the shortcut across," Ray Goode said.

His companion, Ridge Parkman, knew that was as close to an apology as he was likely to get from Goode for insisting that this was the trail they should follow. "But at least we're saving all that time," he said. "What do you figure, Ray? Maybe five or ten minutes, if we can keep ourselves from falling down the side of the mountain?"

Goode didn't answer, which was probably for the best. He was the one who was supposed to know this territory, and the one who speculated that, this far into the spring, they weren't likely to ride into any leftover winter weather. Taking a chance on the high trail was all his doing.

A cluster of clouds passed in front of the moon, casting the men's small realm into pitch blackness for a moment. Then the clouds drifted on, and moonlight dimly bathed the trail again with its life-saving glow. But more clouds were on their way.

"Damn that Alex Moody anyway for stirring up a mess like this," Goode grumbled, trying to pass the blame.

"We don't know that. We won't know for sure what happened to him until we get down to Payday Gulch and find out for ourselves."

"I know, but it's easy to believe the talk that he took off with a Cheyenne woman. He never was that dedicated to our line of work anyway, and he always seemed to be chasing after the next pair of pretty ankles that came along."

"I'll give you that, Ray," Parkman said. "But didn't those teamsters tell us she was Cherokee, not Cheyenne? Seems more likely in these parts."

Ray Goode, riding in the lead, didn't take the time to answer. He pulled his horse up short, and his hand dropped to the hilt of his holstered revolver. Parkman did likewise, although he wasn't sure yet why they were being cautious.

"What is it, Ray?" Parkman kept his voice low.

"Something in the middle of the trail up ahead."

"Is it moving?"

"Nope."

"Man or beast?"

"Some kind of wagon, maybe. A little one."

Goode dismounted and dropped the reins. He had only purchased his mount a few weeks earlier during a stopover in Denver to visit his daughter, but someone had obviously trained the animal. They were still getting used to one another.

The moonlight was about to fail them again, flickering between the passing clouds like a lantern burning up the last of its fuel. Parkman's boot sole slipped on the icy rocks as he stepped to the ground. He waited for his companion, who had moved forward a few steps, revolver drawn, to report back.

"It's one of those two-wheel carts," Goode said. "But you need to come on up here and see what else." Ray Goode already had the body turned over by the time Parkman got there.

The young man lay stiff and straight on his back in front of the cart, his open, lifeless eyes staring up at the sky with what seemed like a sense of wonder.

"No bullet holes, and no blood that I can see," Goode said. The scene puzzled both men.

"Seems like he fell dead behind the yoke like a worn-out ox. Maybe he decided to take the shortcut like we did, to save some time . . ." Parkman paused to let the jab soak in. ". . . and it was too much for him."

"He's a fine-looking boy. What would you say, Ridge? Twenty maybe?"

"Not much more," Parkman said. "And a stout frame, too. Look at those shoulders."

"Pulling that cart along for a thousand miles or so from

wherever he came from would have built him up like that. Probably took most of the winter getting here."

As the clouds thickened, the moon was giving up any pretense of sharing its light with them. Parkman folded back the stiff, oiled buffalo hide covering the cart and rummaged through the dead man's belongings until he found a kerosene lamp. It took three matches to get it lit.

Goode was bringing the horses up. It would be a miserable, hungry night for them because about all their riders could do in these narrow confines would be to unsaddle them and tie them off.

"What did he have in there?" Goode asked, nodding toward the cart.

"About what you'd expect. A dabble of food, flour, coffee, bacon, and suchlike. A change of clothes and a heavy coat. Prospecting tools." Parkman began pulling the dead man's belongings out of the cart and piling them on the side of the trail. "He didn't have a tent, or even a length of canvas to sleep under. I figure we can flip this cart over and make some kind of shelter out of it."

"For our top halves, at least," Goode said. The bed of the cart was no more than four feet long and three feet wide. "Now aren't you glad I figured out that we could shorten the trip by riding over the crest?"

That was one of the things that Parkman liked about Ray Goode. He wasn't such a proud man that he'd let a good laugh get away just because the joke was on him.

They woke the next morning stiff and half frozen. While Goode made coffee, Parkman dragged the dead man's carcass off to the side of the trail and covered it with rocks. There was no use trying to dig a hole in this rocky, frozen soil.

He had been a handsome lad, Parkman thought, as he wrestled a slab of rock over the young man's awe-stricken face.

His hair was blond and long, almost down to his shoulders, and his thin, youthful beard was well-trimmed. He had probably made the hearts of the girls back home flutter when he smiled, and planned to marry the prettiest girl in town when he went back home with his pockets full of Rocky Mountain gold.

"I don't see that there's much worth taking here except the food," Goode said, stirring through the dead man's belongings.

"Leave the rest for somebody who can use it," Parkman agreed. "Did you come across anything that says who he was?"

"A few letters."

"Bring them, and maybe I'll find a chance to get word back to his people when we get someplace where I can send mail. No use for his mother to pine away the rest of her days wondering what became of him."

There was nearly a foot of snow on the southwest stretches of the trail. But when they reached the crest of the mountain and started the descent on the other side, they found it warmer, and the snow was melting quickly in the morning sun.

"Have you got any idea what it's going to be like when we get over yonder to Payday Gulch?" Parkman asked his companion.

"Like all the other fresh-strike camps, I suppose," Goode said. "A few hundred gold-hungry lunatics, living like animals, most of them near to starving while they dig around their claims like convicts, dreaming every second about what it's going to feel like to be rich. I've been to a few of these camps since I started working out of Denver, and I'll tell you, Ridge, it's the damnedest congregation of crazy, greedy men you'll ever want to see."

"Any law there?"

"Probably not, unless Alex Moody is still sporting the badge," Goode said. "Which I doubt."

CHAPTER TWO

The two strangers riding fast and noisy along the trail through the trees didn't seem to know that you couldn't push a horse that hard through country like this and expect anything good to come of it. Fortunately, Parkman and Goode heard them coming soon enough to stop and brace themselves for whatever might come barreling around the curve in the trail ahead. Their presence caught the two riders completely off guard, and they instinctively made a bad decision.

One of the men fumbled a hand gun out of his holster and started firing wildly ahead, while the other made a clumsy attempt to raise a shotgun to his shoulder and fire it with one hand while his other hand kept ahold of the reins.

Ray Goode got one shot off before his horse spooked and nearly bucked him out of the saddle. But his aim was true. As Parkman drew and fired, his own horse scarcely flinched at the noise and confusion. Good training counted for everything, and General Grant had been through this kind of dust-up before.

In the next moment, Parkman and Goode first watched the two men topple to the ground, then looked over at one another with the same question in mind.

"I wonder what in the devil that was all about," Parkman said. He reached around and drew a cartridge from his belt to replace the one he had fired.

"Beats me," Goode said.

One of the men on the ground was still alive, moaning and

pawing weakly at the hole Parkman's bullet had made in his chest.

"Least I got mine clean," Goode noted.

"Yeah, but see there? You nicked his horse's ear doing it. That's why I shot high, so I'd hit my man and not his horse."

Both of them dismounted and walked over to the two strangers. The one who hadn't died yet looked up at them with puzzlement and despair. Fresh blood was quickly spreading across the front of his shirt, and his eyes were starting to glaze over.

"Why did you have to open up on us like that?" Goode asked. "You must be a pair of idiots. We'd have let you go on by, and you'd still be alive now."

The man opened his mouth, probably wanting to ask for help, but all he managed to do was gag and moan. Pink froth seeped from his lips.

"It's a hell of a thing," Parkman said, shaking his head. He gathered the reins of the men's horses and led them a short distance back down the trail so they wouldn't be stepping on their former passengers. He had holstered his Colt, but dropped his hand to its hilt when he heard the sound of more horses coming up the trail.

"More company coming, Ray."

"I heard them, but at least we've got some time to get ready this go-round. Maybe it won't turn out so ugly." They went back to their own horses and tied them off in the edge of the forest. Then they holstered their handguns and drew their Winchesters out of their scabbards.

"I guess we'd better pin the hardware on," Parkman said.

"Yeah, I suppose."

Ridge Parkman dug into his saddlebag and took his badge out of a cloth bag of personal items, while Ray Goode fished around in his pockets for his. They pinned them on their shirts, then each took a position on either side of the road, partly concealed behind a tree. The wounded man lay flat on his back a few yards away, still moving his head around lethargically as if trying to record his last moments on this earth.

Eventually four more riders appeared around the bend in the trail, riding more cautiously than the first two, and each with a firearm ready. They had heard the shots and understood that there was trouble up ahead. When they saw the two loose horses, and the bodies beyond, they stopped their horses and began looking around to see if they could locate the danger somewhere nearby.

"United States marshals," Parkman called out. He saw the gaze of all four men turn his way, and they all seemed to tense at the unexpected announcement. "We're not looking for trouble. Those two didn't give us any choice."

One of the men dismounted and took a couple of steps forward, the barrel of his rifle lowering as he drew nearer. He was tall and sturdily built, with a high-crowned black hat and a thick, wooly beard draping down his chest.

"You only saved us the trouble," the man said, his voice deep. "They had it coming."

"Well, if you wouldn't mind putting the artillery away," Goode said, "we'll step out so we can talk man to man."

The bearded man noticed that one of the men on the ground was not quite dead yet. Almost casually, he swept the muzzle of his rifle in that direction and put a second bullet into the wounded man. "All right, boys," he called out over his shoulder. "Let's holster our iron and see what these lawmen have to say."

As the tension melted away, Parkman and Goode stepped into the open and started forward.

"I'm Marshal Ridge Parkman, and my companion here is Marshal Ray Goode," Parkman said. "We came over from Denver on assignment." No handshakes were exchanged.

"I'm Daniel Zimmer, from Cape Girardeau, Missouri, and

those are my partners. Do you need their names?"

"I don't suppose it matters," Goode said. "But what about these two?"

"The one I finished off is Walter something. A fancy name. Like Chesterfield, or Chestnut, or Chesterton. Something like that. He was a school teacher back in The Cape before he decided to come out prospecting with our company. The other joined up with us somewhere along the Platte, and we just called him Bull. None too smart, but stout as a bull for sure. We signed him up because he agreed to work for food, and a half share."

"Why were you after them?" Parkman asked.

"Thieving," Zimmer said. "We've been panning out some pretty good colors, sometimes fifty dollars' worth a day over in Payday Gulch. But these two decided there was easier ways to get rich."

Parkman had been watching Zimmer's three companions go through the packs on the dead men's horses and turn their pockets inside out. In a moment, one called out, "I found it, Dan'l. Feels about right, like it's all there." He held up a leather drawstring bag for all to see.

Zimmer and the others gathered together for a moment, and seemed to agree that their wealth remained intact. Parkman heard the words "four pounds" mentioned during their discussion, which was, he had to admit, a considerable sum at sixteen dollars an ounce.

"Gold will make a man do things he never thought he would," Goode said, staring down at the two corpses lying in the middle of the trail. Since the four prospectors didn't seem interested in burying their two companions, the law men weren't either.

After riding through what was more or less virgin Rocky Mountain wilderness for the past three days, it was eye-opening for Parkman and Goode to top a crest of rock and see Payday

Gulch sprawled out below them. Springing up practically overnight like a blight on the land, these explosive, ramshackle, greed-infested mining camps were a new phenomenon to Ridge Parkman. According to Zimmer, two months ago Payday Gulch had been a solitary, nameless mountain gorge populated only by the local wildlife, and the nearly-as-wild nomadic Indian bands and trappers who hunted them to survive.

But now, Zimmer claimed, nearly two thousand half-starved, gold-crazed dreamers from all corners of the nation populated the stream beds and rocky hillsides, living in tents, wagons, tiny ramshackle cabins, and stick lean-twos.

"Funny thing," Zimmer told the two marshals. "Some of them are already packing up and moving on, while a whole new batch keeps pouring in. Durnedest thing I ever saw. But I guess I can't say much because here we are, right in amongst them."

Far off to the left, Parkman saw the stream of wagons, carts, mounted men, and foot-sore walkers, all lined out on the dusty track that wound through the broad valley that swept up from the south. And as Zimmer had pointed out, the lines moved in both directions, some coming and others leaving.

"Talk's already started about another big strike south of here. Some place called California Gulch. They say a man can reach down in the stream and come up with a handful of nuggets. But I say, if that was so, why would any man want to cut loose and come up here bragging to us about it? As for our little company, we're staying put and hoping we come across a vein on our claim."

The bulk of the population in Payday Gulch had set up their primitive housekeeping near the banks of the tumbling stream that flowed between the rocky slopes on either side. Farther up the sides, there were a few crude cabins and tents, and even the dark holes where some were taking their search for gold underground.

Smoke rose everywhere from cooking fires and tilting stone chimneys, giving the impression that a midday fog had rolled in. The virgin forest was already ravaged halfway up the hillsides, and higher up on both sides, men were harvesting what trees were left for mine timbers, cabin walls, and evening fires.

"So, are you marshals here to bring some law to Payday Gulch?" one of Zimmer's companions asked. He was an old man, fifty at least, with some kind of back problem that made him sit crooked in the saddle.

"Lord knows we need some," another man back in the line grumbled. "But with the shootings and stabbings going on all around for every little thing, it's not a job I'd take on."

"I can imagine that this place could use some law," Goode said. "But it won't come from us. We're on our way to Utah to mix it up with some outlaws over there. But our captain in Denver told us to swing up this way and see if we can find anything out about another marshal that hadn't reported in for a while."

"What's his name?" Zimmer asked.

"Alex Moody," Goode said. "Handsome fellow, dark hair, about my height. Dresses kind of fancy, and always seems to be chasing after one female or another. Smiles most all the time, so you might think he's your new best friend. But he's nothing but a braggart and a jackass when you get to know him better."

"He was sent up here with a warrant, but he never came back to Denver with his man," Parkman said. "The talk is that he took up with an Indian woman, which is easy enough to believe, knowing Alex."

"Anything could of happened to him," the old man said. "Life don't count for much in a place like this."

The trail snaked back and forth down the mountainside, depositing them at last into the midst of the sprawling gold camp. With Zimmer in the lead, their first stop was at a

Conestoga wagon, where a shifty looking man in a shabby seersucker suit was peddling liquor out of a large barrel on the tailgate.

"You men come to the right place," the man said enthusiastically. There was something about him that made Parkman's skin crawl. "I got the best whiskey this side of the great divide. I hauled it over myself from Tennessee, at great personal peril, I might add. Dollar a snort."

"Don't believe it," the old man said. Somewhere along the ride, Parkman had heard the others call him Brasfield. "Around here they call that stuff Taos Lightning. It's like swallowing lit coal oil, and it'll turn your guts upside down and inside out. But it gets the job done." He produced a battered tin cup from somewhere and fell in line behind his companions.

Parkman looked over at Goode, who simply shrugged his shoulders and started digging around for his cup. They both got in line for their share. A dumpy, bored-looking woman sat farther back in the wagon, swaddled in a mountain of petticoats, cleaning her toenails with a paring knife.

Zimmer paid in gold for all their drinks, closely watching the peddler as he weighed out something less than a thimble of tiny gleaming flakes.

Several shots from at least two guns sounded to the west, far enough away that nobody seemed to concern themselves over it. They sipped from their cups as they gathered up the reins of their horses and started walking east, up the gulch. The first gulp Parkman took scoured its way down the back of his throat, seeming to light little blazes behind his eyes. He coughed and took another swig. "Lives up to its name," he said, his voice raspy.

"You fellows might as well spend the night at our camp," Zimmer said. "Nobody's had time to build a hotel here, and the boarding tents are noisy and stinky. The lice there will pick you up and carry you off."

"We'd be obliged," Goode said.

"There's no room for you in the cabin, but it looks to be a clear night for sleeping under the stars."

Supper that night was beans, spiced with a hunk of bacon that Parkman donated to the cause, and biscuits that seemed hardly more than a few days old. The food was cooked and served by another member of their company who had not gone along on the chase. He performed his chores like somebody was holding a gun to his head, and only grunted anytime somebody spoke to him.

The small cabin Zimmer mentioned was located about thirty feet up the hillside from their claim, with roughly cut logs for walls, and a large tarpaulin spread across the top for a roof. The entrance was a gaping dark hole in front without a door, and there were no windows. The two marshals rolled out their blankets outside behind the cabin and took their turns, along with the others in Zimmer's company, standing guard and watching the horses as they grazed on a patch of grass and weeds higher up the hillside. No man was trusted here.

The next morning Parkman shared the coffee he had taken from the cart of the dead man up in the mountains. It was a welcome treat to the men, who hadn't had real coffee since their own supply ran out.

"So, what's your plan now?" Zimmer asked.

"None yet. We can't stay around here long looking for our man," Parkman said. "There's a band of hard cases that migrated up from west Texas into Utah, and they're raising havoc over there. Things must be getting pretty bad, because those Mormons out there have men of their own who handle these things, and they don't usually ask for outside help. But they've sent a call out for federal help, and our captain in Denver is sending us over to join in the fight. Seems like the army is scattered thin in those parts, and what they've got are busy farther north along the Mormon trail and on up into the Tetons and Northern Rockies."

"If it was up to me," Goode added, "we'd be pushing on west right now instead of taking the time to stop off here. I never did like Alex Moody and wouldn't waste five minutes of my own time to fish him out of a river."

"Moody?" the sullen cook mumbled. Both marshals looked over at him curiously, because it was the first real words they had heard him speak. "Alex Moody, you say?"

"That's our man. Do you know him?" Goode asked.

"Well enough to wish I could bash his head in with a shovel."

"Do you know where he is?"

"With that bunch up in Horsefly Gulch, the talk has it. But before that, he was bodyguarding a couple of crooked three-card monte dealers. Three or four weeks back, they cheated me out of every ounce of gold I had, and me too stupid drunk to know what they was up to."

"Winston there keeps drawing on his share and going out on benders," Zimmer explained to the marshals with clear disgust. "And him with a wife and three little ones waiting back in Cape Girardeau for him to come home with hard cash money in his poke. I'd have cut him loose a long time ago if he wasn't married to my sister."

"A man's got to have something to pass the time out here," Winston grumbled.

"You're nothing but a sorry, worthless sot, too drunk most times to even work the sluices," Zimmer said.

"But what about our man?" Parkman said, interrupting their squabbles. "You said he's in someplace called Horsefly Gulch? Is that near here?"

"It's northwest of here, not too far," Zimmer said. "Word is there's a gang that's come together up there who are up to no good. Waylaying travelers along the road, and coming down here to Payday Gulch to kill and plunder. There's been talk about putting together some vigilantes, but so far nobody's done anything. I'm sure sorry to hear your man might be among them."

"And so are we," Parkman said.

"But it doesn't surprise me," Goode added. "I never liked the man myself."

CHAPTER THREE

"I tell you, Ridge, it nearly broke my heart to only spend three days with my girl before the captain came up with these new orders," Goode said. "I got back to Denver after two months away, and I promised Alice I'd spend at least two weeks with her this time around."

They had ridden far enough away from Payday Gulch to outdistance the ravaged landscape, filth, greed, and stench of the gold camp. The countryside around them was still in its natural state. Parkman found himself hoping that no prospector would wander up this way and pan out any trace of gold in the creeks and streams nearby. It was too beautiful and wild up here to be destroyed by all that nonsense.

"I told the captain that next time I get home, I plan to spend a full month with that daughter of mine, and he can have my badge if he doesn't like it. And I mean it, too. What scares me is that she'll grow up to be a real young woman without me being around to see any of it. And, besides, I think I get too heathen and ornery when I'm out like this. I need the company of the womenfolk to balance things out sometimes."

"So how does Alice get on with her Aunt Tilda?" Parkman asked.

"Better than you might expect for a headstrong gal like Alice, with a daddy that's moving around all over the country most of the time. She got rebellious after her mama died three years ago, but she's grown up a lot since they moved out here to

Denver. Tilda says she couldn't keep the bakery going if Alice wasn't there to help."

When they reached the bottom of the gorge they were riding through, they dismounted and stopped long enough to let the horses graze on the ankle-high grass and weeds that covered the banks like a fresh green blanket.

"I've seen that Tilda a couple of times, Ray, and she's a right handsome woman. Have you ever thought about . . ." Parkman paused, not quite sure it was his place to ask a question of that sort.

"It's crossed my mind about me and Tilda a few times, and I expect she'd have me if I asked her," Goode admitted as they settled in the shade of an aspen to relax. By habit, Parkman took out his Colt to check the action and make sure the barrel was clear.

"She's nearly forty," Goode went on. "An old maid, some would say, and set in her ways. Still a looker, like you said, but I keep thinking maybe it wouldn't be fair to give her the same kind of life her sister had. Since Grace died, I've spent a lot of time thinking about the life I gave her. Moving to someplace new every few years, being gone weeks at a time, and her never knowing for sure whether I'd come back to her on a horse or in a coffin. You know how it is when you're out on the trail too long, thinking about too many things and talking to yourself."

"I talk to my horse a lot," Parkman said with a chuckle. "He's a good listener, but never does offer much of an opinion about things."

After they rode out of Payday Gulch that morning, they had sketched together a new plan for themselves. This excursion north, off the main trail, had cost them four days already, and they were still heading north instead of west, as they should be if they were aiming at Utah. From all reports, their help was badly needed out there in Mormon country, and they were beginning to feel a sense of urgency to get headed back in the right direction.

Parkman and Goode agreed that their real assignment was not taking on the nest of highwaymen ahead. There were hundreds of men back in Payday Gulch capable of dealing with that problem if it got bad enough. Up ahead in Horsefly Gulch they would find out what they could about Moody, if anything, and then get back on the trail west to Utah. No matter what they might discover about Moody—whether he had made himself a highwayman, or was living with an Indian girlfriend, or had turned to smoke and blown away—they would report the news back to Denver, as instructed, and then be on their way.

But still it galled both of them that one of their own might have turned sour and betrayed the badge. Without saying it out loud, both Parkman and Goode thought that if they did ever come across Alex Moody, they would feel compelled to call him to account for what he had done.

When the horses were fed and watered, they started on their way again. Back in the gold camp, few of the prospectors and miners knew much about this part of the country, other than the trails they followed on the way to these western Rocky Mountain slopes, and the rocks and dirt they were digging in now. But the marshals had finally located one greasy old mountain man who gave them rough directions to where they were going. He was drunk at the time, and they could only hope that his memories were accurate enough to get them to where they wanted to go.

They rode on in silence for a while, doing their best to make sure their horses chose the best pathway up the steep rocky trail ahead of them. Clearly Goode's thoughts were still on his dead wife and the small family he had left behind in Denver.

"Alice is thirteen now, already beginning to bud out, but still as innocent as a colt. What plagues my mind most, I guess, is that someday I'll ride back in and find the boys swarming around her like honeybees. I can't say how I might act when that time comes."

"God help you," Parkman said, unable to hold back a grin. "And then the next time, they'll be postponing the wedding 'til you show up."

"Thanks for giving me one more thing to worry about."

Parkman held back from saying more, knowing that his particular flavor of humor might not be welcome when Ray Goode was in such a nostalgic mood. There was a time to talk and josh and needle, and a time for a man to keep his mouth shut and listen.

The old man back in Payday Gulch had told them that when they got about this far, they would see a ridgeline ahead, curling around east-northeast. But soon they discovered that there were actually two. As expected, Ray Goode began to cuss and complain, starting a list of all the things he would do to that old codger when they got back to the mining camp. But of course, that would never happen. They would most likely never set eyes on Payday Gulch again.

In the midst of Goode's rant, Parkman held up a hand and cocked his head to the side. "Hear that? Sounds like gunfire, away off somewhere." His hearing seemed to be a little better than Goode's, but his companion took his word for it.

Near the crest of the ridge ahead, they dismounted, each drawing out a rifle, and moved on up on foot. Once at the crest, it took only a moment to sort out what was going on below. It wasn't a pleasant sight. Beside the stream below, a gaggle of men were huddled behind their wagon bed and a couple of boulders nearby, taking serious punishment from a scattering of hidden shooters on the opposite slope of the gulch. Only a couple of the men by the wagons were making even an attempt to shoot back, and they might as well have saved their cartridges, because it was clear that they were firing wildly in panic.

"Don't these greeners from back east know anything?" Goode said with disgust. One of the men pinned down below was already splayed out on the ground, not moving. As the marshals watched, another of them rose and started stumbling up the hillside behind them, but he caught a bullet in the back and went down howling.

"See if you can't spot some of those shooters," Parkman said. "I'm going back for the Sharps."

By the time he returned and stretched out on the ground beside Goode, two more of the men below had been hit. One lay in a crumpled heap behind the wagon, and the other was leaned against a wagon wheel, staring down at his body as if something incomprehensible had just happened. It seemed like they must be too green to even know that the lumber of a wagon wouldn't stop a bullet.

Parkman laid a handful of long, serious .50-caliber cartridges on a rock beside him, then adjusted the rear sight on the Sharps to the estimated distance. "Give me a target, Ray."

"Those two rocks about halfway up that look like they were stacked one on the other. One of them is hiding back there."

Parkman rested the barrel of the long, heavy rifle on the ground, tilted his head behind the sights, and waited for his target to reappear. In a moment he saw a man step out into the open, raise his rifle to his shoulder, and take aim. But he never got to fire before Parkman's bullet slammed into him, tossing him back like a mule kick.

"Okay, the next one's a little higher, and maybe twenty yards to the right. There's a sort of *V* between two rocks," Goode said.

Parkman shifted the rifle, found his target, and waited. Down by the wagon, another man caught one in the shoulder. He dropped his handgun, then picked it up with his other hand and tried to shoot, but he was too shaky and clumsy to fire it.

As soon as Parkman saw a rifle barrel ease out between the *V* in the rocks, he squeezed off another round. He wasn't able to see what damage he had done, but a muted, desperate scream of pain rose from that direction.

He was able to get off one more round before the attackers on the other side figured out that this fight wasn't going to go well for them now that reinforcements had arrived. One by one they began to break cover and claw their way up the hillside. Parkman counted eight bushwhackers still left.

Goode took up his rifle and joined the fray. "We could of made a good team back during the war. We'd have given them Rebs what-for."

"I expect so," Parkman said. "But they had some fine marksmen on their side as well, and some good rifles, too. I had one of those Spencers for a while, but I sold it after I got my hands on this Sharps. Three rifles are too much iron to lug around on horseback."

The fleeing outlaws were at the far end of the effective range of Goode's Winchester, but he was a fine rifleman as well. He managed to give one of them a bad limp and toppled another forward just as he reached the crest of the rise. Parkman ended the fight for a couple more of them as well.

"Come on, Ridge. Let's kill them all," Goode said. He rose to his feet and began feeding cartridges into his empty Winchester. His blood was up, and Parkman could tell by that granite look on his partner's face that he was a hundred percent lawman right now.

"I'd agree with you if I thought we could catch up with them, but they'll be running now like the devil was after them. We might trail along for days and never catch sight of their dust. Or they might set up an ambush of their own and settle the score."

"At least two of them looked to be Indians. Renegade Apache or Cherokee, maybe. But I saw one of them that looked like Moody," Goode said, staring off in the distance as if he was still looking for somebody to shoot. "It was a long way off, but he stopped at the crest of the hill for a second and looked back, almost like he knew it was us over here. I could swear it was him."

"Could have been. And he might have gotten word up from the mining camp that we were in these parts asking around for him."

They mounted up, keeping their rifles laid across their legs now. They topped the rise and started down, following the winding, rocky trail. Below, the survivors of the attack were beginning to stir around, realizing that the fight was over and that their rescuers were approaching. About half of them were either dead or headed that direction.

"You remember what we agreed on when we started our ride out here," Parkman said. "From all we've been told, they need us pretty bad out there in Utah."

"I know. I know," Goode said stubbornly. "But can we stand to let Alex Moody ride away from something like this and not do anything about it? Don't he need to be called to account for his wicked deeds?"

CHAPTER FOUR

General Grant was a large, heavy horse, a powerhouse of strength and stamina on more solid, level ground. But on these steep slopes where footing was unsure and any stone his hoof went down on might decide to slide away, he moved slowly and deliberately. Parkman let him move along at his own pace, understanding what kind of trouble he would be in if his horse were injured this far out into the wilderness.

It was the morning of his second day of tracking Alex Moody, former U.S. marshal turned squaw man, turned outlaw, turned murderer, and Parkman was beginning to realize that this could turn out to be a long trek. After the attack on the prospectors, the trail of the attackers had not simply led back to some kind of remote camp up in the mountains. Instead they had headed straight north and didn't yet show any signs of stopping.

Outlaw or not, Moody was a crafty rascal, savvy to the ways of the frontier. He had witnessed the skill and precision with which Parkman and Goode had reduced his gang to less than half in only a few short minutes, and even if he didn't know who had done it, he would have understood that he wasn't dealing with a couple of ordinary greeners.

Parkman had the same realization. He had been around Alex Moody long enough to know that this was a man to be reckoned with, and if he was riding with Indians, they might have their own bag of tricks to haul out at any unexpected moment.

After the shoot-out in Horsefly Gulch, Parkman and Goode

had ridden down to see how bad things were for the prospectors below. There wasn't much the two marshals could do for them except to advise them to bury their dead, and then hightail it back to some more civilized, or at least more populated, place. Then as they topped the ridge and saw that the outlaws had hightailed it, Parkman and Goode came to a difficult decision.

They had decided that one of them had to make a try at running down Alex Moody and ending his devilment, while the other pressed on toward Utah. For various reasons, each of them thought they were the one who should go after Moody, but Parkman won the toss. Or maybe he lost it, Parkman now thought grimly.

Late in the afternoon of that first day, only a few miles north of where the ambush had taken place, Parkman had come across the man that Ray Goode had wounded as the outlaws scampered over the crest of the hill earlier. He was a young man barely into his early twenties, and none too bright looking, which might be why he fell into the outlaw life. The round from Goode's Winchester had caught him a few inches below the hip, and the bloody rag tied around the wound had done little to staunch the bleeding. With proper care, the young outlaw would probably have pulled through. But the others he was with were on the run from two sharpshooting riflemen who had already cut their number in half, and none were likely to care much about saving the life of a companion, perhaps at the price of their own.

Judging by the lethargic look in the young man's eyes, and the alarmingly large pool of blood beneath him, it was clear to Parkman that the man had nearly bled out already. His horse was nearby, grazing calmly, but it was clear that this fellow wasn't likely to ever climb into a saddle again.

Parkman paused his horse and stepped to the ground. The wounded man seemed to be giving in to drowsy delirium. He looked up at the marshal blankly but made no move to reach for the revolver lying on the ground beside him. Still, Parkman kicked it away. He could not bring himself to feel any pity for this young outlaw, who only a few hours before had been shooting down prospectors like targets in a carnival sideshow. He turned away and removed the saddle and bridle from the horse, then sent it away with a slap on the rump. As he remounted his horse, the dying man only stared up at him, eyes dull and mouth sagging open, without even enough strength or comprehension to plead for salvation.

Later in the day, as the evening light began to fade, Parkman came across the spot where the remaining four outlaws had split up. Three sets of hoofprints turned west, down the mountainside, while the fourth continued on alone, heading north-northwest toward the higher elevations. Of the set of three hoofprints, one horse was shod and the other two were not, indicating that two of those riders were probably Indians. The single set of tracks heading off in the other direction was made by a shod horse.

Parkman took a few minutes to roll a smoke and ponder what this might mean. It could be some kind of trick, an ambush perhaps if they knew someone was tracking them. But if they planned to ambush him, there was nothing to be gained by splitting up. It might be that they simply couldn't agree on which trail to take and had finally gone their separate ways.

Or it could be, Parkman thought, that Alex Moody had decided that he stood a better chance of escaping if he was on his own up in the high country. Although he probably couldn't have explained it to anyone else's liking, the marshal's instincts told him to continue on after the single set of tracks.

Wisely, the man's trail never roamed above the tree line. Higher up, it was bitter cold nearly all year round, with no wood to build a fire for cooking and heat, and little or nothing for his horse to eat.

By the fifth day on the trail, Parkman thought he might be close to catching his prey. He had pushed hard, riding each day from sunup to last light, and it was taking its toll on both him and his horse. But he thought he was gaining ground and hoped that soon he could put an end to this ordeal.

Eventually he came to a well-traveled wagon road that wound through a pass due west of Denver. It carried another scattering of the usual gold-hungry pilgrims. Rumors must have spread about a new strike somewhere to the west, and the usual traffic of prospectors, merchants, whiskey vendors, fallen doves, crooked gamblers, and all-around ne're-do-wells was heading in that direction. It was only a trickle now, but soon enough it would become a flood.

He paused long enough to talk to a band of four prospectors who had stopped their wagon off the trail and were tending to the wounds of two of their own. They told a sordid tale of a lone gunman who had caught them unaware as they were breaking camp that morning. He shot two of their band who had gone for their guns but were a little slow about it, then helped himself to their stocks of food and forage. He seemed to disappear as quickly as he had arrived, heading north, leaving them befuddled, frustrated, and angry.

After a quick look, Parkman thought one of the wounded men would probably make it, with only a stiff shoulder and ugly scars, front and back, to give him lifelong bragging rights. The other, shot straight through the belly and bleeding out, would most likely end up somewhere close by under a pile of rocks when his companions moved on toward the fortune they hoped awaited them.

When Parkman announced that he was after the man who had committed these crimes, they reluctantly sold him some supplies, but none offered to ride along. The gold fever still burned hot and relentless in their veins.

That night, Parkman camped in a gulley that he hoped would lessen the piercing mountain winds and conceal his evening fire. He turned General Grant loose to forage for whatever he could find in a nearby meadow.

He hadn't counted on having to deal with this kind of cold, and hadn't brought along the right clothes and sleeping gear. He built his fire near one vertical wall of the gulley so that the heat reflected off the stone, and he felt like he spent half the night keeping the fire blazing. But he did manage to get a few welcome hours of sleep.

He was back on the trail at first light, riding with his blanket draped over his head and shoulders until the sun rose high enough over the mountain ridges to give off a little warmth. A dusting of snow had fallen during the night, but soon melted away. His hands and feet eventually thawed, and he thought it was going to turn out to be a decent day after all.

From time to time he lost Moody's trail, only to pick it up again on up ahead. His tracking skills had never been as good as those of some other men he knew. But, fortunately, Moody was traveling in more or less a straight line north. In fact, after a while the ex-marshal seemed to become almost predictable. He was staying within the top regions of the tree line for safety, and any time a rock formation or impassible drop-off blocked his way, he invariably took to the western, downhill side to get around it.

At one point, pausing his horse at the edge of a broad open meadow, Parkman thought he might have caught a glimpse of his prey far away on the other side, passing into a line of stunted pines. The sighting was ever so brief, made out of the corner of his eye. He knew it could just as well have been one of the elks or mountain goats that inhabited these higher regions. But he had to take the sighting seriously and be on his guard.

"I wonder where in the devil he's going to?" Parkman said, mumbling the question out loud.

There were new mining camps somewhere to the north, and a couple of small towns that had managed to survive the boom-to-bust cycle. And, even farther away, well up into the northern Rockies, there was talk about new gold strikes. For a man of bad character who was good with a gun and none too particular about how he used it, there were always opportunities.

Then again, maybe Moody was simply riding in a straight line north to put some miles between himself and the trouble he had stirred up down around Horsefly Gulch.

Parkman sat for a while, surveying the tree line on the distant side of the meadow, looking for any movement and trying to turn each shadow into the outline of a man on horseback. But he saw nothing and started General Grant across the stretch of open ground.

A few miles further to the north, Parkman came across a spot where Moody had stopped to cook a meal and boil some coffee. He had probably been nearly out of food and other essentials before he robbed the prospectors, the marshal thought. The coals of the outlaw's fire still glowed red hot beneath a layer of ashes.

Parkman decided that if he managed to take Moody alive, which was his reluctant intent, he would take him back to Denver and turn him over to the authorities there. With any luck, they might be able to hold a trial the same day he arrived so he could tell his story, and he wouldn't even bother to stay around for the hanging. He had seen enough men die with a noose around their neck that hangings no longer held any fascination for him.

Ray Goode was probably clear of Colorado Territory by now and turned northwest toward Salt Lake City. It was rough going out that way, Parkman thought, with more mountains to cross, and long stretches of empty, arid land that fried a man's skin to a crisp, and roasted his brain and his vitals.

But it couldn't be any worse than what he and Goode had gone through a few years back when they joined up with a band of Texas Rangers and a few soldiers to go after a lawless piece of frontier trash named Duff Joseph and his ragged collection of murderers, thieves, rapists, rustlers, and renegade Comancheros. By the end of that long running battle in some of the worst country Parkman had ever experienced, fewer than half the law men who rode in with such high expectations made it out again. The only reason Parkman had survived was because Ray Goode had refused to let him die and hauled him out to civilization again, mostly dead and delirious.

But the worst of it all was that they never caught up with Duff Joseph. The soulless old scoundrel was probably still down there today, robbing whenever he could get away with it, stealing women, children, and livestock, and killing randomly at the slightest provocation. Sometimes it didn't make much sense why God put certain people on this earth.

When the first rifle bullet whined past, striking a rock wall behind him, Parkman realized immediately what a fine place Moody had selected for his ambush, as well as the disadvantage it put him in. He bailed out of the saddle and scrambled behind a nearby pile of rocks, only realizing after he found scant shelter that he had neglected to grab either of his rifles out of its scabbard. But he had given General Grant a hard slap on the rump so he would bolt away. Moody didn't shoot the General, probably thinking he would like to have a second horse when this was all over.

Another shot chipped at the solid rock wall beside Parkman and went singing away. It gave him a better sense of which direction the shots were coming from, although he had yet to spot his attacker. All he knew for sure was that the bullets were coming from higher ground, which made his situation even more perilous.

For a moment the marshal lay still, as flat as he could make himself, waiting for the jitters to subside and trying to chase away that empty dread that could afflict a man when he realized that death was coming for him. He turned his head to one side, trying to get a better feel for his situation.

No more than two feet away, a sun-bleached skull stared back at him. It was no great chore to tell how the man had died, because an arrow with a flint head still violated his skull from ear to ear. The rest of the man's skeleton was scattered randomly about.

"Parkman? Ridge Parkman? Is that you?" In these ragged surroundings it was hard to pinpoint what direction the shout was coming from, but it was loud enough to let the marshal know what peril he was in.

"It is, for a fact," Parkman called out. He was lying flat on his back, not wanting to risk raising his head enough for Moody to settle his sights on it. He figured Moody must be somewhere along the bank on the far side of the gulley, maybe fifty yards north and thirty or forty feet higher than he was.

"I spotted you two, maybe three, days ago, away down my backtrail," Moody said. "It was too far to make you out, but I sure recognized that big handsome roan you ride. That's one fine animal, but probably not the best for the kind of riding we've been doing lately."

"He's done all right so far."

"Well, I'll be proud to call him mine when this is over."

"It ain't over yet," Parkman said. Moody was a prideful man and squeezed off another couple of rounds to let Parkman know who still held the winning hand. But the bullets didn't land close enough to do any damage. Parkman thought Moody might not want to kill him yet because he wasn't finished boasting and blabbering. He always had too much rooster in him for Parkman's liking.

Looking down past his feet, Parkman could see that the gulch opened onto a broad, steep expanse of land. If he got up and took off in that direction, he'd be like a scared jackrabbit racing across a pasture.

"What in the devil are you doing way out here anyhow?" Moody asked.

"Cap'n Mullins hadn't heard from you since he sent you over to Payday Gulch, and he thought something might have happened. He sent Ray Goode and me out looking for you."

"Then it was you and Goode that shot us up down there north of Payday? In all my days, I've never seen a gang put out of business so fast as that. My compliments."

"A Sharps will do that in the right hands."

Although he couldn't look right now, he remembered that the gulch narrowed and deepened higher up. There would be plenty of cover for him in that direction, but no way to get up on top and deal with Moody except to climb a ragged rock wall.

"Where's Ray now? Did he decide to take off after that other bunch when we split up? If he did, they're probably roasting his entrails over an open fire about now. Them Utes aren't a hospitable people."

"Naw, I told him he could stay back in Payday and drink his fill of rotgut 'til I got back," Parkman said. "I didn't figure I'd need him to scoop up a pile of barnyard flop like you. The captain only wanted us to find you so we could get that badge back. He said he wanted to pin it on the shirt of another man that had the guts and grit to do the job."

"You might want to take another look at who's likely to die here, Parkman. That's hard talk from a man whose death certificate is already signed."

"It's only turned out this way because you're not man enough to go at it face to face," Parkman taunted. He figured his only hope was to get Moody stirred up enough to make a mistake. "Everybody in the outfit knew you were yellow as a Tennessee warbler, and what you've been up to lately only proves the point. They used to draw cards to see who had to ride out with you, and I wish you could have heard some of the nicknames you had. The one I like best was . . ."

A barrage of gunfire interrupted Parkman's tirade, as he had hoped it would. For several seconds bullets peppered around him, slinging up handfuls of gravel and dust, and ricocheting off the rocks nearby. And then Moody's rifle was empty.

Parkman leaped to his feet and sprinted for better cover. He crossed the gulch and ended up plastered to the stone wall on the opposite side. In Moody's perch directly above, there was no way he could lean out far enough to fire again at Parkman. It was closer to being a fair fight now. He drew his revolver from its holster and blew the dust out of the barrel, then spun the cylinder to make sure it rotated freely.

Now it was time for Moody to start worrying.

"You only said all those things to get me riled," Moody exclaimed angrily from somewhere above. "None of it ain't true, and if you was standing in front of me right now, I'd tell you to your face you're a sorry, no-good lying weasel." His voice was loud and righteous with anger, which is what Parkman had intended. A man that fought mad didn't usually fight smart. "I can outdraw and outshoot you any day, and you know it."

Parkman knew better, but didn't answer. Moody no longer knew exactly where he was, and the marshal wanted to keep it that way. He picked up a few fist-sized rocks and tossed them up and down the gulch, hoping to draw fire from Moody, but it didn't work. There were only two directions to move at this point, and he chose upward between the narrowing rock walls.

"You're so high and holy about the job you've got," Moody said. "You and your laws, and all your preaching about what's right and what's not, when it's okay to kill a man and when it ain't. I'll tell you what's right, Marshal Ridge Parkman, and that is to kill a man when he gets in your way, and take what you want from him after you done it."

In his frustration, Moody began to kick small avalanches of loose stone down from where he was, but they arced too far out to do Parkman any harm.

As he waited, Parkman began to notice the trail of bones scattered up and down the gulley. Some were human, and others were probably from horses. This wasn't the first ambush within these steep, rugged, stone walls. He imagined that some fight long, long ago, had probably unfolded in this same place much like this one had—attackers up above on the rim, and vulnerable prey down below.

He couldn't help but wonder if his own bones might soon join those of the other fallen warriors here.

"You and me, Parkman, out here like this, we ain't no different than the other wild animals that live in these mountains, the bears and cougars and wolves and snakes and all the rest. They fight to live and don't leave nothing but rotting meat behind when they move on to the next battle. You've got to be strong and hard and as cold in your soul as a block of ice to survive on the outlaw trail. I don't apologize to no man for taking it up. It was my choice."

As Alex Moody continued to rant, his voice grew a little quieter, more introspective. He's trying to justify his evil doings, Parkman thought, but he's talking to the wrong man. The marshal slowly worked his way up the gulch, hugging the irregular stone face and watching the crest of the wall above to make sure that his adversary's head didn't loom out unexpectedly. Once in a while he threw more rocks to keep Moody confused about exactly where he was.

Parkman began to feel a dull ache above the knee of his right leg. When he glanced down, he was surprised to see his pants leg soaked with blood. He decided that a bullet fragment must have nipped him earlier when Moody was shooting at him. But the pain was still mild, and he had more important things to deal with now. Staying alive was foremost.

He came finally to a crack in the rock wall, about a foot wide, barely enough for him to slip his body into. Looking up, he saw that the crack widened to about three feet at the top, with precious little to use for foot- and handholds going up. But he knew that the best way to deal with Moody was to get up there where he was.

As he climbed carefully, Parkman was annoyed by the soggy feeling as his right boot began to fill with blood. By the time he reached the top, little needles of pain were beginning to probe into his knee and down his leg. He needed to close the wound soon. Losing too much blood could make him weak and addled. But he didn't dare pause to take care of it yet. Moody could be anywhere by now. He rose to his feet, then staggered from the unexpected jolt of pain that shot up his leg as he placed his weight on it. This was a mess, and getting worse all the time.

Parkman's thoughts began to shift from tactics for finding Alex Moody and either capturing or killing him, to what he needed to do to survive the next few minutes. He staggered away from the lip of the gulch, into a roiling tangle of boulders and thick, shoulder-high brush. There were more bones up here, as well as a dry-rotted long bow with the string missing, and a decaying quiver with a few arrows still left in it. That must have been as desperate a fight as this one.

Limping back into the rocks and brush, he reached a clear narrow space no more than three feet wide and five feet long.

He half fell, half dropped to the ground and crawled behind a bush that provided him with a scant bit of cover. There were more bones where he sat, smaller than the others. This was where they had hidden their children, but it hadn't made any difference in the end.

Parkman drew his Colt, checked it again, and laid it across his lap, clear of the blood. Then he wrestled his right boot off and drew his sheath knife out. He sliced open his left pants leg from thigh to ankle and folded it aside. The wound was in the meaty side of his leg, above his kneecap, less than an inch long and looking more like a stab wound than a bullet hole. Blood was still oozing out in a steady flow, and he knew it must have punctured a blood vessel.

"Well look here, won't you?" Alex Moody's voice, coming from no more than thirty feet away, seemed filled with confidence and delight. "It appears that Marshal Ridge Parkman has left me a bright red trail to follow."

Parkman wiped his bloody hands on his shirt, then picked up the Colt. This was the moment, and he'd be glad to get it over with.

"Seems like I wasn't just whistling Dixie when I was cutting loose with all that lead down into that ditch," Moody gloated. "At least one shot connected."

Parkman thumbed back the hammer of his Colt, which Moody might have heard if he wasn't still blabbering. The marshal heard the scuff of his boots on the ground as he approached the jumble of rocks.

"Are you dead yet, Parkman? If you ain't already, I'll be pleased to take care of that shortly." His arrogance was beginning to get downright annoying, and Parkman would have liked to answer back, just as cocky, but silence and stillness were his allies now. "But don't you worry. I'll take good care of that tall horse of yours. And the Sharps."

Through the foliage of the bush beside him, Parkman saw Moody ease into view, stop for a moment, and then come on. Moody still held his rifle in both hands, pointed forward with his finger already on the trigger. That was a mistake, Parkman thought. A handgun was the tool for close-in work like this. He fired three rounds in succession, in case his aim was off or the bush deflected any of his bullets. Moody muttered a harsh "Uhhh" like a man punched hard in the gut. He toppled forward, no more than ten feet from his executioner, and lay still.

"Are you dead yet, Moody?" Parkman said gruffly. He put one more bullet in the top of Moody's head for caution's sake. Sometimes a man pretended to be dead when he wasn't.

The wound in his leg was still leaking blood, and Parkman was about to tear up his shirt for a bandage. Then he had a better idea. He struggled to his feet and, with two fingers over the hole in his leg, hobbled over to Moody's body. The dead man's shirt was splattered with blood from Parkman's first three shots, but he had died so fast that there wasn't time for it to be soaked in the stuff.

He put together a decent bandage from strips torn from Moody's shirt and tied it snug around his wound. Then he fished around in the dead man's pockets and came up with a small leather bag of gold dust and nuggets, no doubt stolen, and the star-shaped badge that the disgraced ex-marshal still carried around with him for some unknown reason.

With the aid of Moody's Winchester, Parkman struggled to his feet again, then used the rifle as a cane, barrel down. He hobbled along the crest of the deep gulley, stopping once to let out a shrill, two-fingered whistle to call in his horse. The last time he had seen General Grant he had been trotting away, into the trees downhill from where Parkman had landed when he bailed out of the saddle. It was important that he find his horse.

It could mean his life.

Parkman limped and stumbled down a steep grade to the trees where he had last seen his horse. It seemed to take forever, and when he got there he sat down with his back to a tree and tried another whistle. He felt weak and helpless and suddenly tortured by an overwhelming thirst. He had lost more blood than a man could spare, and he obviously had not stopped the flow, because the bandage was soaked through already. His head was swirling. He understood that he might sit here and die, the same as that young outlaw he'd come across, if things didn't turn around soon.

Parkman whistled one more time and was rewarded with a snort from the nearby woods.

CHAPTER FIVE

As Parkman felt himself slowly waking, he fought to return to the dream he had been having, realizing that it was far preferable to the reality that awaited him when he woke up.

In his dream, he was standing at the bar in the Chuck-a-Luck saloon and dance hall in Denver, or someplace like it, surrounded by a gaggle of friends and fellow marshals, chugging whiskey from a shot glass that never seemed to be empty. He was the center of attention, spinning a preposterous saga about how he had tracked down Alex Moody and his gang of ten, or fifteen, or thirty thieves and killers, wading into the fight unafraid, and not stopping the slaughter until the last of them lay dead or dying around him. Of course, none of the men around him believed a word he said, but still they celebrated the actual demise of Moody himself, and the ritual return of his disgraced badge to Captain Mullins.

Ray Goode was there in the saloon with them, standing aside, grinning and shaking his head with amusement each time Parkman belted out another grandiose lie.

Waking fully at last, Parkman folded back his blanket and surveyed the rough camp around him, realizing that the reality of the day would bring no such pleasures and pleasantries as those in his dreams.

He felt better this morning, and his worries about simply passing out and dying alone and unawares up here on a nameless mountainside were beginning to fade. He had no doubt that the timely arrival of General Grant yesterday had saved his life.

With no particular plan or destination in mind, Parkman had kept his horse headed downhill all day yesterday, and today would be much the same. Denver was too far away to try for, and Payday Gulch was even farther. But he felt sure that somewhere down below he would come across a trail to someplace, or run into a band of prospectors, or even find a town of some sort where he could get help and care.

The wound on his leg both tortured and puzzled him. During a midday stop yesterday, he had removed the makeshift bandage and washed the dried blood away to have a look. Blood was still oozing out, but not as bad. He had poked around for a while until the pain made him stop, and he began to think that it might be a shard of stone instead of a bullet. Whatever it was, it was lodged into a bone, and he didn't think he could get it out without some knife work, so he left it there. It had to come out eventually, but he decided it would be better for now to close the hole and stop the bleeding.

He had decided to cauterize it with powder from a couple of .45 pistol rounds. The pain from that sudden little flash was overwhelming, and the scream he cut loose with had startled General Grant and caused him to scuttle away in surprise. But the bleeding had stopped, and eventually the agony of the reddish black, silver-dollar–sized burn began to ease. He had done that kind of thing before, to himself and others, and had a good idea what to expect. It would leave another ugly scar to add to his collection.

This morning his leg was swollen, and the area around the burn was crimson red. But that was all part of his body healing itself, and he figured it would diminish over the next few days. It could be worse, he reminded himself. That could be him lying up there on the mountainside, getting gnawed on by a pack of wolves or a wandering bear, another scattered jumble of bones to join the other dead warriors there.

He ate a breakfast of cold biscuits and jerky and drank water until his stomach bulged. Building a fire took too much energy, so he mounted up and rode away without that first pot of coffee that always seemed to start a man's day right. Water was the thing he needed now to fight the fever that he felt coming on. Thankfully, it was all around him in abundance in the tumbling creeks and streams.

General Grant seemed to sense that all was not well, and most of the time he chose his own pathway down the mountain. Parkman was content to let the horse have its way, because he didn't have much of a notion of where he was going anyway. Just down. Down where the riding was easier. Down where it was warm, and he wasn't likely to wake up in the morning half buried in last night's snowfall. Down to what passed for civilization in these parts, where he could find a town or a camp, or at least other human beings, where he might find someone who could tend to his wound and save his life.

By dusk that day he had descended to the foothills. He found a decent place to spend the night at the edge of a wild meadow where the General could graze, with a patch of woods alongside where he could find deadfall to build a fire and start the coffee boiling. His world was slowing down, and it was getting harder to herd his thoughts together so they made any sense.

He'd stopped a couple of times during the day to loosen the bandage when it got too tight around the swelling wound. The pain went back and forth from bearable to excruciating, but it seemed now as if he simply forgot about it from time to time as his mind swirled away into a vague fog of confusion and nothingness. Something like dreams floated across his consciousness even while he was awake, and occasionally he felt like he was someplace else, or even someone else.

One minute he trembled from the cold, and the next he was sweating, blazing hot. He took the bandage off and saw that the redness and swelling were spreading. The white bubble of pus nearly covered the spot where he had cauterized the hole in his skin. At great expense in terms of pain, he pricked the spot with the point of his knife, then squeezed out what he could before washing it and tying the bandage back on.

He had seen this kind of thing before, fairly often back during the war, and knew too well what it meant. His leg was putrefying. Wounds like this were common after a battle, and if a man didn't get medical help reasonably soon, the odds of survival were poor. Next would come the long, black lines of rot, creeping up his leg like spiderwebs, and when that started, the rest was all too predictable.

He drank two cups of coffee, unpleasantly strong because he let the pot boil too long, but he didn't feel like going to the bother of eating. He curled up on the ground and went to sleep, his blanket spread haphazardly across him.

General Grant was standing a few feet away when Parkman began to stir the next morning. Shafts and splashes of sunlight lit the ground around him, and a cool morning breeze was welcome on his clammy flesh.

He lay there for a while, drifting in and out of awareness as the last of his confusing, befuddled dreams seemed to dissolve away. For a while he hardly had a grasp on where he was, or what was going on around him, or even who he was. But at least the sight of his horse provided him with a vague reassurance. He wasn't alone, and he wasn't dead yet.

The pain returned as soon as he tried to roll over, boiling up from his entire leg, and seeming to overflow into his right hip and lower gut. He decided not to take another look this morning, dreading what he might see.

Parkman had little awareness of where he was, or what he should be doing long about now, but one thought did manage to make its way through the fog and brambles of his mind. He had to get on that horse or die.

Chapter Six

Strong arms wrapped around Parkman's chest and lifted. A second pair of hands slid under his rear end, and another held his good leg.

"All right, cut the rope around that horse's neck, but hang onto that bridle so he don't run off."

"That's fine, boys. Now let him roll off into our arms. Lower him easy."

He heard grunts, and he felt like somebody had set his bad leg on fire as it dragged across the saddle. Then he was being carried somewhere.

"Put him on that patch of grass over there, and then we'll have a look."

Parkman was lowered to the ground. He tried to see what was happening around him, but the sunlight hurt his eyes. Everything was blurry and confusing, so he closed them again.

"What do you figure happened to him, Hugh?"

"Must have got shot. Some time ago, I'd say, and couldn't tend to it proper. So now the fever's got ahold of him."

"His skin's burning up, and he smells like a dead possum. 'Specially that leg."

The sky was blue above Parkman, flanked on either side by tall, slender pine trees. He saw kneeling shapes around him, but couldn't make out faces clearly. A hand lifted his head from behind, and water flowed into his mouth from a canteen. He choked at first, then drank greedily.

"He knew he was passing out and tied himself to his horse. Smart move. Elsewise he would have fallen off someplace and probably never been found."

"That's one fine animal he was tied on. Tall and strong, and smart looking, too. Maybe if this fellow don't make it, I'll lay claim to that horse for myself."

Parkman wanted to protest but lacked the ability. His arms felt like lead, and his voice wouldn't work.

"Let's take things one at a time, Jubal. After all, he might make it, and if he don't, he might have people around here that would have first claim to the horse. We can sort it all out when we get to Weatherby's Lode."

"All right. But if he does pass on, and if he don't have any people . . ."

Several steps away, Parkman saw the blurry shape of a wagon of some kind, with tall wooden sides, piled high on top with cargo.

"Where do you intend to put this man, driver?" That came from somewhere out of Parkman's line of sight.

"On the floor of the coach, I suppose."

"But the coach is packed full with seven people already. If you put him in there, there won't be any place to put our feet except on him."

"We'll have to make do. There's room on the driver's seat for one more, and maybe we can put somebody up top on the luggage and gear. And one man might ride that horse if it'll let him."

"Why don't you tie him on top? He's so far gone he won't know the difference. He'll be dead by the time we get to Weatherby's Lode."

"Mister, how would you like to ride into that town with a fat lip?"

The water began to trickle into Parkman's mouth again. He

swallowed some, and the rest leaked back out. When he opened his eyes again, he felt like he was looking through cheesecloth, and when he tried to say something, it only came out as slurry gibberish. He felt himself fading away and gave in to it.

Blurry forms of people came and went above him, speaking words that he recognized but did not understand. Sometimes glaring light scorched his eyes, and other times the darkness was so dense that he felt hopelessly lost in a void of nothingness. Sometimes he was so miserably cold that his whole body quivered uncontrollably, and other times he was bathed in sweat, feeling as if liquid fire flowed through his veins and leaked out through his flesh.

It was frustrating to exist in such a confusing condition. He was unable to control even the simplest movements of his own body. Raising an arm or leg was like trying to lift a log, and yet there were times when his limbs flailed and shook without command. When he was aware, the pain was relentless, and he welcomed that dark delirium that always followed.

At one point he was back up on the mountain, talking to Alex Moody as the blood flowed from his lifeless corpse and the wolves stalked in the shadows around them. Moody cursed Parkman roundly for killing him, swearing he would never give up his badge and would take it on down to hell with him just for spite.

In another fevered vision, he was down in the gulley where he had rolled out of the saddle as Moody's bullets sang past him. It was full of screaming, frantic, painted Indian warriors now, hacking and stabbing at one another in frenzied battle. The fight was going on as far as he could see up and down the gulch. Nearly naked men swung war clubs and horribly wounded one another with lances, knives, and crude stone hatchets. Up along the rim, where Moody had been, lines of braves shot their arrows indiscriminately into the bloody throng below. The shrill war cries of the living blended with the agonizing screams of the dying, mixing into a terrifying pandemonium of fury and pain.

Parkman was among them, witnessing horrible atrocities and feeling the blood and sweat of the warriors splatter on him. But, somehow, he was not a part of what was happening all around. None raised their weapons against him or even seemed to acknowledge his existence among them. The hail of arrows from above passed harmlessly through him.

The victors, if there were any, would carry their fallen tribesmen away, and the remaining dead would lie where they fell until their bodies returned to the earth beneath them.

And then he was back in the Appalachian foothills of western Virginia, only a boy not yet in his teens. He was watching a twelve-point whitetail at the edge of a clearing, majestically standing watch over his herd of does and fawns. The boy that was him raised the long, heavy rifle to his shoulder, and his finger found the trigger. But a ponderous dread, something like guilt, came over him as he contemplated killing such a splendid animal.

The pain brought him back. The forms stood beside him again, talking to each other as one of them folded the blanket back and began to cut the bandages from his wounded leg.

"I didn't want to do it, but we needed the meat," Parkman muttered, assuming that they would know what he was talking about and understand the necessity.

"What did he say?" It was a man's voice, and through the haze Parkman made out a scraggly beard on a weathered face. "He needs some meat?"

"Just more jabbering." He saw a tired, freckled face and a shock of thick, red hair, graying at the temples. "But the fever seems to be down today. He might still make it."

Parkman saw a rough wooden table suddenly overturning in

front of him and felt the tin cup of whiskey he was holding splash in his face as he toppled backward out of his chair. All around him guns were firing, but he couldn't find his. It had slipped out of the holster, and he had the dreadful feeling that if he didn't find it soon, he would join the dead around him.

A face hovered above Parkman's. It was simple, sincere, and just starting to wrinkle. Thick, red hair was pulled back and tied somewhere behind. He had seen this woman before. She wasn't what you'd call skinny, but her no-nonsense frame looked lean and healthy. She wore a simple blue dress, faded from many washings, and a dirty apron hung down the front. A smile spread across the woman's face as she watched his eyes flutter open.

Parkman's thoughts seemed clearer than they had been in a long time. He had the feeling that he was really where he seemed to be, and what he saw was real as well.

"Well, it looks like you're coming back to yourself. It's about time," she said.

Her eyes told her story. They were gentle and caring, but at the same time they seemed knowing and seasoned. Parkman, still only half awake, tried to smile back at her, but wasn't quite sure he pulled it off.

"Ma'am, is there any chance you know what happened to my horse?" His voice was raspy from disuse. Even the act of talking seemed to cost a measure of energy he didn't have.

The woman laughed heartily, her head tilted back, mouth wide open. It seemed like a release of tension that she needed.

"Here you are, just now stepping back from death's door after four days out of your head, blazing with fever, and nigh onto losing a leg, or your life. And you want to know about your horse?"

"Well, he's finer than most, ma'am," Parkman said. "And I remember some man saying he might lay claim to him."

"Don't worry about your horse, cowboy. He's boarded down at the livery barn and doing fine. Your guns and the rest of your gear are in a pile over there in the corner. And in case you're interested, your leg's doing better, too. It took four men to hold you down while I dug this out." She picked up something from a table beside his cot and put it in his palm. It was a slender, jagged piece of limestone about an inch long.

"By the shape of the hole and the way it felt, I thought it must be a rock instead of lead," Parkman said. "But it was stuck too hard in the bone for me to dig out myself. I couldn't stand the pain of it."

"Ricochet?"

"Yep." He didn't have the energy to start going over his fight with Alex Moody up there in the mountains, and she didn't push him for details. The time would come for that.

"After we got that hunk of rock out, I cleaned the hole as best I could and then turned you over to the Lord's good graces. Seems like He decided to leave you here amongst the living a little while longer."

A breeze blew in the open doorway, sweeping over Parkman, soothing his still fevered body. The woman folded back a corner of the blanket that covered him so she could take a look at the bandage around his leg. She smiled and nodded her approval. "The swelling is still going down," she reported.

"Seems like I'm not wearing much under this blanket, ma'am," Parkman noted. She grinned with amusement.

"You're naked as a peeled onion. But don't worry, cowboy," the woman said without embarrassment. "I grew up with three brothers in a two-room shanty. I've been married twice and come close a few other times. I've seen the elephant."

She covered Parkman's leg back up and leaned over to fluff his pillow, then stood up and started for the door. "I've got work to do, but I'll be back a little later. And, by the way, my name is Hattie O'Shea."

"Pleased to meet you, ma'am. And I do thank you for all you've done for me, Miss Hattie O'Shea. I'm Ridge Parkman."

"All right, I'll bring you some supper when I can. And don't you even think about getting up from that bed 'til I get back."

"How about bringing my britches back when you come?" Parkman couldn't help but ask.

"I burned them. They weren't much but bloody rags, and I couldn't stand the stench," Hattie said. "But if you're going to go all shy on me, I'll see what I can scare up for you. I burned your shirt, too. But Cyrus cleaned your boots and oiled them down, so they should still be fit to wear. When you're ready."

After she was gone, Parkman tried to move his legs off the bed and at least sit up. Between the sudden pain in his wounded leg and the overall weakness of his limbs and body, it was an impossible task. He spotted his holstered revolver on the stack of his belongings across the room and thought he would feel better if it was in reach. But for all the good it did him, it might as well be on the other side of the Rocky Mountains. He laid his head back on the pillow, feeling utterly exhausted.

Parkman decided he liked this woman, this salty, sassy Hattie O'Shea, but she sure was a puzzler. She came back later with a platter of food in one hand and a bucket of water in the other. She lifted him up with one strong arm under his shoulders, then raised a dipper of water to his mouth.

"I brought you some of Cyrus's elk stew. It's mostly meat, but that's what you need right now. You haven't swallowed much of anything but water for four days, and we've got to get you fattened up again."

Parkman didn't feel hungry until Hattie shoveled that first spoonful of stew into his mouth, and then he ate greedily.

"So your husband does the cooking for you?" Parkman asked. "I've got nothing bad to say about the stew, but a man cooking?

Isn't that backwards of the way it usually is?"

Hattie laughed at his question. "Shoot, that whiskery old pile of bones is not my husband," she said. "He's my cook. I run a café on the other end of this building. Right now, we've got you bunked down in the storage room."

"So how did I end up here? The last I clearly remember, I was up on a mountain someplace, tying myself to my horse so I wouldn't fall off if I passed out. And then I sort of recall that there were some men cutting me loose and carrying me someplace."

"That was Hugh Bushworth and Jubal Flatt. They brought you in on the weekly stage over from Denver," Hattie explained. "I took you in 'cause nobody else would, and I figured you wouldn't last more than a day or two anyway. If I knew you were going to hang on this long and make such a nuisance of yourself, I might have thought twice about the whole thing." Her smile showed that she was playing him along.

"Well if you hadn't burned my britches, I'd get up right now and cease being a burden to you."

"I bet you've already tried," Hattie chuckled. "A man like you would have to take a stab at it."

For a while Parkman concentrated on eating until his belly began to swell and ache. Then Hattie lowered his head back to the pillow and set the food aside. It seemed to Parkman like the simple effort to chew and swallow had drained away what little energy he had.

"I found your badge," Hattie said. "Two of them, in fact. So you're a U.S. marshal, then."

"One's mine, and the other belonged to a man that decided to go into another line of work."

"I guess it didn't pan out for him, then?"

"Not hardly."

Parkman began to feel an overwhelming need for sleep, and

he lost the fight to keep his eyes open. He was out before Hattie reached the door.

CHAPTER SEVEN

"When they first brought you in, Cyrus thought he might be able to cut that leg off for you," Hattie said. "During the war he was an orderly in a field hospital in Tennessee and Mississippi, and he said he'd seen it done many a time."

"He wouldn't have been doing me any favor," Parkman said. He imagined what it would be like to end up one legged, like so many of the wounded war veterans. Those urgent, clumsy battlefield amputations seldom healed well, and a lot of the recipients still died. It just took longer, and involved a lot more suffering. He had family back in Missouri who would take him in and care for him, but how the devil would he ever get there?

"I told Cyrus that seeing and doing are two different things, and I wasn't about to let him give it a try. I don't know much about it myself, but I do know there's veins that need to be tied off in there, and bones to be sawed, and other things that neither of us know the first thing about."

After a week in the tiny storage room, eventually getting up and hobbling around with a makeshift crutch that Cyrus had cobbled together for him, Parkman had insisted on going outside and learning to get around on his own. One of his motivations for pushing himself so hard to get out and about was so that he could make it to the outhouse on his own. It had become too embarrassing taking care of his business inside into a bucket.

He and Hattie were sitting now on the front porch of her

café. Parkman had a certain feeling of accomplishment that he had been able to mount the two steps onto the porch, sit down, and hike his leg onto another chair without help. He didn't show what all that cost in pain, lest Hattie start trying to revise the rules for him again.

"I've never cut off a limb myself either, but I have tended a few bullet holes," Hattie went on. "I know that when one starts to fester like yours did, you have to open it up and let it heal inside out. We tied you to the bunk and opened it back up with a peeling knife. The hole drained for two days, and us pouring grain alcohol over it every few hours trying to keep it from starting to rot again."

"Alcohol is good for such things. I normally carry some, but my partner got into it on the trail."

"I wish you could have seen yourself when you were out of your mind, bucking and howling and fighting like a wild man. We poured water into your mouth 'til we thought we were drowning you, but you swallowed a good bit of it, and that helped, too. By the third day we thought things were turning around, and you started being yourself again long about the fifth."

Parkman took a taste of the half-inch of whiskey that Hattie had poured for him in a chipped coffee mug. The cool evening breeze blowing up from the west felt good on his still warmish skin. The sun was setting, and the western sky was ablaze with layered shades of red, orange, and yellow. He felt privileged to still be alive, and still two legged.

"Why'd you do it, Hattie?" he asked. "There must be men getting hurt and dying all the time in a wide-open town like Weatherby's Lode. You can't take them all in like you did for me."

"I couldn't say for sure. Maybe it was on a whimsey because you're so doggoned handsome," Hattie teased.

"I wouldn't be around long if I had to get by on good looks," Parkman said.

"Truth told, maybe that horse of yours had something to do with it."

"My horse?"

"When they pulled you out of that stagecoach floor and laid you out on the ground, your horse came over and lowered his head down to you. He smelled you and licked your cheek like a dog, and then nuzzled your shoulder like he was trying to wake you up. It touched something in me, and I can remember thinking that somebody who can build that kind of bond with a dumb animal must be a good man, one worth saving."

Parkman pondered that for a moment. He could picture General Grant doing something like that. "Well, in any case, I want to pay you back for all you did for me," he said. "I came across a pouch of gold a ways back that its owner didn't need anymore. I'd like to give you some of it for your time and trouble and tender mercies."

"You can keep your damned gold, cowboy," Hattie said, sounding almost offended. "Tender mercies aren't for sale." He considered that and didn't try to convince her otherwise.

Parkman's eyes settled on a man walking up the hill toward the café. He was small and flustery and moved with a kind of brisk urgency, as if his errand was highly important.

"Evening to you, Mrs. O'Shea," the man said as he approached, touching the brim of his hat with unnecessary formality. He wore a dusty, wrinkled suit that seemed entirely out of place in a ramshackle settlement like this. "And I assume you are Marshal Parkman, sir."

"Ridge Parkman, meet Claude Bondoro. He runs the telegraph office down the way and is also the agent for the stage line."

Parkman nodded a greeting and said, "What can I do for

you, Mr. Bondoro?"

"I have a telegram for you, marshal," the man said. "Just came in from Denver." He handed over a sealed yellow envelope.

"Much obliged," Parkman said.

After Bondoro was gone, Parkman slid a thumbnail under the flap of the envelope and tore it open.

A few days before, as his mind cleared, he had realized that he needed to send a message over to Captain Mullins to let him know what had happened to him, and to report the result of his encounter with Alex Moody. He also asked the captain to get the word of his mishap over to Ray Goode in Utah so his friend would know what became of him. He asked Hattie O'Shea if she would write a letter for him, but she had proudly informed him that telegraph lines had been run into Weatherby's Lode last fall by the same crew that built the stagecoach road.

Parkman took the folded piece of paper out and read it, then passed it over to Hattie. He knew she'd be curious.

Glad your recovery. Goode reports
hard fighting Utah. Go when can.

"Your boss is loaded down with sympathy about how you nearly died, isn't he?" Hattie said.

"The captain's a hard man with a hard job."

"Maybe he needs to face some facts, and the same for you, Ridge. If that leg of yours stiffens up or starts to fester again, it might be a long time before you can ride out to Utah and do any kind of hard fighting yourself."

Parkman turned his head away, not willing to continue this particular conversation. It annoyed him that Hattie was pointing out the very same things that he himself was trying to ignore. His own plan was to get that leg working again, and then head for Utah. But his leg didn't seem to want to buy into the plan.

Up on the hillside to the north, the miners were beginning to file out of the gaping mouths of the mines after their day's work deep beneath the mountain. Even at a distance, Parkman could see how exhausted they were from their grueling twelve-hour shifts underground. These were the unfortunates who had come west chasing dreams of wealth, but ended up instead digging some other man's gold out of narrow, dangerous tunnels for slave wages. Some headed toward the tent city across the tumbling stream from Weatherby's Lode, and others started for the log footbridge that would lead them to the more built-up part of the town.

Parkman choked back the remaining whiskey from the cup as Hattie rose to go inside. Some of those men would want a full meal before they went down the road to waste their meager salaries in the saloons and gambling halls scattered along the main street of the town.

"I saw the scars on your body, Ridge," Hattie said before leaving, "and I nursed you back to life when you were leaning over your own grave. You're not an old man yet, but maybe it's time to start thinking about such matters. There's a lot of things to live for besides riding around the country with a badge on your shirt."

"Generally, I keep it in my pocket," Parkman said, trying to lighten things up. But Hattie was in no mood for it and turned away with a determined stride and a last swish of her skirts.

After he watched her go inside, Parkman's eyes roved over to the shiny glass window pane by his shoulder, and he studied his features for a moment. He didn't have the sort of good looks that most women noticed right away, but there was something about his crinkling eyes and his relaxed half smile that made most people feel comfortable around him, unless they had reason not to. He was only of middling height, but he had the solid build that ran in his family. Even though a peppering of gray hair was starting to show up on his temples, he never had given much thought to the notion that he might be growing old . . . not until recently at least.

It had been a long time since Ridge Parkman had contemplated any other sort of life except the one he lived. But there were other things out there, he supposed. Raising horses might not be such a bad life, even for a man with a crippled leg. General Grant would be his prized stud, of course.

The days and weeks passed slowly in Weatherby's Lode for a man who was used to staying on the move most of the time, and living a life of purpose. This wasn't much of a place to be in for a man who wasn't chasing gold, cared little for gambling, and knew, usually, when to put the cork back in the bottle.

He'd been shot and knifed and beat all to hell before, but never like this. He'd always healed eventually and come out the other side nearly as good as ever. But this time it was different. There was something about that knee that didn't want to get better, and he began to think that that little sharp-edged rock must have done permanent damage to his knee cap, or sliced into muscles and tendons that might never heal completely.

Sometimes at night, when he'd settled into his tight little quarters in back of the restaurant, he would pick up that small sliver of stone, no longer than the last joint of his thumb, and wonder at the fact that something so insignificant could interrupt a man's life so much.

With time on his hands now, he'd written a letter to Captain Mullins, and another to Ray Goode, explaining his wound and the frustration he felt at being tied down like this in the middle of no place. It was hard to think that they would believe him when he wrote that he gimped around like an old man, or that he could scarcely ride a mile without feeling like somebody had laid his leg across a fire. It was embarrassing and frustrating.

The worst, he thought, would come when he met up with

Ray Goode again. This was the same Ray Goode who had once ridden forty miles, with a bullet in his shoulder and an Apache arrowhead stuck in a rib bone, to get help for a stage waystation under siege, then rode back with the troop of soldiers and still claimed his share of the fight. Parkman knew his friend would show him no mercy when they met again, especially if Parkman was unwise enough to show him the little piece of rock that had laid him low. He would be living it down for years, and every time Goode told his story for him, the rock would get smaller and his vacation in Weatherby's Lode would get longer.

It was late spring now, a pleasant time of year in these elevations. The trees were leafing out, and the open meadows at the lower edge of Weatherby's Lode were awash with a sea of colors. The nights were still chilly, but the daytime hours were comfortable, and the winds were moderate.

Parkman had been out that morning giving General Grant some exercise. He still mounted up inside the livery barn so no one would see the milking stool that he needed to get into the saddle. He was hobbling up the steep slope of the main road now from the barn to Hattie's café. He had switched from the crutch to a cane, mostly out of embarrassment, but still swung his stiff right leg awkwardly as he walked. Hattie had seen him coming and brought a cup of coffee out on the porch for him.

"I heard there was trouble west of town at the Judas claim," Parkman said as he mounted the porch steps and took a seat at the table. "The talk is, the owner of the Judas hole, some fellow named Grimes, dug far enough in that he got under the claim beside his. So, a man named Perkins, who owned the other claim, pitched some sulphur pots into the Judas hole and suffocated half a dozen miners. Then, of course, there was a shootout after, and more dead."

"That must have been the shooting we heard down that way yesterday evening. It seemed to go on forever."

"I suppose." It felt odd to Parkman to be passing along gossip about that kind of thing instead of being right in the middle of it, trying to stop the killing. But that wasn't his job here. Not anymore.

The regulars in town knew that Parkman carried a badge, but he made no pretense of enforcing the law in Weatherby's Lode. In his condition, it seemed almost a silly thing to try. He left that business up to the embattled miners, the angry mobs, and the gaggles of hooded men who sometimes roved at night, enforcing their own interpretation of the law, or simply righting the wrongs that had been done to them.

He still kept his pistol belt strapped on, mostly because it felt right, and practically every other man he passed on the street carried some sort of firearm. There was no telling what kind of ruckus might flare up from one minute to the next.

"How did the leg do today?" Hattie asked. They had fallen into the habit of referring to his wounded limb almost as a third entity among them.

"Better, I think." It was always "better," another habit. "I stood up in the stirrups for a while and let the General have a good run. It's starting to bend a little, and it's taking longer before the deep pain starts to set in."

Hattie took a drink of coffee, looking at him but saying nothing for a minute.

"After you go back to work," Parkman said, "I think I'll finish up that letter to my mother and family over in Missouri. She likes to know where I am and what I'm up to from time to time, even though I don't usually see her letters until I get back to Denver. I don't think I'll tell her about this leg business right away. She worries enough as it is, and there's always things I don't bother her mind with."

"You said she's got a farm over there, didn't you?"

"Yes, she took over my grandfather's place up north of Kansas

City after he was killed near the end of the war. And I've got other kin in the area, too. We're a big family."

"It's pretty country. I came through there with Roger when we were making our way west. Rolling hills, decent weather, and rich farm land as far as your eyes can see." Roger was her second husband, who had drowned crossing the Platte River before they reached Denver.

They watched a group of four men walking up from town toward the café. They would probably be Hattie's first noontime customers, and for the next three hours the stream of hungry men would be steady.

"Time to go to work," Hattie said. "Are you up for a walk a little later?" It had become their routine to take an afternoon walk when Parkman's leg felt up to it.

"Sure. I'll be close by. It's not like I plan to wander off someplace."

Two hours passed as Parkman finished the letter. Some of Hattie's customers stopped to chat coming and going, and he paused sometimes to stare up the mountainside, considering what he should put in the letter and what he should leave out. It wasn't as if his mother was a delicate flower who didn't understand and accept the dangers of frontier life. But he was her son, her only son, and no mother was completely immune from worry.

He folded the letter and slid it down into an envelope. Eight pages was a pretty good product for him, and he knew she would forgive him for the ink splotches and bad penmanship. He didn't get much practice at this sort of thing.

With his chore finished, Parkman planted his feet up on another chair and tilted his hat down over his eyes so he could take a little snooze. It occurred to him that, despite his problems, he felt more at peace at that moment than he had for a long time. That should tell him something, he thought.

He woke a little later when Hattie came out for their walk. They followed a path behind the café, over to the edge of the broad gulch where the majority of the local mining and prospecting took place. It had rained the night before, and the runoff tumbled and surged down the middle of the gulch, slowing where the gulch grew wider, and speeding up where it got narrow and steep.

The pathway meandered through a multitude of stumps, and Parkman imagined how different it must have been along here when the virgin forest grew thick and wild almost down to the water's edge. As the path arced to the right, the grade became steeper, and their pace slowed.

"Sometimes I wonder how I ended up in a place like this," Hattie said, "and I wonder, if I had my druthers, what kind of life I might want to live for the rest of my days." Parkman was not surprised by her words. These walks gave them the leisure to talk about so many different things.

A stone rolled under his right foot, and he staggered sideways, but the cane kept him from falling down. Hattie looped her arm through his and slowed her pace a little. She smelled like boiled meat and cabbage, the lunch special today.

"I've been here in Weatherby's for over a year now, and I've done all right, but I've about had my fill of this frontier life."

"You're a pretty good woman of business, Hattie. If the mines keep producing and the town thrives, in another few years you could own half of Weatherby's. You could be set for life." He was half teasing, although what he said might be true.

"I never pined for more money than I need to live comfortable, Ridge. And besides that, this isn't the kind of place I'd like to live in over time. There's no children around, nor hardly any women of the type I could associate with. I don't believe I've laid eyes on a church steeple since we left Lawrence."

Down in the gulch Parkman saw two men squatting at the

water's edge. Newcomers, he thought. Otherwise they would surely know that the sand they were panning in search of the precious golden flakes had already been harvested by others long before. They needed to go out into the wilds if they wanted to do any real prospecting.

"So where would you go, Hattie?" he said.

"Roger and I lived in St. Louis for a few years, and I like Missouri. Kansas is too flat and dry for my liking, and I don't think I'd like to go back down to New Orleans where I grew up. My parents are both dead, and my brothers have scattered who knows where, so I've got no family to go back to. And anyway, the summers are so hot and damp you can hardly catch your breath, and every couple of years the yellow fever comes along and kills half the population. Yes, I think Missouri would suit me."

The pathway took another turn to the right and became steeper for a few dozen yards. Hattie held his arm securely as they trudged up to easier ground. Then Parkman stopped there to let the aching in his leg drain away.

"Look there, Ridge," Hattie said. She pointed toward the footbridge farther up the gulch. "They've hung another one. It seems like not a week goes by without some poor sinner getting his neck stretched off that bridge."

Parkman looked up and saw the body turning slowly in the afternoon breeze. His wrists and ankles were bound, and his head was cocked oddly toward one shoulder because of the thick hangman's noose alongside his head. His clothes were simple and worn, and his feet were bare. Someone had probably claimed his footwear before they tossed him off the side of the bridge.

"I've seen more than a few men hanging there," Hattie said, "but it's still something that's hard to tear your eyes away from. It gives me the shivers to think about dying like that."

"Looks like a young fellow, maybe no more than twenty, I'd guess. Does he look familiar?"

"I don't think so," Hattie said. "If he'd taken a meal in my place, I'd remember him."

"I haven't heard any talk about it. I wonder what he did."

"Probably the usual. Claim jumping, or stealing quartz out of somebody's mine." Tearing her gaze away, she turned her back on the dangling corpse. "It would be a real delight to live where this isn't such a common thing."

They took a different route back, crossing a large meadow south of town before circling around and heading back. Parkman's leg was giving him plenty of trouble by then, but he tried not to hobble so Hattie wouldn't know. Of course, she did anyway and suggested that they sit for a little while and catch their breath. She was still in a pensive mood.

"When I was fifteen, I married for love," Hattie said, "and when I was thirty-four, I married for security." She stared off into the faraway distance, as if she might be seeking a glimpse of her future somewhere out there. Miles of low hills and flatlands lay before them, and beyond that was another range of mountains. It seemed almost like a person could see to the edge of the world.

"I'm forty-one now. I figure I've got one more marriage in me, and maybe it isn't too late to pop a couple of babies into the world, even though most folks would say I'm too old for that." She paused and turned her gaze back to Parkman. There was something in her look that stirred a ripple of discomfort, as if he were learning more about this woman than he wanted to know. "I'm not looking for that hearts aflame kind of love anymore. I'm leaning more toward practical things this time. I want a good man of high integrity, a man I can respect, and a man that can be as much a friend as he is husband and bed partner."

It was Parkman's turn to stare out over the broad vistas now.

"Have you ever been married, Ridge Parkman?"

"I came close a time or two, but I always managed to make it out of the corral before the gate closed." Wasn't it the man who was supposed to be doing what Hattie was leading up to now?

"Well, you're not moving quite so fast these days, are you, cowboy? It's something to think about."

★ ★ ★ ★ ★

PART TWO

★ ★ ★ ★ ★

Chapter Eight

The dark, towering thunderheads swept relentlessly eastward, flashing and glowing with powerful internal energy, smothering the peaks to the west, turning day to night beneath them, pounding the forests and mountain meadows to the west with rain and hail. The rush of wind in advance of the storm was heavy with the damp scent of the impending downpour. It shook trees like switches, stripped the drying laundry from clotheslines, and rattled plank buildings on their fieldstone foundations. The temperature plummeted remarkably in a matter of minutes.

Ridge Parkman sat on the wide front porch of Hattie O'Shea's Café, tilted back in one chair with his bad right leg propped up on another, witnessing the storm's inexorable approach. The leg had been predicting the coming storm since yesterday, or so it seemed to Parkman.

Something about the approach of dramatic weather—whether it be a dust storm on the prairie that blotted out the sun and robbed men and horses of the breath in their bodies, or a mountain blizzard that could bury a cabin in half a day, or a spring thunderstorm like this that bore the power to topple hundred-year-old trees and toss a grown man through a barn wall—always sent a surge of primitive excitement through him.

It looked to Parkman like this storm had drawn a bead on the isolated little mountain town of Weatherby's Lode. They were definitely in for it.

He drew his pants leg up and gave the ugly four-inch scar

above his knee a good scratching. The itch was aggravating, so demanding that it sometimes woke him in the middle of the night. But at least he still had a leg down there to scratch.

As he leaned back, the telegram slipped out of his lap and fluttered to the porch planks. He retrieved it and started to read it again, then changed his mind.

This would be the first time he ever had to tell Captain Mullins no. Parkman hadn't actually sent his badge back to the captain yet, because he hoped to do that in person when he felt at least in good enough shape to take the stage over to Denver. But after this refusal of a direct order, he thought Mullins might demand the return of both his badge and the one he had taken from Alex Moody up in the mountains.

Down the long dirt track that split Weatherby's into two long lines of ramshackle homes and businesses, the townspeople were preparing as best they knew how for the storm's onslaught. Merchants carried their wares in from porches and boarded up their windows. Women gathered kids and chased chickens and turkeys into flimsy shelters. The liveryman herded horses and cattle into the barn. Up on the mountainside the miners were taking down their flimsy tents and either making their way down into town, or taking refuge well into the scattered mines. In these mountain regions, sudden spring thunderstorms like this one could be a rollicking experience. If poorly situated, an entire town the size of Weatherby's, along with all its residents, could be washed away within minutes when a gentle, tumbling stream became a churning, unstoppable torrent.

Hattie O'Shea came out of the restaurant with two mugs of coffee and gave him one. She sat in a chair near his with a heavy sigh. It was the slack time between lunch and dinner, her best chance to relax for a few minutes before it all started again. Clearly there would be no afternoon stroll today.

She scanned the approaching storm clouds and said, "Good

thing the supply wagons got back from Denver before this one hit. Zada Pass Road is bound to wash out again."

"It looks like a humdinger," Parkman agreed, glancing over at her. He thought her eyes were her best quality. They seemed to find shades of humor in just about all of life's experiences and reflected the wisdom and patience that her difficult life had taught her.

Down the street a man was tying down an outhouse to stakes driven in the ground around it. The first fat raindrops started puffing the dust in the street, and west of town the trees started to thrash. Parkman had thought about walking down the hill to check on his horse, but he knew the liveryman would already have moved him inside the barn, which was as safe as any place else right about now. General Grant would have to take his chances like everybody else.

A gust of wind slapped the side of the outhouse the man was trying to anchor down and over it went, losing its roof as it slammed to the ground. The man threw up his hands in disgust, then turned and scrambled for the back door of his business.

The air blowing in was heavy with moisture. Torrents of rain followed close behind, quickly obliterating the buildings at the far end of town from sight. Hattie and Parkman got up and went inside the café, taking their chairs with them. While Hattie went back to refill their coffee cups, he stood at the open front door watching the sheets of rain sweep over the town.

"Sure glad I'm not out on the trail in that," he said. "There's a lot to be said for town living on a day like this." He closed the door, having to shove it against the wind, then went to a nearby table to sit with Hattie.

Small and lean or not, Parkman had to admire the way she handled herself in a rough environment like this. Just the past week he had seen her lay out a drover with one solid punch after he slid his hand across her backside while she was serving his dinner.

"Cyrus heard down in town that you got another telegram from your boss over in Denver," Hattie said.

Parkman grinned tolerantly. Not much went on in an isolated little community like this that everyone didn't hear about.

"He's asking if I'm fit for duty. Some weasel got his hands on a stock of stolen military ordnance over in Utah, and he's headed northeast toward the northern Rockies with it. Probably looking for some kind of trade deal with the Indians. There wasn't much detail, but I'm guessing it must be some of the same bunch that Ray Goode's been scrapping with lately. I wonder if Ray ever got my letter so he knows what happened to me?"

"So, are you?" she asked.

"Am I what? Fit for duty? Probably not. But it doesn't matter anyway. You and me made other plans, didn't we? I've already ordered a suit from Kansas City."

"And if there's one thing I know about you, Ridge, it's that you're a man of your word."

"That's right, Hattie. And without complaint." He patted her hand and tried to smile reassuringly, but he could see that she was still wrestling with conflicting emotions.

"I wouldn't try to stop you from going, Ridge."

Parkman took a drink of coffee, looking at her above the rim of his mug. There was no selfishness in the clear, brown eyes that looked back at him.

"I pinned my first badge on when I was twenty-two, Hattie. A few years before the war started," he told her. "That's been my life ever since, in one form or another. After I left Virginia, the closest thing I ever had to a home was a rented room someplace, or a bunk in a barracks between assignments.

"I knew it was going to take some time to get used to the notion of not being a marshal anymore. But I like the idea of sinking some roots over in Missouri, around my family, and seeing what kind of horse breeder I can make of myself. And I want to see if I can't make you a good husband, too. It's a good plan, Hattie."

Hattie O'Shea smiled, her eyes glistening, and she raised her hand to stroke his stubbled cheek. "Did you lose that razor of yours again, cowboy?" she teased.

The storm hurled everything it had at Weatherby's Lode for the next two hours. After a bolt of lightning struck so close that it shook the wall of the café, Parkman pulled on his slicker and stepped out onto the porch. The wind nearly tossed him off into the muddy darkness before he grabbed hold of a support post.

Lamplight glowed in a few windows down the darkened street. Bolts of lightning stitched across the sky every minute or so, and by their light, Parkman got a first impression of the damage. A loblolly pine had measured itself across the saddlery, nearly mashing it in half, and a new house down by the livery barn was missing its roof.

No one came for supper that night. It wasn't worth the soaking, not even for a bowl of the thick deer stew that Cyrus Tate, Hattie's cook and handyman, spent all afternoon preparing.

Later in the evening Cyrus got out his guitar, and they passed some time singing a few of their old favorites. Parkman had once heard his singing voice compared to a saw blade scratched across a tin roof, but he gave it a shot because Hattie liked for him to sing along. Her favorite was "Beautiful Brown Eyes," although he had to make up parts of it because none of them could quite remember all the words.

Later they struck up a card game, playing for dry lima beans instead of money because Cyrus was such an unapologetic cheat.

Eventually the thunder and lightning lessened in intensity, and the rain began to slacken as the storm moved on to clobber other regions to the east. Cyrus completed his last chores in the kitchen, and Parkman stacked chairs on tables as Hattie gave the floor a final sweeping.

When the front door unexpectedly slammed open it startled all of them, and Parkman reached instinctively for a sidearm that he wasn't even wearing. A drenched man in a dirty, gray apron rushed into the café, his eyes large with excitement.

"You gotta help me, Marshal," he huffed, his eyes fixed on Parkman. He was hatless, and the rainwater made his bald head shine in the lamplight.

Being called "marshal" caught Parkman off guard. Since the day when the weekly stage delivered his half-dead carcass into Weatherby's and Hattie had begun the touch-and-go process of saving his life, and his leg, no one had called him that. He didn't even remember where his badge was—probably in his kit somewhere.

"What's got you so stirred up, Helmut?" Hattie asked. "You come running in here like your pants was ablaze, which isn't likely in weather like this."

"I need the marshal here," the man said. His name was Helmut Werner, and he was the unlikely proprietor of what passed for a saloon here in Weatherby's Lode, perhaps the most disreputable of the several drinking establishments in the town. "Skunk Murphy's gone and drug Christabelle off into the woods right in the middle of this cyclone." There was a note of aggressiveness and anger in Werner's tone that rankled Parkman, as if he might somehow bear responsibility for not stopping the abduction.

The sorry kind of life he'd led was written all over Werner's face. His eyes were the color of lead, and when he focused them on Parkman, they seemed as cold and absent of humanity as pebbles from a mountain stream. Besides his trade in liquor and beer, Werner also kept a couple of fallen doves in the back of his place, so Parkman had heard. He had also heard that Werner treated the women none too well.

"Who's Skunk Murphy?" he asked.

"He's one of them heathen prospectors from over on the western slopes. He wanders in every few months to drink up his dust and get his ashes . . ." He stopped short and cast a cautious glance in Hattie's direction.

"I say it serves you right, Helmut Werner!" Hattie scolded him. "You shouldn't be keeping those sad, sorry women over there anyway. I bet between the two of them they've got every disease and critter known to mankind, and maybe some that hadn't even been named yet."

"This ain't the time to argue that, Hattie," Werner fired back. "I need the marshal here to go get Christabelle back before that crazy half-wit prospector does something awful to her."

"Everybody in town knows I'm stove up with this leg, Werner."

"Plus, he's getting out of the marshal business," Hattie said.

"Nobody will go after them if you don't. Are you going to just sit around here while that heathen lunatic drags Christabelle off to a life of pain and degradation? Like I said, that old man's crazy as a bat."

Parkman was surprised that he was actually considering the request. Old habit, he supposed. He didn't figure he would cross the road to spit on Werner's grave, but with a woman involved, it was another matter. "Do you know what direction they went?" he asked.

"I heard Skunk telling somebody that his base camp was down along Split Creek. It ain't far, only a few miles southwest. He'd probably take her there."

Parkman looked around at Hattie, as if she might help him judge whether it made any sense at all to light out on a fool's errand like this, late at night in a steady downpour. She shrugged her shoulders and gave him that little amused grin of hers.

"All right, I'll help you go after them," Parkman decided. "Let me get my slicker and my weapons, and we can meet at the livery barn."

"We?" Werner asked, glancing warily at the sheets of rain that still raked the porch outside. "I ain't no lawman, Marshal. I'm nearsighted, and a piss-poor shot, which is why I didn't light out after them in the first place. I won't be no use to you."

"She's your woman," Parkman said, "and you know this country a lot better than I do. What did you expect, that I'd ride out of here alone in the pitch dark while you sat dry down in your saloon watering your whiskey down with coal oil? Either we both go, or nobody goes."

"Well, hell!" Werner grumbled.

"Maybe it's true love, Helmut," Hattie said with a chuckle. "Maybe she went off with him of her own choosing."

"She's a whore, Hattie!" Werner said, his temper rising again. "It she run off with a man, it would be some fellow with gold jingling in his pocket and a mouth full of sweet-sounding promises. Nope, ol' Skunk, he took her by force for sure."

"Are they afoot?" Parkman asked.

"Skunk only has the one mule for his gear."

"Then it shouldn't take long to catch up to them. Swing by the livery stable and tell Hoot to get our horses ready. I'll be there in a little while."

Werner left, and Parkman went to retrieve his gear from the back storage room where he slept. He checked out his Winchester rifle and his two Colt revolvers carefully, deciding that there would be no need to take the Sharps along. None had been fired for weeks, but he'd kept them clean, dry, and loaded. He found his badge, wrapped in a fold of cloth with the guns, and pinned it on.

Hattie had a bundle of food and a canteen of coffee ready for him when he came back out. He watched, amused and grateful, as she poured a generous measure of whiskey into the canteen before sealing it with a wooden stopper.

"To keep the chill out of your bones," she explained with a grin.

Dawn broke chilly and damp as they rode down a hillside trail into Split Creek Valley. Even under his slicker, Parkman's clothes were so wet that he felt like he was wrapped in washrags. A thick, damp fog lay on the land like cotton flocking, limiting visibility to a few yards ahead and behind. Patches of pine, fir, and birch were interspersed with sloping, green meadows, and there was no trail to speak of, although Werner seemed to know the way. Parkman imagined that it would probably be a pretty spot if he could see much of it.

"This is it," Helmut Werner said. "Skunk told some fellow that his camp was about two miles down below the rim into Split Creek Valley. But exactly where in here, I don't know."

"If he's here, we'll find him when the fog burns off," Parkman said. " 'Til then we need to be quiet. It'll be easier to take him if he doesn't know we've come looking for him."

The rain had stopped a couple of hours after they left Weatherby's, and the sky eventually cleared. Through the night they had made their way slowly southward, navigating cautiously by the stars and a quarter moon. Werner had bitched and carped for most of the ride, grumbling about how sleepy and hungry and miserable he was, vowing to take it all out on Skunk Murphy's stinking hide when they caught up to him.

When they came to a swift, swollen little creek, Split Creek, Parkman imagined, he stopped General Grant and eased carefully out of the saddle. His wounded leg was numb, and it nearly failed him when he tried to put his weight on it. Jolts of pain shot up from his knee to his groin like hot wires shoved up through his veins. He wished he had thought to bring his cane along.

Werner dismounted and turned away to take a nip from the flask he didn't think Parkman knew about. But that was okay. Parkman wouldn't have put that flask to his mouth if there was gold dust in it. He limped to the creek and took a drink upstream from where General Grant was drinking. He had to grab a stirrup to get back on his feet.

What the hell kind of way was this for a man to get around, he thought. It was a lucky thing they were only chasing after a drunk, lonely, dim-witted prospector instead of some truly dangerous scofflaw.

"You all right, Marshal?" Werner asked skeptically.

"Being gimpy doesn't affect my aim any," Parkman replied irritably. "I can do my job."

But there was a nagging doubt in Parkman's mind, a dread he was unaccustomed to experiencing when danger was near. He broke out the meat and bread Hattie had bundled up for him and gave Werner part of it.

"The way I see it," Parkman told the saloon keeper, "there's no use stumbling around in this fog. Murphy knows this valley better than we do, and even if we did luck onto his camp, he'd hear us coming and be ready. This fog should burn itself off in two or three hours, and then we'll have more choices."

"Suits me I s'pose," Werner grumbled. He stuffed the food into his mouth like a starving animal, then went on talking while he chewed. "But it grates my gizzard to sit and wait now that Skunk's probably gone to ground. Crazy as he is, he might start working Christabelle over, and I don't want that gal scarred up none. She's got the prettiest skin you ever saw, Marshal. Soft as peach fuzz, and pale as clouds. She makes me twice as much as that other one I got, Della."

"This ain't about protecting your investment, Werner. I need to tell you straight out, I've got no respect for a whoremonger. I'm with Hattie on that. You shouldn't be making them women do what they do."

Werner laughed out loud. "Hell, Marshal, I don't have to make them do nothin'. They both came to me saddle ready and liking it fine. I do believe some females are born to it."

Parkman decided to let the matter drop, although there was plenty more he felt like saying. There were men like Werner all over the frontier, all over the world, no doubt, who always found a way to make a dollar off another man's baser needs.

Werner spread his slicker by a tree and promptly fell asleep. Parkman hobbled around for a few minutes, trying to stretch the stiffness out of his leg, then spread his own slicker and settled down with his back against a tree to wipe down his weapons and check his loads. He didn't plan to go to sleep but soon began to nod off and on. Despite the sleepless night in the saddle, it seemed like his leg wouldn't allow him to get any real rest. At that moment, he felt like he hadn't made an inch of progress in healing, which only reinforced his decision to make big changes in his life.

He finally drifted off into a shallow, restless sleep, waking every few minutes to the throbbing drumbeat of pain. Nearby, Werner was snoring like a rooting hog.

The abrupt, unexpected yell of an aggravated woman in pain echoed toward Parkman and Werner through the fog, jolting both of them awake in an instant. It came from somewhere west of them, across the creek, and seemed unexpectedly close. "Durn your stinkin' hide, Skunk," a half-mad, half-scared woman exclaimed. "Don't you know a single thing about this sort of goings on? It hurts when you do that!"

"That's her. That's Christabelle!" Werner announced urgently.

Parkman raised his hand, fingers splayed, to shut Werner up, but it might already be too late. They rose and came together.

"What's over there?" he whispered, pointing across the creek.

"I ain't too sure in all this fog," the saloonkeeper admitted. "But if I remember right, it's probably a straight rock face, with jumbles of stones at the bottom. Must be where Skunk made his camp, where he took Christabelle. Come on, we got to get over there before he ruins her!"

Without waiting for Parkman, he turned and splashed into the knee-deep waters of the creek, his rifle in one hand. On the other side he plunged into the fog at a labored trot. Another mistake, Parkman knew.

Knowing he couldn't run like that, Parkman pulled himself up into the saddle, ignoring the jolt of pain that shot up from his leg. He pointed General Grant across the creek at a walk, Colt drawn, following the sound of Werner's huffing, stumbling, noisy progress through the fog. Soon he began to hear the woman again, not talking as loudly now, but still angry. A man's voice answered, quieter and more cautious.

Perhaps a minute passed, then a single shot sounded ahead, a rifle, probably Werner's. The echo rolled down the valley and died away. Then there was silence. Parkman tugged the reins slightly, slowing his horse even more.

As a clearing materialized ahead, it took Parkman a moment to piece together the scene before him.

The apparent target of their search, Skunk Murphy, was kneeling over Helmut Werner, trying to dislodge a sheath knife buried deep in the saloonkeeper's chest. It seemed stuck there, and each time he tugged at it, Werner, not yet dead, moaned and writhed in pain. A woman approached them cautiously, pulling her bodice together as she came. For the moment, neither of them seemed aware of Parkman's presence.

"Gawda'mighty, Skunk," the woman complained, still the shrew. "Now you've gone an' killed Helmut." Werner was indeed close to death. Blood flowed freely from the wound, and his movements had diminished to an occasional spasm.

"Didn't mean to," Skunk Murphy said. He spoke like a child in trouble. "But he come at me."

"Mean to or not, you've killed him all right. And now we got to get out of here in case he didn't come alone." Apparently familiar with her employer's person, Christabelle slid a hand inside Werner's jacket and drew out his wallet, then retrieved his watch from the fob pocket of his trousers.

"I guess it might be a little late for that," Parkman announced, thumbing back the hammer of his revolver.

Skunk Murphy and the woman looked up, both seeming more puzzled than surprised to see a mounted man sitting there with a gun in his hand. Slowly a look of recognition came into the woman's eyes.

"Say, you're that marshal fellow that's been staying up to Hattie O'Shea's," Christabelle said. Murphy looked stricken and afraid, his hand still gripping the knife stuck in Helmut Werner's chest.

Christabelle inclined her head toward the prospector and said something too low for Parkman to hear. It seemed to take Skunk Murphy a few seconds to absorb the words. Then suddenly he let go of the knife and moved his hand down beside Werner's body. When he raised the hand again, he held Werner's rifle.

"It's a fool's play, Murphy," Parkman warned him. "I've got you cold! Don't try it!"

But the end of the incident seemed preordained, perhaps by the words the woman had whispered to the prospector. Now the conclusion only needed to be acted out. Murphy swung the muzzle of the rifle around toward Parkman while his finger, still slippery with blood, fumbled to find the trigger guard.

In shoot-out terms, Parkman had plenty of time. His first bullet caught Murphy in the center of his chest, where long experience had taught him to instinctively aim, and the second went in high on the man's left cheek beside his nose. The dead man crumpled unceremoniously across his own victim.

Parkman's gaze met the woman's across the clearing. She appeared neither distraught nor afraid. She looked put-out at the inconvenient outcome.

"What in blazes did you say to him that made him do a fool thing like that?" Parkman demanded.

Christabelle slid sideways on the ground, away from the piled up dead men, and retrieved a ruffle of her skirt that was too near the growing pool of blood.

"I told him if you took him back to town, they'd hang him for killing Helmut," she said defiantly. "It's true, ain't it? You know it is."

"I've half a mind to go ahead and spend another bullet on you," Parkman said with disgust.

"You could do that, and nobody would know or prob'ly care," Christabelle reasoned, her tone softening, "or you could take me to that pile of blankets over yonder and . . ."

"Get yourself put together, woman," Parkman interrupted. "You're going to have to help me load these two bodies up so we can start for town."

CHAPTER NINE

Outside the small window in the storage room where he slept, the sky was pale blue and cloudless as Ridge Parkman swung his legs around and sat up on the edge of the cot. He stretched his right leg tentatively and tried to bend it, with little success. He massaged his wound and the muscles around it before trying to put his weight on it. The pain was more of a nagging ache this morning, an improvement from the shafts of fire shooting up through it yesterday after the long ride.

On the other side of the plank wall, Cyrus was clattering around in the kitchen preparing breakfast for the first of the early risers. The odor of biscuits, fried meat, and coffee encouraged Parkman to pull on his clothes and go out.

Hattie served him breakfast but had no time to sit and chat. After eating and enjoying a smoke with his second cup of coffee, Parkman went outside to get a look at the storm damage. Reluctantly he took his cane. The leg didn't seem any too reliable this morning, and he didn't want to suffer the embarrassment of having it go out from under him in public.

During the long ride back to town yesterday with the two bodies, Parkman had quickly grown to despise Christabelle, his traveling companion. Riding astraddle Skunk Murphy's sturdy mule, with him tied on behind, she whined and complained endlessly about Skunk's death, and all the other losing hands life had dealt her. Rather than kidnapping her, Murphy, it seems, had persuaded her to go with him by promising her a share of his latest gold strike. But if such a strike existed, Murphy ended up dead before he could share its location with her. She showed no remorse for the death of either man but was distraught that riches had seemed so near, and now she had to go back to the scarlet life.

When everything else failed, Parkman vowed to gag her if she didn't shut up. The world might have been better served, he thought, if Christabelle had gotten in front of one of the bullets that had been flying around back there in Split Creek Valley.

They parted wordlessly, and she headed for the room behind the saloon where she slept and conducted her business affairs. Parkman left General Grant at the livery, then led the horse and the mule, each bearing a corpse, down to Elliott Mayhune's carpenter shop. Mayhune kept a few simple pine coffins in the shed behind his shop for unexpected circumstances such as this and was, by default, the town's undertaker and grave digger.

Few of the buildings in Weatherby's Lode had escaped the storm's destructive passage. The bakery was little more than a pile of kindling, and a ramshackle plank building behind the livery barn, used as a two-bit flop house by miners and transients, had fallen flat like a house of cards. Other structures lost roofs, porches, windows, lean-tos, and so on.

But the townspeople would recover and rebuild. Little settlements like Weatherby's sprang up along the fringes of the frontier in remarkably short time. It couldn't be harder to rebuild the place than it had been to throw it together in the first place. All over town people were pulling nails, stacking lumber, and salvaging whatever soggy belongings they could pull from the wreckage.

He saw a wagon starting out from behind the carpenter's shop. The team pulling it consisted of Helmut Werner's horse and Skunk Murphy's sorry old pack mule. Apparently Mayhune figured they were his property now, and who was there to argue the point? Only Werner's women might try to take them, and they would be too busy claiming ownership of their dead boss's saloon to worry much about a horse and a mule.

Parkman followed the wagon as it started up the stony pathway to the cemetery south of town. By the time he got there, Mayhune and his nearly grown son had unloaded three coffins beside three open graves.

Parkman glanced down into the shallow graves, each no more than three feet deep.

"My boy Bob dug these this morning," Mayhune said. "Can't go too deep in this stony soil, but we try to plant 'em deep enough that they don't smell later."

"Who's in the third coffin?" Parkman asked.

"Blacksmith," Mayhune said.

"Jeremiah something?"

"Strong. Jeremiah Strong," the carpenter said. "Always seemed to me like a good name for a smithy."

"But he wasn't strong enough to keep that roof from squashing him flat," Mayhune's son offered up. "You shoulda seen him, marshal, when we was scooping him up to put him in the box."

"Mind your tongue, boy," Mayhune told his son sharply. The young man glanced at his father and Parkman, then ducked his head in embarrassment. "Jeremiah was our friend," the carpenter said, "and the town's going to miss having a good blacksmith around. Not like these other two," he added coldly. "I expect we'll get along fine without them."

"Which is which?" Parkman asked.

"That's Werner," Mayhune said, kicking the end of one coffin. "For my part, I always despised the man. He watered down his whiskey, he fleeced the drunks, and he treated them saloon girls like farm animals."

Parkman watched as father and son slid the other coffin,

presumably the one containing Skunk Murphy's remains, into one of the open graves. It landed on its side, and neither of them took the trouble to climb down in there and right it.

"I sure hated taking that man's life away from him," Parkman said. "He didn't seem like the sort that deserved it. He was all confused, an' that Christabelle convinced him to make a bad play."

"Didn't know the man," Mayhune said dryly. He and his son moved to the second coffin and put it in a grave, then the third. It was just another day's work to them.

Bob, the carpenter's son, took out a soiled handkerchief and wiped his forehead. "But ain't you a lawman?" he asked. "Surely you've drilled your share of men. Seems like one more wouldn't make no difference to you."

Parkman stared at the youth and said nothing. How could he communicate the fact that they all mattered, even when you had to do it?

The carpenter took a shovel and tossed a scoop of dirt into the nearest grave. Then he paused and put words to the knotty confusion Parkman felt in his chest.

"Sometimes life is cheap as dirt out here in the high country, son," he said. "But every life has a value. To our Lord in heaven, and especially to the man who loses it."

Picking his way down the stony hillside toward town, Parkman listened to the sound of dirt falling on the wooden coffins behind him. He thought there was no sound on earth quite so bleak and final as that one.

Killing had never been something he enjoyed, even when the need was clear and his choices were narrowed down to only that one. Some men he'd known did grow to like it, Alex Moody for instance, which Parkman thought spoiled him for the job he'd taken. But Parkman did kill when necessary, and, for whatever stupid reason, Murphy had left him no other choice.

So why this nagging regret, he wondered?

Maybe it was the look on Murphy's face that last instant before his death—simple, befuddled, desperate, and disbelieving. It would take a long time for that look to leave his memory.

He skirted wide around the spot where Herm Morgenstern was starting to reconstruct his privy, not wanting to make small talk or re-hash the shooting. He passed down an alley between two buildings and stopped when he got to the main street, wondering whether to head back toward Hattie's or give his leg a little more exercise.

"There you are, Marshal Parkman," a voice called out from one side. Parkman turned and saw a squat tumbleweed of a man approaching at a clumsy trot. It was Claude Bondoro, the telegraph operator.

"I was at the restaurant looking for you," Bondoro huffed. "You have another telegram from your captain over in Denver."

"Is that so?" Parkman said. "I figured that storm probably took the lines down."

"They usually do. But we got lucky this time." Bondoro handed the telegram to Parkman, and Parkman gave him ten cents for his trouble. He stuck the telegram in his vest pocket without looking at it.

"Ain't you going to read it?" Bondoro asked. "Might be something important." Of course, the little peckerwood knew exactly what was in it because he was the one who received it and wrote it down. In an hour or so, half the town would know its contents as well.

"I'll read it when I find the time," Parkman said casually to annoy the little bald man.

"Are you going out with the rest of them to look for the strike?" Bondoro asked, changing the subject. "Just because you're a lawman don't mean you wouldn't like to be rich."

"What strike are you talking about?" Parkman asked.

"Why, Skunk Murphy's strike, of course. The one he promised to share with Christabelle. Out there somewhere in Split Creek Valley. Word is it's a rich one. Big chunks of quartz laying around a' glittering with gold."

"That's a lot of hogwash," Parkman declared disgustedly. "I was right there in Skunk's camp, and I didn't see any quartz or gold or anything else. The only thing laying around that place was dead men."

"Well, you can't blame them for having a go at it," Bondoro reasoned. "Mite near every man in this town came west hoping to get rich. And now here they are working themselves half to death at one dull thing or another, like they did back in the states. We haven't had an outbreak of the gold fever in six or eight months now, and it kinda stirs a man's blood like the old days. I might even give it a shot myself if it wasn't for this cursed gout."

"I guess it doesn't hurt anybody. Maybe one of them will stumble on it," Parkman said, still skeptical.

"Sure, and if someone does, he'll have a bride waiting back here in Weatherby's. Christabelle swears she'll marry any man that finds Skunk's strike."

Parkman was chuckling to himself as he turned away and started up the street. He'd rather stay poor than hook up with that one.

The breakfast rush was nearly over by the time he got back to Hattie's Café. An old drunk miner, possibly still up from last night's bender, was asleep at a table, his face partially buried in a plate of steak and eggs. Two other men lingered over their coffee, talking big talk about the lumber business they planned to start.

Parkman sat in a corner by the serving counter and took out the telegram.

Before the storm and his unexpected trip to Split Creek Valley, he intended to send Captain Mullins a telegram of his own, explaining that his leg was slow in healing and that he had to turn down the assignment. Then he planned to follow up with a letter, explaining things in greater detail. Now that he had made up his mind to resign, it was only a matter of when and how.

But this new message from the captain sent his thinking down an unexpected fork in the trail. All his plans were thrown into the wind by what he read.

"What's the matter with you, cowboy?" Hattie asked as she came around the counter. He had grown accustomed to the nickname she gave him, although he'd never worked with cattle in his life. "You look like you swallowed a mouthful of coal oil."

"That might be better than having to deal with this," Parkman said. He handed her the telegram.

Hattie read the message, then looked back up at him, her face etched with concern. "This marshal who was killed. Ray Goode. That's the friend you talked about, wasn't it?"

"The same one," Parkman said dourly. The whole notion of attempting to accept his friend's death was like trying to swallow a rock. It went down hard and got stuck somewhere along the way. "We rode many a mile together," Parkman confirmed. "I guess if I ever had a best friend, he'd be the one."

"What about this other man, Duff Joseph? The one with the guns."

Even as she waited for him to answer, Hattie saw a hardness creep over Ridge Parkman's face. His eyes narrowed, and his lips tightened into a grim expression. The kind, easygoing, agreeable Ridge Parkman she planned to marry had withdrawn to some other place, and a hard, almost frightening, being replaced him. Finally, he answered her.

"Have you ever known someone, Hattie, that was so rotten, deep down in their soul rotten, that they scarcely deserved to be a part of the human race? Yep, I know Duff Joseph, all right.

Who would have thought that old bastard could live this long? But I reckon he lives still, and now he's killed another good man worth a hundred of his kind."

Hattie took one of Parkman's rough hands in both of hers. He accepted the affection with a tight, forced smile. She knew what this message meant.

"Years ago, Duff Joseph ran guns and whiskey into the badlands of west Texas and eastern New Mexico Territory." Parkman looked past her, out the front window, as he spoke.

"He sold his goods to outlaws, Comancheros, and every other kind of lowlife you can imagine. Even to the Comanches, when they had gold to pay. He liked to steal women, too . . . whores, saloon girls, and sometimes the wives and daughters of storekeepers and settlers. It never was pretty what happened to them.

"I rode into that wilderness half a dozen times trying to catch up with Joseph and his bunch. But he was crafty as a coyote, and he knew every rock and snake hole out in that wild patch of territory.

"Once we went in after him with five marshals, half a dozen rangers, and two sharpshooters the army loaned us. We were well mounted and supplied, and we had fresh information on his whereabouts. There was a feeling amongst us that this would be the time when old Duff Joseph finally got his.

"After three days, with us hard on his trail, he started leaving prisoners for us to find. Each one was half dead from hunger and thirst and hard treatment. And each time we had to make a decision. Do we risk them dying by taking them with us, or do we dilute our numbers by sending men to take those poor souls back out to safety?

"The first two captives we found were women, and we sent two men apiece out with them. Next was a little girl about ten, a scrawny, pathetic snippet of a thing that jumped like she was burned every time a man came near her. One of the rangers who was snake-bit, and his brother, who was also a ranger, knew the girl, and they took her back.

"That left only seven of us, and I s'pose Duff figured the numbers were even enough by then to stand and fight. He set up an ambush, but one of the soldiers sniffed it out so we didn't ride into the middle of it. We fought off and on for two days, sometimes with him on the run, and sometimes hunkered down behind rocks and trees whaling away at each other.

"By then we were out of food and water, nearly out of ammunition, and there was only four of us still alive. Or sort of alive. So, much as we hated to, we skedaddled. By the time we reached Yankee Wells, I hadn't known where or who I was for a night and a day. It was Ray Goode that tied me to my horse and got me out of that hellish place."

His story told, Parkman slumped back in his chair, feeling drained by the recollections. Hattie brought him a cup of coffee, then added a healthy slug of bourbon to it while he built a smoke. He lit the cigarette, took a drink of coffee, and smiled his crooked smile.

"I s'pose this changes everything, don't it?" he said. "All our plans."

"We'll make new plans when you get back," Hattie said.

"I won't lie to you and say I'm sure I can pull this off, Hattie. Something's gone out of me. I could feel it when we were out there looking for that crazy miner. I ain't the man I was back then, nor even the man I was when I last rode out of Denver with Ray."

"I don't know about that, because I didn't know you back then. I'm not sure I even know you that well now. But I do know you well enough to understand that you'll be leaving me now."

"I'd be no man at all if I didn't."

Chapter Ten

Late May was a fine time to ride through the high country of the northern Colorado Rockies. In the distance the Gore Range loomed, still capped with ice and snow in the upper reaches. In the lower elevations the spring thaw was well under way, and the headwaters of the Colorado River that Parkman was now trailing due west churned and tumbled on their steep downward path.

When he started at dawn that morning, General Grant had been rambunctious and hard to handle. The big, strong-willed roan wasn't used to so much time spent in corrals and barn stalls, and he seemed to hold it against Parkman in a personal way.

The other thing that was certain to bother the General was the pack mule that now trailed behind them. Parkman wasn't too fond of the notion himself, but the fact was that he had brought along too many supplies to tie across the rump of his saddle horse. Not knowing how long he'd be gone, he had stocked up particularly well on coffee and tobacco, which were not only necessities, but also helped a man make friends quickly on the trail.

After a tedious diet of dry hay for the past few weeks, General Grant was enthusiastic about the array of fresh grass and wildflowers in the meadows they passed. His tastes seemed to lean toward the columbine, bluebells, and honeysuckle, while leaving the milkweed, geraniums, and black-eyed Susans alone.

The mule appeared to be a little less particular and seemed willing to eat about anything that sprouted up out of the ground.

Parkman was glad to pause from time to time and let the horse enjoy his simple pleasures. After each hour or so in the saddle his leg would begin to ache and stiffen, and he didn't want to overdo it now, at the very start of what promised to be a long, difficult journey.

Based on the scant intelligence Captain Mullins provided, Duff Joseph left the vicinity of Salt Lake City ten days ago, heading northeast into Wyoming Territory. That made sense if he had guns and ammunition to sell and wasn't particular about whose hands they ended up in.

The various Indian tribes up north in Wyoming Territory, and farther up in Montana country, were stirring up as much mischief as they could manage as the encroachment of civilization pushed them farther and farther back from their ancestral lands. But to do that, or even to survive in the wild mountains and plains they still laid claim to, they needed rifles and powder and lead. Duff Joseph had made it his life's work to supply desperate men such as these with the killing tools they needed.

To reach Indian territory, Parkman figured Joseph was probably backtracking along the old Mormon Trail. The trail, which originated in Missouri, spanned Nebraska and Wyoming, and terminated in Utah, had fallen into relative disuse in recent years. The great Mormon migrations to their promised land, Utah, were nearly over, and much of the territory the trail traversed was no longer safe for civilian travelers.

But it would serve Duff Joseph's purpose nicely. The advantages of all those old westward trails were that they were passable by wagon, followed navigable routes through the mountains, and passed water sources often enough to keep people and animals alive.

Parkman knew almost nothing about this part of the country,

and nobody in Weatherby's Lode was much help. He did find an old curmudgeon who had been as far north as the Wind River Range with a party of prospectors, but he had trouble drawing any useful information out of the rusty bucket that the old frontiersman used for a brain. All the old guy wanted to talk about was the scrapes they had with the Indians, during which he apparently killed prodigious numbers of Sioux, Cheyenne, Utes, Apaches, Blackfeet, and any other tribes that came to mind.

That left Parkman doing what he had often done in the past in unfamiliar regions. He read the natural features of the land, navigated by the sun and the stars, and gathered what information he could from the occasional people he encountered.

Near the spot where Muddy Creek flowed into the Colorado, Parkman turned north. The Gore Range loomed forbiddingly to the west, while the broad valley to the north offered the prospect of easy riding, plenty of cold, clean water, and possibly an occasional rabbit or coon for the evening meal.

Within two days Parkman found a pass that allowed him to traverse the forbidding mountains to the west, and beyond lay open country with far more navigable hills and valleys. Much of the country was open and virgin, although signs of mankind were occasionally scattered about. He encountered a few travelers, some helpful and some not. A little shared tobacco tended to loosen most tongues, and he continued to gain a growing understanding of the country ahead.

The Double-W Ranch, a few miles south of the Snake River in northwest Colorado, looked more like an experiment in wilderness survival than it did a working cattle ranch. According to its owner, a weathered old relic named Hezekiah Wooten, it had been a hard winter, both for the cattle and for the five-man crew who tended them. Between the wolves and bears and the small marauding bands of half-starved Utes who called this country their own, his herd had actually diminished in numbers since October.

In that same time, he had lost one ranch hand to fever, another in a bear mauling, and two more had given up and struck out south. That left him only five hands, and two of them were getting up in years and probably only stuck around because they had no better prospects.

The Double-W headquarters consisted of an odd assortment of sod-roofed log buildings and ramshackle corrals. Parkman accepted the rancher's invitation to supper, and soon after his arrival he had joined the crew at an outdoor table. The cook served up a thick beef stew with red beans, wild onions, and some kind of salty, bitter greens that Parkman took to be dandelions. The biscuits were hard enough to drive nails with, but softened in the thick broth of the stew.

Wooten and his crew were starved for news from the outside, and Parkman obliged them as best he could. Colorado Territory had ratified a constitution, and there was talk of statehood this year or the next. Women had won the right to vote in a couple of states. Ulysses Grant was still the president. Denver was turning into a railroad hub, and there was talk that gas lamps would soon be installed on some of the streets. Up north in Montana and Wyoming, the Sioux, Cheyenne, and some of the other tribes were refusing to go back on their reservations after suffering through a harsh, humiliating winter of starvation, abuse, and disease. The U.S. Army was going in to convince them otherwise.

"Can't say I blame them Indians any," one of the older hands named Paul Reeder said. "I seen one of those reservations once when I was scouting for the army, and it was pretty bad." He had rolled himself a smoke from the tobacco Parkman broke out and was savoring it like a fine cigar.

"The people lived in little stick and mud houses, and most of them were skinny as lodge poles. Hardly any of the beef and supplies the gov'ment promised ever got to them. They were sick with every kind of disease you could name, and oftentimes they died from something that wouldn't be no more than a nuisance to a white man. I guess if somebody made me live like that, I wouldn't see that I had much to lose by hightailing it neither."

"But the gov'ment ain't gonna let them go back to their old hunting grounds," Wooten pointed out. "Right or no, there's too much gold in them mountains, and too many white men ready to stampede in there once the red men get run out."

"Or wiped out," another of the hands, a lean, sallow-faced youth named Lem Grubb, added grimly.

"Well, maybe they wouldn't get themselves wiped out if they'd settle down and live like normal folks does," chimed in a cowboy that the others called Spud. Parkman easily recognized the twangy drawl of a northern Arkansas man. Back during the war, they were known as some of the most resilient, relentless fighters for the Southern cause, although few had any real understanding what started the war or what was at stake.

"I been around Injuns all my life," Reeder said, "and I can tell you, it ain't in their nature to settle in one place."

"The Cherokees done it in Tennessee," Spud said, "and the Creeks in Mis'sippi an' Alabamie done it, too. When they seen it waren't no use fightin' no more, they tamed down an' took to the plow. Some of 'em even owned slaves back before the Rebellion."

"But the government gave them land worth farming, and they had more time to get used to the new way of things," Reeder said. "Hell, twenty-five years ago these red men laid claim to about everything west of Missouri, and the buffalo herds was so big they'd run past a man for half a day with no end in sight." He paused and chuckled to himself, then explained, "I was trying to picture a wild, proud, scalp-taking widow-maker like Red Cloud following a mule's backside across fresh broke ground." He laughed again, and the others laughed with him, even Spud.

"I've heard of Red Cloud," Parkman said. "He's a Sioux chief, isn't he?"

"One of 'em," Reeder confirmed. "He's a war chief of the Oglala Sioux. But there's other chiefs that have strong medicine, too. There's Crazy Horse with the Lakota, and Red Sleeve and Little Wolf with the Cheyenne. And then of course there's wily old Rides Between the Clouds, who's lived through many a fight and prob'ly took more scalps that his lodge pole could hold."

"Sounds like a bloodthirsty bunch."

"Might be you'll find that out firsthand, Marshal," Hezekiah Wooten commented dryly, "if you're still of a mind to ride up into those parts."

Eventually the ranch hands wandered off to the bunkhouse. Parkman and Wooten made their way to Wooten's cabin, where Parkman was invited to sleep that night.

Fumbling around inside the pitch dark but familiar cabin, Wooten lit a small fire in the stone fireplace. Even in late spring, the mountain air was chilly enough to make the blaze welcome. Producing a small flask, Parkman poured a finger of whiskey for each of them into metal cups.

"What can you tell me about the Mormon Trail?" Parkman asked his host. "If I ride due north, will I recognize it when I come to it?"

"I'd say so," Wooten said, tasting the whiskey and smiling his approval. "In a lot of places, you can still see the ruts the wagons wore down in the hardpan, and there's other signs as well. Worn out wagons and burned ones, busted wheels, ruined barrels, and old furniture—all the things you'd expect folks to cast off because they was busted up, or used up, or because the load needed lightening. And there's graves, too. Plenty of those."

"What about Fort Bridger? Is it still there?"

"It was the last time I heard," Wooten confirmed. "The Mormons burned it to the ground a few years back when they was trying to set up their own country, or some nonsense like that. But the army rebuilt it and has a garrison there still. A small one, though, so I heard."

Fort Bridger was located in the southwestern corner of Wyoming, and Parkman had vague hopes that the garrison there might help in his pursuit of Duff Joseph. But Wooten's next statement doused that expectation.

"A company of surveyors that passed through these parts last fall before the snow set in said there wasn't but a handful of troops at Fort Bridger, an' most of them green recruits. Hardly enough to take on a good-sized Sioux hunting party."

So, there would be no help from the army for his reckless escapade, Parkman thought grimly.

Wooten slept in a brass bed in a small back room of the cabin. Parkman spread his blankets on the dirt floor in front of the fireplace and was out before the crackling flames died down to embers.

He was back on the trail at daybreak, carrying a flour sack of dried beef jerky and a couple of enormous fresh steaks. In return he left behind a little coffee and some tobacco. Luxuries were scarce out here at the edge of nowhere, which made them all the more enjoyable when they came a man's way.

CHAPTER ELEVEN

Parkman found a narrow twisting pass to get beyond a line of forested hills that from a distance appeared impassible. Riding around them would have taken a day or more, and he was eager to continue his due north course, believing he would intersect the Mormon Trail any day now. At the north end of the pass he followed a game trail that led toward a broad, lush valley below.

This could be it, he thought. The Mormon Trail would follow a general east-to-west direction and would have to be passable to the heavy Conestoga, freight, and prairie schooner wagons that used this route. The valley ahead filled the bill in all particulars.

The afternoon sun was low near the western horizon, and his leg was beginning to telegraph to his brain that it was long past time to stop. As soon as he could find clean water, a little dry wood, and a patch of grass for General Grant and the mule, he resolved to make his camp. Supper that night would be a pheasant he'd killed that afternoon with a snap shot that he wished someone had been around to witness.

Off to the left a few hundred yards from the trail, he noticed that buzzards were riding the wind currents in slow circles no more than fifty feet above the ground. He paused for a moment, noting their slow spiraling descent, then pointed General Grant in that direction.

As he neared the horse carcass that would soon become a feast for the ugly, black, crook-necked scavengers, he fired a shot and yelled out to scare the few that had landed already, or at least force them to retreat a few yards.

The dead horse was a lanky gray bag of bones with a saddle, bridle, and bedroll still strapped to him. When the horse went down either the rider was too hurt himself, or in too big a hurry, to retrieve his gear from the animal.

Scouting the area, Parkman soon found the answer. The man lay face down and still in a small depression a few feet past the dead horse. His body and limbs were twisted in grotesque and unnatural directions. He had a ragged, ugly wound low on one side that had soaked his clothes and the ground around him with blood. The blood was a muddy, reddish brown, some of it nearly dried. It was a wonder that the buzzards hadn't already gone to work on him.

Parkman realized he had a grave to dig. It would be rough going in this stony soil, but he had always felt like most men and a few good horses deserved a decent burial when it was possible.

He found a sturdy stick about the thickness of his wrist and began gouging and scraping at the soil. It was sandy and not as hard going as he expected. With any luck he could get this fellow planted and still have a little daylight left to find a decent camp site away from this carnage.

A raspy moan issued unexpectedly from the man Parkman was about to bury. It startled him, and he stumbled back, then tripped and sat down hard on the ground, revolver in hand.

"Is somebody here?"

Hearing words from that damaged, twisted, motionless body was downright eerie. Parkman hadn't actually checked earlier to see if the man was still alive, because he looked so damned dead.

"Yup, I'm here. Name's Ridge."

"I'd be much obliged for some water," the voice rasped. "I'm parched."

Parkman fetched his canteen, then knelt and touched the man's shoulder tentatively. "It might hurt when I turn you over," he said. "You're shot in the side."

"Go ahead," the man said. "I don't feel nothing anywhere. But I sure need a swallow of something wet."

Rolling the man over was like turning over a sack of wet grain. He didn't move a muscle, didn't wince or groan. Parkman had a pretty good idea what that meant. He raised the man's head and poured some water into his mouth. Relief seemed to flood his dusty face, and Parkman gave him another, longer drink.

"Looks to me like your neck's broke, mister," Parkman said, not knowing how to temper the bad news. "I took you for dead when I rode up. I was digging your grave when you spoke up."

"Guess you can keep digging. Seems like I'll be needing that grave soon enough." The skin of his face was tough and brown like old leather, and his thick mop of hair was streaked with gray. His eyes shifted to the canteen, and Parkman gave him more water.

"So, what happened here?" Parkman asked.

"I don't rightly recall," the man admitted.

"Your horse might have throwed you and broke your neck. But that don't explain that bullet hole in your side, nor why the horse is dead, too."

"Probably them teamsters shot him, and he throwed me as he fell dead. Must have shot me, too. I knew I should've stayed clear of that bunch. But I smelled coffee, and meat cooking, so I hailed their camp, and they waved me in."

"What about these teamsters?" Parkman asked.

"Four big freight wagons, loaded down, and maybe two dozen outriders. Pretty big party for so few wagons, I thought."

Alarm bells clanged in Parkman's head.

"While I was drinking my coffee an' eating a plate of meat an' beans," the man went on, "one of them fellers laid back a corner of canvas on a wagon. I saw some crates with "U.S Army" stenciled on them. I axed if they was hauling guns to Fort Bridger, an' they said yes they was.

"But then I figgered out that warn't so, because them wagons was pointed east, and Fort Bridger was maybe forty miles west along the Mormon Trail."

So, the Mormon trail was nearby, Parkman noted.

"I got on my horse and lit out of there soon as I could, but I guess they came along behind and put us down, me and old Plug. That's the part I don't recollect so well."

Over the next hour as darkness fell, Parkman made camp and did what little he could for the injured man. He gave him all the water he wanted, and even managed to get a few scraps of biscuit into him. He built a small fire and covered the man with a blanket, although the poor fellow was clearly beyond feeling the nighttime chill.

The boss of the freight wagons, Parkman learned, was an old man, stoop shouldered and evil eyed, with dark skin like an Indian or a Mexican. That could easily describe Duff Joseph, who was thought to be the offspring of an enslaved Yaqui woman and a white Texican preacher turned highwayman and scalp hunter.

It pleased Parkman to realize that fortune might have put him so close on the trail of the bunch he was after, although it sure was hard luck for the man who delivered the news.

Late at night Amos Pruett's breathing became a harsh rasp, and he started fading in and out of consciousness. Sometimes he spoke to Parkman as if Parkman were his wife, Lena, instructing her to sell the milk cow if she needed money, and advising her to bar the door and keep the shotgun handy at night.

At other times Parkman became Pruett's son Abe, whom the dying man had apparently come north from Colorado to find. "Son, there warn't no need to run off like that and join up with no army," Pruett advised at one point. "Murder or no, we could've hid you out 'til the trouble blew past."

During a lucid moment, Pruett asked Parkman if he would end it for him, and Parkman promised he would if it still needed doing by morning. But sometime in the night Parkman woke and realized that Amos Pruett's labored breathing had stilled.

It was a relief to the marshal. He hadn't looked forward to the promise he might have had to keep in the morning.

CHAPTER TWELVE

Early the next afternoon he found what he took to be the Mormon Trail. Despite years of disuse, the deep, hard-packed wagon ruts were still easy to spot, and the hardy prairie grasses had yet to obliterate the evidence of countless westbound wagons heading to the vast American promised land.

Ongoing Indian uprisings had made the trail too dangerous for any but the most heavily armed expeditions. Even bands of prospectors and fortune hunters could no longer make the trip through Indian country with impunity, and tales of bloody massacres were common.

Military outposts were too scattered and understaffed to provide even a semblance of security. Seldom did garrisons like the one at Fort Bridger venture more than a few dozen miles from the safety of their stone walls and fortified log strongholds. Only bands like the one led by Duff Joseph stood any chance of crossing this country safely. Word had undoubtedly spread that he was abetting the Indian cause, and orders from the war chiefs had probably gone out to let him pass unmolested.

Out in the open, in the trough of a long valley through which the trail coursed, Parkman felt as vulnerable as a rabbit. Even a small band of warriors could easily run him down and kill him.

But he figured his skills and good sense might improve his chances. After all, this was far from the first time he found himself riding down dangerous trails, and even Duff Joseph himself had led him into hostile territory before. Sometimes it was easier for a single man to navigate through situations like this than it was for a larger, well-armed band.

He would stick to the cover of the trees and rocks along the mountainsides as much as possible. If he could spot his adversaries in the valley floor before they saw him, it would give him valuable time to hide or run or fort up, whatever the situation seemed to require.

After his stop at the Double-W Ranch, he never gave serious consideration to seeking help at Fort Bridger. Riding there and back would cost him two or three precious days, and the chances were slim that the commander there would commit a substantial portion of his garrison to a risky expedition into the wild country.

He was on his own with this one, and only cunning and caution would get him through it. If he did happen to encounter troops in the field, they might be willing to go after Joseph. But rumor had it that most of the larger commands were on the move far to the north and east, in Big Horn Mountain country.

Before burying Amos Pruett that morning, the only things he had taken from the dead man were a battered revolver and a heavy wool blanket. His old rifle looked too unreliable. The night before, Parkman had promised to notify Pruett's wife of her husband's death if he ever had the chance, although he couldn't imagine when he might pass through the prairie lands of western Kansas again.

His skills at reading trail sign were not the best, but he estimated that Duff Joseph's wagons probably had a two-day lead. That was not a problem unless Joseph was near his destination. Despite the pain and stiffness in Parkman's leg when he stayed too long in the saddle, he resolved to ride long hours until he caught up with the wagons, then plan from there. He had brought along a few little homemade surprises for Joseph, if he could get close enough to use them.

The south Wyoming country he was riding through was so enormous, so lush, and so desolate that it was sometimes hard to understand why the westering American settlers and the native Indians, who could lay claim to being the first Americans, fought so furiously to deny each other the right to live and prosper here.

But as nomadic hunters, the Indians needed vast amounts of land to maintain their way of life. They probably had no concept of the uncountable numbers of people far to the east who were ready to rush to the frontier seeking new opportunity and new beginnings. But they had learned that wherever a white man stopped to dig a prospector's hole, or break the virgin soil with a plow, or raise a cabin, or graze his cattle, more always came soon after.

Ridge Parkman spotted his first small Indian band a couple of days later. It was only a man and a half-grown boy, both mounted on lean, compact Indian ponies, followed by three women walking along a few dozen strides behind. One of the women led a horse, which pulled a travois piled high with their belongings. Both the man and the boy were armed with bows, and the man carried a lance as well. A considerable expanse separated them, but Parkman saw no evidence of firearms.

Parkman remained in the edge of the tree line until the party moved out of sight. Then he continued his eastward progress through the trees another few hours until full darkness arrived. By the light of the moon, he dropped down into the trough of the valley and scouted around until he found the trail again.

Even in the pale moonlight he could make out the clear sign of Duff Joseph's passage—the wagon tracks and hoofprints of many horses. It was encouraging to know that he was still on their trail, but their numbers were daunting.

Retreating back up into the trees, he made a cold camp that night, dining from the bag of jerked beef that Hezekiah Wooten had provided him days before. He felt pretty ragged. By the time he spread his blankets to lay down, his bad leg was giving him so much trouble that he broke out the whiskey and took a couple of long slugs. He slept that night with the leg parked on his saddle. Sometimes that helped.

The next day, after several hours of steady riding, the countryside started to flatten, and the patches of trees began to diminish. Riding out in the open was not to his liking, but he had to take the chance. He was unwilling to give up the progress he had already made toward actually catching up to his old adversary and his friend's murderer.

That afternoon, still riding due east, parallel to the Mormon Trail, Parkman was surprised to find evidence that Joseph's band had left the trail and was now moving north toward a forbidding mountain range in the distance. It didn't make any sense, but the signs were clear. He pushed on north with renewed determination but still hadn't come in sight of them as darkness fell.

That night he camped once again in the pitch darkness, without even a cup of coffee to blunt the nighttime chill. Lying on the ground with his slicker under him and his blanket pulled up, he tried to make up his mind about exactly how crazy this escapade actually was. Despite the deceptive barrenness of this country, there was danger all around, from red men and white, as well as from the variety of wild animals that roamed free hereabouts. Even the treacherous terrain offered up its own dangers. He had been fortunate until now, but how long could he count on that luck holding out? Another day? Another hour?

General Grant huffed in the darkness a few feet away where Parkman had hobbled him and the mule so they could graze while he rested. But it was an ordinary snort, not a sound of alarm. All was well, at least for now.

★ ★ ★ ★ ★

The cabin was nestled in a small grove of trees tight against a rock wall that would provide it with protection from the harsh winter winds that raked these parts. Ridge Parkman would not have even noticed it if the wagon tracks he was following had not led him right to the open front door. There was abundant sign that Joseph's party had spent at least one night here. The ashes of several small fires cluttered the open area outside the cabin, and empty food tins and whiskey bottles were strewn about haphazardly. The leftover carcass of a butchered elk hung from a tree branch, black with flies.

Pausing out front to take in the surrounding territory, he had to admire the spacious view of the sweeping, open valley below. Whoever had chosen this spot to make their home must not have selected it only for its inconspicuous and sheltered location, but also because of the sprawling panorama that surrounded it. Pines and birch trees had grown up close around the cabin, and the sheer cliff behind would provide some buffer from the worst of the windy winter storms.

The cabin was about ten by sixteen, with a steep roof to shed the snow and a crude stone chimney at one end. Once it was probably sturdy and tight, but decay and the elements had done their work. The roof sagged ominously, and much of the mud chinking between the logs was gone. The chimney looked like it might fall away into a long jumble of useless stone any day now, and even the logs themselves showed signs of softening and rot.

At first the place seemed abandoned, but on inspection there were signs to the contrary. A fresh raccoon skin, stretched tight on a wooden frame, hung on the front wall. The odor of wood smoke and cooked meat drifted out of the front door. On a crate beside a hand-made chair on the front porch sat a battered tin cup with coffee stains, or at least some frontier equivalent, in the bottom. A large brown stain on the porch beside the chair indicated that spittle from many a chaw had landed there.

Mostly to satisfy his own curiosity, Parkman drew his revolver and stepped inside. He found about what he expected—a crude cot, a small table, another chair, a cook pot, a water bucket, and all the random tools and implements it took to maintain a simple frontier lifestyle. The stale air in the cabin was stifling, a mixture of more unpleasant odors than he chose to consider. What he didn't see inside was any sign of food. Joseph and his bunch had probably taken care of that.

An unexpected bullet whacked into the door frame as Parkman was starting back out, and the noise of the distant shot reached his ears. It sounded like a long gun. He dodged back into the dim interior of the cabin and peered in the direction of the shot, trying to spot some movement. There were no windows, and he saw nothing through the open doorway.

Long minutes passed. Unable to spot the shooter, he had no choice but to wait and wonder. The cabin had a small back door, which he figured led to a privy close by, but who was to say another gunman wasn't waiting out there. It was an old trick.

Finally, a voice called out, seeming closer than the shot had been.

"That ball could just as easy have hit your gut instead of the wall by your head. I'm a sharpshootin' son-of-a-bitch when the situation calls for it."

"I don't doubt it. But why shoot at all?" Parkman yelled back.

"You ain't gettin' that horse," the voice announced. "Even if you was to get me, he's hid so far back in the canyons you'd never find him."

"I don't know what horse you're talking about," Parkman insisted. "I got my own saddle horse and pack mule out front, as you can see, and that's plenty for me."

"You're so full of bear hockey I can smell it clean out here," the voice complained. Then, for emphasis, another bullet came singing into the cabin. It ricocheted off the stone face of the fireplace and embedded in the cabin's back wall. Parkman tipped the table over and hunkered down behind it. The shooter might not be able to see inside, but he might still get lucky with a random shot.

"I knowed one or two of you was likely to double back. I seen you riding up the valley, and I been out here waitin' for you."

"Who do you think I am?"

"One of them, come back to take my horse and finish me off."

"No, you've got it wrong. My name's Parkman, from down Colorado way, and I'm travelling alone. Have been for nearly three weeks now." He started to add that he was a United States marshal on official government business, but he wasn't sure enough of his audience to make that announcement yet.

"If that's true, then come on out an' show me some proof," the voice ordered. "I won't shoot you 'less you provoke me."

Parkman weighed his options. He could go out the back door, but because of how the cabin was situation, that would only mean that he would be trapped behind the cabin instead of in it. And there was still that second-man thing to worry about.

"Come on out, I say," the voice repeated.

"No, I guess not. I don't trust you any more than you trust me."

"Well hell! What do we do now?"

"Beats me."

For the next few minutes the only sounds Parkman could hear outside were the breeze blowing through the birch trees, and an occasional snort from General Grant, who was grazing unconcerned outside the cabin. The mule brayed out once, irritated that he was tied to a branch and couldn't reach the eats. Parkman built a smoke, lit it, and waited.

The next time the man spoke his voice was much closer, right outside the cabin in fact. "Look here, mister . . . What did you say your name was?"

"Parkman."

"Look here, Parkman, I'm only a gimpy old man living out my time in this little log house. I probably ain't got no more than a couple of cold North Rocky winters left in me, but that don't mean I'm in any danged hurry to head on upstairs."

"I swear I've got no plans to bring that day any closer for you. But you're the one doing all the shooting."

"All right then, I'll be coming on up now. You meet me outside, and we'll see what happens."

The old man that Ridge Parkman saw approaching from the trees was about what he had expected. Dressed head to foot in animal skins and carrying an ancient Hawken, he was a living relic of decades past when men like him had plunged westward beyond civilization in search of furs, freedom, and untamed places that no white man had ever laid eyes on before.

The old mountain man managed to display a smile underneath his wooly thatch of gray whiskers, and he reached out a hand for a shake. Parkman thought it was something like shaking a grizzly's paw might be. The same roughness, and the same power.

"Name's Samuel Lyons," he said, parking himself on the porch boards beside Parkman with a satisfied grunt. "I'm pleased to make your acquaintance. The Crows called me Skunk Hunter for reasons I do not care to discuss, and the Sioux burdened me with Woman Beater because of the shrewish squaw I chose to share my blanket with for a spell. But when I give up living with the tribes, I went back to plain old Sam again."

"You can call me Ridge, or Marshal Parkman if you'd rather. Fact is, I'm on the trail of that bunch that passed by this way a few days ago."

"A marshal, huh?" Sam said, eyeing him skeptically. "So, where's your badge, boy?"

"In my kit someplace. It makes too good a target sometimes."

"We're all targets out here in the high country, son," Sam said with a chuckle. "Eat or be et. Just meat a'walking."

"So how long have you lived out here alone like this, Sam?"

"Don't know for sure. The seasons come and go. I built this cabin myself awhile back, and you can see what shape it's in now. But it should last me on out, and if someday a blizzard brings the whole thing down on top of me, well, there's worse ways to go."

As he talked, Sam raised up his powder horn, drew out his ramrod and bag of shot, and started reloading his old gun. It reminded Parkman of the ancient long gun that his grandfather had brought west with him from Virginia to Missouri. He couldn't even begin to imagine how much blood it must have spilled.

"So, you're figuring to taking on that whole bunch by yourself, huh?" Sam said with a chuckle. "Sounds a mite optimistic to me, son."

Parkman grinned at him sheepishly. "I can't say I've got that part quite figured out yet. But I was the only law man close enough to have a chance at catching up with them. Or at least the only one crazy enough to try."

"Well, there's times that a man alone can do the most harm," Sam conceded. "Back in the forties, a bunch of no-goods caught me unawares and stole my whole winter's take of hides. They thought they killed me, but they hadn't, and I lit out after them soon as I was able. Every time I got my hands on one, I left him like the Sioux would, not quite dead but wishing he was. By the

118

time I caught up with the last one, over toward the Yellowstone, he blew his own brains out with his last load, as a smart man might before the Injuns got holt of him." He paused and leaned his musket against a porch rail, then concluded his message. "But there was only five of them, and the bunch you're after is more like five times five at least. And bad men, too. They shot down Jackson, my mule and my good friend, just for sport."

"That's a shameful thing, but about what I'd expect," Parkman said. "They killed a friend of mine, too, Ray Goode, a man I rode many a mile with, and owed my life to more than once. I didn't know there was quite that many when I started out, but that doesn't change anything. Mostly I'd like to get my hands on their leader, a worthless heap of steaming manure named Duff Joseph. I'd like to haul him back to the nearest fort and let the army hang him."

"They told me they was prospectors, headed over Bozeman way. But it was clear enough that they was lying."

"So you didn't see what they were hauling in the wagons?"

"Nope, they was only here one night. As soon as I had a chance, I grabbed my gun and horn, slung a rope over my horse's neck, and slipped off."

"They're hauling a load of army rifles and ammunition to sell to the Indians. Spencer carbines, I figure, or maybe Winchesters."

"Probably looking to hook up with the Sioux or Cheyenne up northeast of here," Sam speculated. "And that ain't good news. Not after all the goin's on over at Fort Phil Kearney. That's been their tribal lands for as far back as their legends go, and they won't give them up easily."

"Well, that's too big a problem for a fellow like me to sort out," Parkman said. "But I will stop Joseph if I can."

That evening Parkman shared his stores of food and tobacco with the old man and reluctantly let him polish off half a bottle of the whiskey he had brought along. He could hardly do otherwise when he learned that old Sam's last visitors had stripped his larder clean.

They talked until well into the night over a campfire that Sam Lyons built in front of his cabin. Parkman relished the yarns the old man spun, set against the backdrop of how this big-sky country must have been decades before the westward flood of miners, settlers, and soldiers began to engulf it.

Despite his solitude, the old man was also surprisingly current on his gossip, and Parkman could sense his conflicting loyalties to the red men and the white.

"I guess it ain't really a matter of who's right and who's wrong," Sam said. "A man could argue either side. But when you cut right down to the quick, it's all as simple as skillet-bread. What's gonna happen will happen."

Despite the nearness of the cabin, Parkman chose to make his bed outside, leery of the stench and parasites of the cabin's interior, as well as the old man's inevitable snoring. By the time he roused an hour or so after dawn, Old Sam had already gone out and retrieved his horse from whatever hiding place he had taken him to.

"I figure to go along with you for a spell, if you'll have me," Sam announced. "I know the country east of here like I know the lines on my hand, and I might be of some use to you. My bones could use a good stretch, and killing old Jackson for no good reason is something I don't choose to abide."

CHAPTER THIRTEEN

"Don't you ever get lonesome living out here like you do?" Parkman asked. "I'm a solitary sort of man myself, but after a while, I sure do get sick of trying to stir up a conversation with my horse."

"You get used to it," Sam said. "The worst times are the winters, when you might go days, sometime weeks, at a time and never set foot out the door, except maybe to dig the snow away and let some breathing air in. I've heard of men going pure loco holed up through the winter like that. But I guess it's about like anyplace else you can think of. The strong ones and the clever ones, and sometimes only the lucky ones, make it on through. The Good Lord sorts the whole thing out when the time comes."

They had veered off Duff Joseph's trail not long after leaving the cabin that morning. All day they had navigated a vague and rocky track partway up a low mountain range that ran parallel to the valley Joseph had no doubt traversed with his wagons. Sam Lyons had explained that this difficult but straighter trail should allow them to gain some distance on a string of wagons that, by necessity, must follow the twists and bends of the long valley below. He also pointed out that a cunning old devil like Joseph would probably have outriders ahead and behind his main band. Parkman knew that to be likely from previous experiences with Joseph down in west Texas and the wild territories beyond. For a fact, Duff Joseph was a shrewd old buzzard and never to be taken for granted. Being so clever and unpredictable was one of the things that had kept him alive for so long. Sheer brutality was another.

Now, in their humble camp high up on the side of the mountain, the two men had spread their blankets in a small, somewhat flat clearing behind a cluster of boulders. They did not risk a fire, not knowing how far away it might be seen, so there was no evening coffee after they ate. Sitting with his back against a wall of stone, Parkman figured that now he was in for another string of frontier stories from Sam Lyon's seemingly infinite library of adventures. But instead the old man seemed to have spent some time thinking about the work at hand instead.

"Judging by their willingness to head straight into lands the Indians claim and protect," Sam said, "I figure they must have some sort of rendezvous already set up, or at least have some half-breeds along who can ride ahead and announce their coming.

"This here's Cheyenne territory we're in right now, and the Sioux lands are farther off to the east," he went on. "But since the army has started pushing them back and back and back, farther west and north, those two tribes have gone on the warpath together to fight for what lands they're still holding onto."

"What about the Crows?" Parkman asked. "Down below, you always hear about them having their own lands somewhere up this way."

"They're farther to the west, and they've never joined up with the Sioux and the Cheyenne. The Crows and the Sioux, especially, are ancient enemies, always raiding and killing each other as far back as their tribal legends go. If you look at any Sioux warrior's battle lance, it's likely you'll find Crow scalps on it. And lately the Crows have thrown in more and more with the army to help them whip the Sioux and the Cheyenne. Besides, the white army scouts like Bowie and Cody, you're likely to find Crows in any scouting party, and they charge right in with the white men when there's a battle shaping up."

"Well, if Joseph is heading for a rendezvous with the Indians, how does he expect the Indians to pay for the rifles and ammunition he's delivering? They must be expecting something better than buffalo hides for their trouble."

"Gold is what they're after," Lyons explained simply. "The Indians in these parts don't place no value in the stuff themselves, and it would never occur to a Sioux or Cheyenne warrior to dig in the ground for it. But they have learned how much the white man cherishes it, and they know that it's powerful goods to have on hand when the trading starts. So, they take it from the prospectors and miners up this way.

"There's always enough damn fools willing to ignore the warnings and orders of the army and risk it all to fill their pouches with nuggets and dust. It's like the siren's song I used to read about when I was a boy back in Pennsylvania. Once a man's heard that singing, he gets all tangled up in it, and nothing else seems to matter, not even his own life. It's that way over around the Bozeman Trail and parts west of there where there's colors in every pan. Or so folks say."

"It's the same down in Colorado," Parkman said. "But you can add silver to the mix down there. And women," he added thinking about Skunk Murphy's ridiculous, needless death in the valley down the mountainside below Weatherby's Lode.

The two men could see their own breath as they rolled out of their blankets the next morning, both feeling stiff and creaky in this fresh, crisp mountain air. They risked a small fire so they could start the day out with coffee, following up with jerky and leftover biscuits from the day before.

The trail began rising once more, in places so perilous that they had to dismount and lead their animals past the worst patches. At the start of their journey, Parkman had worried that the ancient old frontiersman would be so aged and rickety that he would slow their progress. But when they were afoot, they made a matched team. His wound was acting up on him today, and if he had been a less prideful man, he probably would have worked in some stops along the way to give his leg some relief. But he thought that if he couldn't keep up with a grizzled old man nearly twice his age, maybe it was time to fold and leave the game.

"For a time, I used to trap in these parts, over on the other side of this range, and on north of there," Sam said. "That was back in the days when there was still trapping to be done, and stuff-shirt Yankees and Englishmen still had a liking for their beaver skin hats." He chuckled, and then added, "I never even saw one of them hats, but I always imagined them looking showy and silly on top of a city man's head.

"The Crow and the Sioux fought some hair-raising battles in these valleys and hills for as far back as any of their legends went. Back then they fought with flint-head arrows, and lances, and clubs."

"I wonder how long they've been here, and where they came from in the first place?"

"Who knows where any of us came from, boy? The tribes have their first-man legends same as we do, but I never put much stock in all of that, red or white. Maybe I'm made different, but it never seemed to matter that much to me."

As the trail continued to twist and rise toward the higher elevations, they had a better view of the long valley in the distance. It was at least three miles away, Parkman figured, still close enough to make out a string of wagons and horsemen if he saw one. But there wasn't much to see down there, except an occasional small herd of buffalo, or a few deer straying out into the open to graze and drink from the stream that wound through the valley.

Sam seemed to read his thoughts. "This trail we're following will keep veering off to the north and won't be much use to us pretty soon. Might be we should cut down to the valley and make sure we're still headed in the right direction. There's a range of mountains at the upper end of the valley and only one pass that a man could even think of moving through with wagons."

"But if he doesn't know this country that well, he might have turned away into another one of these canyons instead," Parkman said. "I'm with you. Let's go down and scout around until we cut wagon tracks. This is the closest I've been to Joseph since back on the Mormon Trail, and I don't want to lose him now. Besides, we need water."

Sam found a winding track down the mountainside, more suited to mountain goats than men and horses, Parkman thought, but eventually they managed to make it down into the rolling foothills that fringed the valley. After a couple of hours of more comfortable riding, they found what they were looking for. The wagon tracks and hoofprints had been made since the last rain, which meant they had passed through here less than two days before, according to Sam Lyons.

It was only another short ride to the broad, shallow stream that snaked through the valley floor. There they let their animals drink their fill, then graze on the abundant sagebrush and prairie grasses nearby. Parkman and the old man settled on the bank to eat and relax. Parkman found a hummock of dirt and raised his bad leg on it to ease the aching.

"Gone lame, huh?" Sam said. "I noticed you starting to limp up there on the trail."

"A few weeks back, a bullet chipped off a piece of rock, and it found my leg," Parkman said. "It wouldn't have been so bad, but it stuck in the bone, and then it started to putrefy before I could reach anywhere to get some help. Nearly died from it."

"Did you close it proper after it happened?"

"Best I could, with gunpower."

"That's some straight-on pain there, ain't it?" Sam chuckled. "Worse than the bullet hole. And it don't go away any time soon."

"Like filling your britches with chili peppers," Parkman agreed. "I've been shot before, even in worse places than a leg, but there was something different this time. I can't say what."

Parkman leaned back and cocked his hat down over his eyes to shield them from the afternoon sun. His thoughts drifted away to Hattie O'Shea. He smiled, picturing her going up aside some hungover prospector's jaw with her balled-up fist because he'd put a hand where it didn't belong, and then setting a platter of fried steak and spuds in front of him. It must be hard on her with him away like this, and never knowing for weeks, or maybe months, whether he would ever come back, or what shape he would be in if he did.

Back during the war, he had similar thoughts many times, when the men marched away and the women stayed home. The men might fight their battles, suffer all the deprivations that wartime required, and even die if their turn came. But even then, their courage and sacrifice seemed no greater than that of the women left behind to wonder and grieve, and to try to keep some pieces of life held together for the men to come home to.

Sam Lyons woke both Parkman and himself with a loud snort that would have done a wild boar proud. Both jolted into consciousness, and both landed their hand on a weapon before they gathered their wits and realized there was no danger.

"It's a danged nuisance, sleepin' so loud," Sam said. He stretched his limbs to get the kinks out, then struggled clumsily to his feet. Parkman could hear his knees crackle. "Back in my squaw man days, no chief would've ever let me ride along on a raid if I made as much noise sleepin' as I do now."

"You even went out on raids with them?" Parkman asked, somehow surprised.

"A few against the Crow. But mostly I went along to see how it rolled out and to tend the horses while they snuck up on a camp. I didn't hate the Crow like the Sioux did. Even lived with them for a spell. But I preferred the Sioux. Prettier women, and they didn't smell so bad, seemed like."

The animals had not strayed far. Parkman removed the hobble from his pack mule and gathered up General Grant's reins, then waited while Sam finished his business in the bushes and got ahold of his own horse. They rode over to the track marks of Duff's Joseph's wagons and turned to follow them.

"I figure we've got about five hours of daylight left, and then if the moon comes up, we can push on longer," Sam said. "Riding out in the open like this sets my nerves a'jangling, but I don't see no other way if we're going to keep on gaining ground on them."

"It's a risk," Parkman agreed. "I don't think they know yet that anybody's coming along behind. But I'm like you. I don't see any better way to go about it. How far away is the head of the valley and the tree line?"

"Four hours, maybe. Less if we run the horses some."

"Do you think he's headed toward the pass you mentioned?"

"Seems like."

They worked the horses hard for the next few hours, alternating between a steady gallop and a slower trot to let them catch their wind. Parkman knew that he could have covered twice the ground if he had been alone atop General Grant, but he had to make concessions. Sam's horse was aging just like its passenger and couldn't have held up at a quicker pace. And the pack mule was as ornery and disruptive as you might expect from an animal of his breed. But still, they had to be gaining ground on Joseph, with all those wagons.

Near dusk, they topped a slight rise on the rolling valley floor and saw the tree line in the distance. It was two or three miles ahead, but still reassuring by its simple presence.

"We'll be fine when we get back into the forest," Sam said. "I always felt better in the deep woods. I figure it's one of the reasons I held on so long. I always stayed clear of the wide-open spaces whenever I could."

The old man looked and sounded exhausted, and Parkman realized how tough the long ride must have been for him. Now that he had a pretty good bead on Duff Joseph, maybe it was time to send Sam Lyons back to his little cabin in the woods . . . if he was willing to go. He decided he would suggest it tonight after they made camp and were settling in for the night.

Parkman turned his head to agree with what Sam had said. But he was puzzled, and then alarmed, by the look on the old man's face. Sam's eyes were glazed, and he looked like he had lost all his senses in an instant. Then he toppled sideways out of his saddle, and Parkman realized what had happened. The shot was fired from so far away that the sound of it had nearly been swept away by the wind.

Parkman swung from the saddle, grabbing his Sharps on the way down, and sprawled flat on the ground. Stabs of pain shot up his wounded leg, but he hardly took notice of it. The horses and mule scattered, but that was okay. It might keep the distant rifleman from taking a bead on them as well. And Parkman knew he could always get his hands on General Grant when he needed to and then round up the other two animals. If he lived through this.

More attuned to the danger, Parkman heard the next couple of shots as he scuttled over to where Sam lay. They sounded like the distant snapping of a twig. As near as he could tell they came from somewhere off to the east, and Parkman figured the rifleman was probably down in the river cut. He and Sam were safer now because the tall grass around them kept them concealed.

Sam Lyons was only halfway conscious, his left hand clamped over a blood splotch midway down the right side of his chest. If Parkman had to describe the look on the old man's face, he would have to call it pissed off. Sam was mumbling threats and curses under his breath and hardly seemed to recognize the marshal's face as he leaned over him.

The wound was a bad one, close enough to the middle of his chest to have passed through some necessary innards. For an instant Parkman thought about Amos Pruett, the broken man he had encountered back on the trail, and he hoped and prayed that Sam Lyons would not ask to be finished off.

"Get him, son," Sam rasped out. "Leave me here. Ain't nothing you can do. Go get the bastard that done this if you can."

"Hell, it's just a scratch, old man," Parkman said.

"I know." The expression on Sam's face was half grin, half grimace. He didn't seem to be in much pain yet. "But let me rest up a bit before I crawl back in the saddle. You've got work to do."

With the Sharps slung across his back, Parkman started crawling clumsily forward through the tall grass. It was rough going with his bad leg, but he forced himself to pass beyond the pain and do what he had to do. From time to time he continued to hear the distant shots ahead, and his confidence grew as he came to realize what a fool he was up against. The horses had wandered back over the crest of the rise, so there was nothing to shoot at, and wasting ammunition out in the wilderness like this could be a deadly mistake. He must be scared stupid, Parkman thought, but all he was accomplishing was to pinpoint his location.

By the time Parkman had made a hundred yards or so of cautious progress, the shooting had stopped. "Out of cartridges, aren't you?" he mumbled to himself. "And now you'll run for it."

In almost every situation, Ridge Parkman was more likely to pull the shorter-barreled Winchester from its scabbard. But there were times that the Sharps was the only tool for the job, and this was one of them. He kept moving forward patiently, sometimes crawling and sometimes walking bent forward. His hope was that the rifleman wouldn't do the sensible thing and withdraw along the river cut until after dark.

When the horse came into view, struggling up the river bank with its rider clinging to its back, Parkman knelt and prepared to make his shot. Sitting on his good leg, he raised the bad one and poised the Sharps across his knee. He judged the distance, then raised the rear sight about halfway. He had plenty of time.

His first shot brought the horse down, squalling and thrashing. Parkman raised the sight slightly, adjusting for the distance based on his first shot. Then he waited, hoping that the man might have been caught under the horse, or even killed during the fall. Instead, in a moment the man scrambled clear from the flailing hoofs, rose to his feet, and started a desperate dash back toward the safety of the river bank. The second shot pitched him sideways like a backslap, but Parkman could tell by the howling that started almost immediately that he wasn't dead. Yet.

The small camp Parkman built a few hundred yards into the woods was a dreary place. He didn't bother to find any sort of secluded spot, because he was convinced that if anybody was out there looking to do some mischief, they would home in on the moans and howls of two wounded men long before they spotted the glow and smoke of a cooking fire.

Earlier he had boiled up something akin to a broth made from beans boiled down to a soft mush and flavored with tads of jerky, hoping that Sam Lyons might take at least a few swallows of it. But all the old man would accept was swigs of water now and then. With remarkable grit, Sam had weathered the jolting ride in from the valley, tied to his horse and choking back horrible pain in the doing. Parkman had wrapped his wounds as best he could, and his bleeding had subsided to a slow trickle. He wished he had a little whiskey to keep the old man distracted, but the last of it had gone down Sam's gullet back at the cabin.

By contrast, Parkman had treated his prisoner much more harshly. After firing the shot that put him down, Parkman had come across the man crawling pathetically back toward the river bank, as if he might find some refuge there. At first Parkman had considered leaving him there to bleed out, but his better instincts prevailed, and he tended roughly to the man's wound. The bullet had smashed the bones in his right forearm before skittering across the front of his belly. Sitting astride him, Parkman had roughly stuffed plugs torn from the man's shirt into the bleeding holes, then tied the remainders of the garment around the wounds. If the wounded man bled on out, at least the marshal would feel like he had done what he ought to.

After the fight, Parkman had tied his prisoner to the carcass of his own dead horse while he went about doing what he could for Sam and gathering up their animals. Then he made the bushwhacker walk the last mile to the woods with a rope around his throat like a bawling steer. After the camp was made, Parkman had given him some water to drink but didn't waste any of his food supplies on him.

When all the chores were finished and the horses were hobbled for the night, Parkman laid a few more deadfall branches over the fire, then sat with his back against a tree and rolled himself a smoke. He sat for a while staring into the flames, wondering what came next, and what kind of plan he might be able to come up with. For now, he decided, fate alone was in charge.

Sam Lyons lay a few yards away on the pallet Parkman had made for him, with his head resting on his saddle. From time to time he mumbled and tossed deliriously, and once he even tried to sit up before the pain overwhelmed him and he fell back again, exhausted.

The prisoner, whose name turned out to be Homer Brad-berry, was tied to a tree farther out in the woods, because he couldn't seem to stop his moaning and jabbering, even when Parkman gagged him. While he was still able to talk, he had sworn to his captor that he didn't have a notion of what he was getting into when he joined up with Duff Joseph, and planned to slip away and report the whole thing to the army as soon as he could. He kept pleading for better treatment for his wounds, but even if Parkman had been so inclined, he knew there was no doctor within two or three hundred miles of where they were.

A particular kind of meanness, which most people never saw in him, came over Parkman when he had to deal with men like this. Maybe that was another reason to give all of this up after he and Hattie jumped the broom. He didn't particularly like that side of himself and wouldn't mind seeing the last of it someday. But right now, out here in the wilderness and a week's ride from any sort of help, he understood that he needed to haul out all the meanness he could muster.

Parkman raked up a pile of pine needles and unrolled his blanket on top. He could hear Sam Lyons snorting and moaning across the way and was glad he was far enough off that the old man's miseries would not interfere with his sleep.

★ ★ ★ ★ ★

Ridge Parkman couldn't say what woke him. It must have been some sound nearby, he thought, the rustling of the tree branches in a breeze, or some small woodland creature, or possibly an enemy nearby slipping up on the camp to do some harm. The moon was up, but he could see no movement in the trees nearby. He slid his finger into the trigger guard of the Colt that lay by his side but didn't thumb the hammer back yet. A large, winged shadow swooped across the patch of open nighttime sky above him, but an owl's hoot was not what had stirred him awake.

He heard a muted grunt of pain, followed by a muffled curse somewhere nearby in the woods. He looked over at the spot where he had settled Sam in for the night and was surprised to see that the old man was not there. He had fully expected to wake in the morning to find that Sam had passed on during the night, but he was not prepared to discover him gone entirely. It crossed his mind that maybe Sam had crawled into the woods to die, like an old dog might, but why go to the trouble? Out here in the wild country, one place was as good to die as another.

When Parkman heard old Sam groan again, throaty and deep like the low growl of a dreaming dog, he started putting the pieces together. The noise came from back in the trees, where Parkman had tied the prisoner to a tree for the night.

He found Sam Lyons lying on his side, up close to Homer Bradberry, or at least beside the bushwhacker's butchered remains. Sam raised his head slightly and grinned at Parkman, weakly lifting something with one hand. It looked like the pelt of a small animal, but Parkman realized it was something more gruesome.

"All right then, there's one problem I don't have to worry about anymore," Parkman said. "You sure done a job on that fellow, old man."

"Wal, it ain't often a man gets the chance to scalp the bastard that killed him." Old Sam chuckled, then coughed wetly. "I would of took his beard too, but I run out of spunk." A rivulet of blood seeped out of the corner of his mouth, and his arm dropped weakly back to the ground. The forest floor beneath him was darkly puddled with blood. He had reopened his wound getting over here, but to him it was clearly worth the effort.

"Looks like you didn't stop at scalping, either." Bradberry's throat was open ear to ear, and his nearly severed head sagged forward, as if he were examining the detached arm between his legs. His other arm was hacked and mangled but still connected, probably because Sam had run out of the strength to do more. The dead man's legs were slashed as well, and there were bloody holes in his bare chest where Sam had shoved the knife home an overly-sufficient number of times.

"It's the Sioux way," Sam explained in a harsh whisper. Then he held out his trophy to Parkman. "You can take the scalp for a souvenir if you're of a mind. Or bury it with me. It don't matter." His eyes sagged closed, and his breaths were slow and shallow.

"You need to take it across with you, old man," Parkman told him gently. "When you get where you're going you can show it around and spin the yarn that goes along with it."

CHAPTER FOURTEEN

The sun was midway up in the sky before Parkman returned to the trail again. It was a beautiful late spring day, with pale clouds as delicate as lace drifting across the vivid blue sky. Snow-topped mountains rose majestically on three sides of him, and a steady breeze stirred the treetops of the forest around him. A man couldn't have asked for a prettier day, nor prettier country than what he was riding through this morning.

But he was in no mood to admire the wonders of nature. He had liked and admired old Sam, envying him for the things he had seen and done during his several decades on this earth. His breed of men was nearly gone now, except for a few grizzled relics sitting around some sutler's stove, trying to snag somebody who was willing to buy them a mouthful of whiskey and listen to their half-forgotten tales.

If we'd stayed up in the hills a little longer, or kept a sharper eye out. Maybe if we'd let the horses graze a little more, or took them down to the stream again for one last drink. If Homer Bradberry's aim had been just a little off . . .

But none of those maybes had happened, probably because it was old Sam's time, and there was nothing that anybody could do to change it. He hadn't realized it at the time, but when the old man was spinning his yarns, some of them probably made up, and most of the rest exaggerated, he was listening to history of a kind.

Now he felt an unfamiliar loneliness, as well as a heightened vulnerability. Who could know where along the trail ahead another bushwhacker might be waiting behind a tree, or down in a creek cut, or flat on the ground, ready to level his sights and take his shot?

He had buried Sam Lyons in the edge of a small meadow near the camp, overlooking the long valley, thinking that the old man would have appreciated the view. He had put most of Sam's belongings into the grave with him, including the scalp, keeping only his rifle, powder, and shot, as well as a few old coins and a sprinkling of gold dust in a small leather pouch. He left Sam's saddle atop the grave and set his horse free.

Homer Bradberry's gruesome remains were right back there where they had been, still tied to a tree. He didn't deserve better, and Parkman didn't want to waste his time digging a second grave, even a shallow one, that the wild animals would get into anyway.

Parkman hoped the guilt he felt would pass on soon. Any way you looked at it, this was a risky undertaking in wild, dangerous country, and a man shouldn't head into it unless he was willing to face up to that. Old Sam had chosen this life long ago, and Parkman figured he'd be satisfied with the way it ended.

This whole incident was proof that Duff Joseph was staying true to his old habits. When he had enough men to manage it, he always sent riders ahead and behind, so he never traveled completely blind. Even the fact that Bradberry never returned would probably tell him something, and he would send out a larger party to try to figure out what happened. If old Sam's estimate of twenty-five strong was close to right, Joseph still had men enough for it.

The land before him rose steadily. Here in the middle of such endless wilderness, Ridge Parkman could gain a better understanding of what had drawn men like Sam Lyons out here so far away from civilization, with its laws and rules and governments, where a man could see brand new places and things, and would survive only if his wits and strength and courage were up to the challenge.

But those times were fleeting now. The Union Pacific Railroad track that he had crossed down to the south was evidence enough of that. Times were changing. They always did.

The trail rose steadily, and the air grew chilly as he approached the higher altitudes of the pass. Parkman slowed his pace and took advantage of the trees any place he could. He kept his eyes constantly scanning ahead, uncomfortably aware of the countless places where a man with murder on his mind could lay in wait for any unsuspecting traveler. He kept the Winchester across his lap and the strap loose on his holster. Even those precautions would not be enough if the first shot was true. But if that first shot missed, or if he spotted the shooter an instant before he fired, there was always a chance.

A fast, narrow stream flowed down along the pass, and Parkman found a couple of places where Duff Joseph's caravan had crossed it to reach flatter ground on the other side. It must have been tough going along here for mules and wagons, but he was beginning to think that Joseph probably had someone along who knew this country—Indians or breeds maybe, or frontier scouts who had passed this way before.

Parkman reached the crest of the pass about dark and paused to take in the broad landscape before him. He was a little disappointed that he couldn't spot Joseph's party somewhere on the trail down the mountain, or on the rolling foothills beyond. He and old Sam had made pretty good time when they started out, and his hopes had been high, but the ambush and the events that followed had delayed him again.

He camped that night in a small clearing where there was a little grass for the animals to feed on, and a sheltered spot where he could build a small fire and lay out his blankets.

It occurred to Parkman as he stirred his cooking pot that he was doing better than he had when he first started out from Colorado weeks before. He was toughening up after the lazy days he had spent recovering from his wound, and even his damaged leg was stronger and less inclined to punish him with sharp bursts of pain whenever he asked too much of it.

His animals were also holding up well, he thought. For a horse as large as he was, General Grant had always been sure footed and seemed to have little trouble navigating this rocky mountain terrain. The pack mule was just a mule, of course, stubborn and plodding, but tireless and resilient even under the heavy load he carried. Somewhere along the journey he had taken to calling the mule Lucky for no particular reason.

Going down the eastern slopes of the pass proved to be more treacherous than coming up the other side. As before, Parkman kept the pace slow, and General Grant was as diligent in choosing where he planted his hooves as Parkman was in watching the rock formations and clusters of trees ahead. As usual, Lucky plodded along behind, complaining only occasionally about this or that.

As they neared the bottom, the mountain pass transformed itself gradually into a winding valley that snaked around the foothills. Despite the added distance, the wagon tracks revealed that Joseph's band had chosen that route to follow for obvious reasons. Parkman relaxed his guard a little now because he could watch farther ahead for any signs of ambush, and he rode in the edge of the trees as often as possible. He would have liked to take some straighter overland route for safety's sake, and to gain a little time on his prey, but decided against it. He had no idea which way the valley might eventually turn, and to get lost in these sprawling hills now could turn into a catastrophe.

In late morning, a hard rain fell for about an hour, complete with coal black walls of clouds, rolling thunder, and shafts of lightning stabbing down from the sky. As the valley stream rose, Parkman moved up into higher ground to wait it out. This could complicate things. Enough of this kind of rain could obliterate the trail he was following, leaving him guessing what direction Joseph had gone. But surely it would take an absolute deluge to erase all sign of a party that big, with wagons, he thought hopefully.

When the storm blew past at last and the skies cleared, he rode back down as close as he dared go to the glutted stream, and was pleased to find the wagon ruts still visible. It was a good sign, Parkman thought.

He camped that night up in the edge of the trees off the trail. It rained again, but not so furiously. As he lay there on his blankets, completely drenched, with only his hat to shield his face from the downpour, he thought it was lucky that he hadn't had to endure this kind of soaking in the chilly altitudes of the pass behind him.

You could nearly always find a little piece of good luck working for you if you looked hard enough.

When Parkman first spotted the half dozen columns of smoke drifting up through the trees a mile or two ahead, his spirits rose. But then he realized that this couldn't be Duff Joseph's bunch. For one thing, they would not have gone so far up a hillside to make their camp. And for another, he hadn't been moving fast enough to catch up with them so quickly. This had to be the campsite of someone else, he realized, prospectors possibly, or even Indians from one tribe or another.

It was risky, but he decided it might be worth moving in closer and finding out who had built those fires. If it was white men, he should be able to find out from them how long ago Joseph's crew had passed this way. And if it was Indians, he would have to find a safe way around them.

When he heard the shooting start, Parkman was no more than half a mile away from the camp, but there was one last hill to keep him from finding out what was going on ahead. As he neared the next crest, he once again drew out the Sharps and dismounted, leaving the horse and mule back out of sight.

Now he was close enough to get a clear idea of what was going on down below. A scattering of tipis indicated that it was an Indian camp, and three or four mounted white men were riding around and through it, firing their rifles and hand guns at anything that moved. None of the Indians were fighting back, and Parkman decided that their men must be away, hunting possibly, or fighting somewhere else.

As he watched, one of the riders raised his rifle and took aim at a young Indian girl who was making a desperate dash for the safety of the woods. When the shot rang out, the girl sprawled forward and lay still.

"Well that don't seem right," Parkman muttered to himself. He raised the Sharps, drew a bead, and knocked the killer out of his saddle. He too lay still as soon as his body splayed out on the ground, and the horse bolted away in fear. That left only two riders that Parkman could see, but they hadn't seemed to realize yet that they were the targets now.

Parkman took aim at another of the raiders, a man in army blues, possibly a deserter, and emptied his saddle. By then the third rider seemed to realize what was happening and spun his horse, heading for the thick woods nearby. Parkman got off another couple of shots but didn't think he hit anything. That would be bad news if these men belonged to Joseph's crew.

He approached the camp carefully, still on foot, drawing his Colt and thumbing back the hammer as he got closer. He saw no signs of life ahead, only a scattering of dead, bloody bodies. Most were women and children, except for one old man who lay dead in front of his tipi with a bow still in his hand.

Why would those lowlifes do something like this? he wondered. There must be little enough to steal in a camp like this, and they hadn't spared any of the women to have their brutish fun with. It had to have been for the pure joy of killing, he decided, and he was glad he had done what he did.

A pistol shot rang out from somewhere nearby, and the bullet passed so close to Parkman that he felt like he could hear it whispering by. He fell to the ground and rolled behind a tipi, not completely sure he had moved in the right direction to shelter himself. He came up onto one knee and checked the loads in the Colt, then started looking around for somebody to shoot back at. Another shot passed through the tipi to one side.

Across the camp, perhaps fifty feet away, Parkman heard a man howl out, then curse angrily. "You bitch!" There was the confusing noise of a tussle of some sort, and then the man called out again, this time with a mortal scream of pain. That ended abruptly, and then there was only silence for the next few seconds. Parkman moved around to the other side of the tipi and risked a quick look around.

He saw an Indian woman across the camp kneeling over the fallen form of a white man, slashing and stabbing at him furiously with a long hunting knife, muttering what must have been curses in her own language as she continued her butchery.

"I expect you can stop now," Parkman said, standing up. "He looks as dead as he's going to get." But still he understood her fury.

The woman sprang to her feet and whirled, still holding the knife threateningly forward. Her dress was torn away in front, but she seemed to pay no mind to her nakedness. Her hair, face, arms, and body were painted with the fresh blood of the man she had slaughtered. She thrust out the bloody knife and grunted, as if inviting Parkman to step forward and feel its bite.

The scene came together in Parkman's mind. The dead man had been in the process of raping this woman when Parkman opened up on his companions. He had taken cover behind a tree as Parkman approached and managed to get a couple of shots off. Then the woman attacked him from behind, and he didn't have a chance to shoot again. The knife seemed to be his own, because the leather sheath on his belt was empty.

The Indian woman stabbed the air in front of her again, her face a mask of pain, hatred, and fury.

"You know I ain't one of them," Parkman said. He knew she would not understand his words, but he thought his tone of voice might calm her down. "I don't mean to harm you. You can see I killed those others." He lowered his gun toward the ground and took a few slow steps forward.

She watched cautiously, unmoving as Parkman drew nearer. He pointed at the knife and then at the ground. This would be all right, he thought. In a minute she would come to her senses and realize that he was the one who saved her.

Her lunge was as quick as a snake, and absolutely unexpected. Parkman was barely able to grab her arm before she could stick the knife in his belly, and the whack he delivered across the side of her head with his pistol barrel was purely reflexive. He collected the knife from her hand as she crumpled to the ground and tossed it aside.

"Well hell!" he mumbled to himself. "You save her from them, and then you lay her out yourself."

But she wasn't dead. Her blood-drenched breasts rose and fell softly, and the cut on her temple was small and hardly bled. She might be okay, he thought, if he hadn't addled her senses for good with that whack on the head.

But what now? he wondered. He didn't want to leave her here, in case the one rider who got away came back with others to finish the job. All he could come up with was to get her away from here, and if she came to later, he'd simply let her go.

For caution's sake, Parkman tied her wrists and legs together with strips of rawhide he found in one of the tipis. He found the dead man's horse tied to a bush near where the rape went bad on him and lifted the unconscious woman on its back, securing her arms around its neck so she wouldn't fall off.

There wasn't much he could do about the woman's torn and damaged deerskin dress, but he found a similar garment in one of the tipis and brought it along as they left the massacred camp. He disliked the thought of leaving so many slaughtered bodies scattered around like that but couldn't think of anything he could do about it. He didn't even know what tribe these Indians were, or what they did with their dead.

After gathering up his own animals and mounting up, he headed down toward the stream that flowed through the valley, thinking that he could at least clean her up. When they reached the stream, Parkman took the woman down from the horse and laid her on a patch of grass nearby. He wasn't quite sure how he was going to get the drying blood off of her because he had already decided that he wasn't about to scrub her down himself. Fortunately, she began to come to as soon as he poured the first bucket of cold water onto her. At first, she fought against her restraints, but when Parkman pulled out his knife, she relaxed and let him cut her free.

Parkman walked up out of the cut where the water flowed, while the Indian woman cleaned herself up and put on the dress he brought for her. The land was fairly flat for at least a mile up and down the valley, and he could see no threats in any direction. They were safe for now, he thought, but only for now. One of the marauders got away, Parkman reminded himself, and if he had cohorts around, they could come back in force.

One of the scenarios that Parkman toyed with in his mind was that the captured man that Sam Lyons had scalped and sliced up back to the west was a rear guard Duff Joseph sent back to make sure his small wagon train was not taken unawares from behind. When the man never returned, Joseph had sent out this bunch to see what became of him. On the way out, the four of them spotted the Indian camp, discovered that they were not defended by full-grown braves, and decided to have some fun.

If that was the case, then the rider that escaped would head straight back to Joseph and make his report. In that scenario, Parkman was in deep trouble when Joseph sent another bunch back this way.

Or, he thought, the four raiders of the Indian camp could have simply been wandering hard cases or army deserters, on the lookout for one sort of opportunity or another. As crazy as it seemed, there were gold-hungry prospectors who wandered these mountains alone or in small groups, willing to face the enormous risks in search of the big strike. And men like the ones that raided the Indian camp would have figured out long ago that it was a sight easier to take somebody else's gold than it was to pan and dig out their own. In that case, he might be safe enough for now.

A noise behind him interrupted his thoughts, and Parkman turned around to see the Indian woman gathering up their two horses and the mule, all of which had taken the opportunity to graze on the grasses that grew alongside the river. He turned around and hurried back, not ignoring the possibility that the Indian woman might decide to make off with all three animals and leave him stranded here afoot. She was an Indian, after all, and no matter what tribe she might belong to, stealing horses was one of the things they particularly liked to do. He only slowed his pace when he was within an easy pistol shot of where she stood.

Now, with the blood washed away, he got a better look at her.

She was short, hardly reaching up to Parkman's shoulder, and looked stout enough to lift one end of a freight wagon. Her skin was a light coffee color, and her face was round and expressionless. Her long black hair was pulled around behind and tied off with a beaded strip of leather. Her eyes were unreadable.

"You can go now if you're of a mind," Parkman said, knowing that there was no real chance that she spoke his language. "And you can take that horse with you." He pointed at the horse, then at her, and then at the broad landscape around them. He had no notion of how to do sign language, but figured that should be clear enough. He pointed at himself and swept his hand in the opposite direction.

He might as well have been reading Latin to her for all the response he got. He tried the same gestures again, but her face remained as blank as the pale-blue sky.

"All right, then do as you please," Parkman said in frustration. He wasn't quite sure how it would work out traipsing around this country with a woman along, but it didn't look like he had much choice for now. She seemed to have attached herself to him, perhaps for safety, or maybe even because she thought she belonged to him now that he had saved her life.

They mounted up, and Parkman led the way upstream, in the opposite direction from where he wanted to go. It frustrated him to think that he was wasting time and daylight, but he was uncomfortably aware that somebody might be on their trail before long. What he was doing wouldn't fool a skilled tracker, but it might confuse an ordinary man long enough for him and the woman to get lost in the vast country that surrounded them.

After following the winding bends and curves of the river for a mile or two, he turned aside at a spot where the banks were rocky and their exit from the water might be less noticeable. He rode straight up the hillside ahead, and into the forest that began a little higher up. He felt some relief now that they were into some cover and couldn't be spotted from a long way off.

He rode about a hundred feet into the trees before dismounting, and the Indian woman slid off her horse when he did. Parkman hobbled the horses and mule, then untied a grub bag from
the mule and set it on the ground. The woman immediately
began going around picking up sticks and kindling for a fire,
but Parkman vetoed the idea. "No fire for now," he said, waving
both hands in front of him, palms down. He didn't know if that
was an acceptable sign or not, but the woman seemed to
understand and dropped her armload of fire makings.

Parkman broke out the jerky, and they both took a handful.
The woman ate the first few pieces greedily, and he figured it
might have been a while since she put anything in her belly. She
followed him as he walked back to the edge of the trees and sat
down, overlooking the vast, wide valley they had just crossed.

The woman settled in several feet from Parkman, and slightly
farther down the sloping hillside. Her eyes fixed on the faraway
location on the other side of the valley where the Indian camp
had been. The tipis were too far back in the trees to be seen,
but a few pale wisps of smoke still rose to mark the spot. He
watched her for a while, wondering what thoughts might be going through that stoic head of hers.

She must have lost friends and family during the raid, and
perhaps even some of her own children. But you would never
know it by her stolid expression, and no tears flowed from her
eyes. After a few moments she began to sing quietly to herself in
a choppy but somehow rhythmic tone, chanting in the ancient
language of her people. Their songs were prayers, Parkman had
been told, and they had one for practically all of life's occur-
rences, even the arrival of their own death.

Feeling something like an intruder, Parkman turned his gaze
away from the Indian woman and swept the broad, open
expanses before them. He watched an eagle swoop down from

the lofty heights like something dropped from heaven. Its wings flared only at the last instant, and its extended talons snatched up some unfortunate furry, landlocked creature. Then its powerful wings began to rise and fall, carrying it back into the sky and away toward its roost someplace in the high country.

Miles away, down on the eastern end of the valley, a grazing herd of buffalo began to meander into view, their heads down, feeding on the spring crop of brush and grasses. A V-shaped gaggle of at least fifty geese crossed the sky from southeast to northwest, honking randomly as they passed almost directly overhead. A few deer wandered out of the trees and began to graze no more than a hundred feet from where Parkman and the woman sat. His first impulse was to down one so they could have some fresh meat tonight, but his rifle was back with the horses, and he knew the deer would be long gone before he could go back and retrieve it.

Much to his liking, the one thing he didn't spot anywhere in the wide-open valley below was mounted men, either of the white or red variety.

The sun was settling down toward the peaks of the mountains to the west by the time Parkman rose and stretched his legs. He thought that if they moved farther up into the forest, they should be able to safely build a fire, which meant cornbread and beans and hot coffee to go along with the boring, ordinary fare of jerky and water. It had been a long, bloody day, full of tragedy and surprises, and he would be glad when it was over.

The Indian woman, who had ended her mournful chants, stood and followed him back up to the animals.

Parkman jolted awake when he felt the cold metal touch his throat, but he had the presence of mind not to try to raise his head or reach for the revolver lying at his side. In the smattering of moonlight that filtered down through the trees, he caught a shadowy glimpse of a scraggly, graying beard and a grizzled head with some sort of animal skin atop it.

"Don't make me do nothin' that I'll wish later I hadn't," the man told him calmly.

"I must be losing my touch," Parkman said. "There was a time when no man could have snuck up on me like this."

"Wal, I've always had a talent for it."

The two men studied each other for a moment in the near darkness. Parkman thought his captor looked not quite as ancient as old Sam Lyons, but old still for this country, and smelled as bad as Sam had.

"I'll sheath this blade as soon as you seem calm and peaceful like," the man said.

"The way I see it, you never needed to take it out in the first place. Not unless you planned to use it."

"I guess I'm the careful type."

As the man drew the blade away from Parkman's throat and moved back a little, Parkman could see that it had been the back side of the knife at his throat, and not the cutting edge. He liked this fellow already.

"Let's have us a little talk," the man suggested. Parkman felt around on the ground at his side for his hand gun, but it was gone. "What do you figure on doing with that woman over there?"

"I don't know what to do with her," Parkman admitted. "I killed two of the men that was shooting up their camp, and she finished another one of them with his own knife. The fourth one got away. Later on, I tried to let her go, but she wouldn't."

"Well she's scared, as you might imagine after what she went through," the man said. "She told me she didn't want to go along with you and don't trust you 'cause you're a white man. But she felt like she didn't have much choice for the time being."

"So you can talk to her?" Parkman asked. "You know her?"

"Her name is Morning Fawn. I was travelling with that bunch, but me and the boy had rode out to get some meat for the camp. We didn't get back until about dusk yesterday and seen what happened."

"And you found us all the way over here in the dark?"

"I'm a pretty fair tracker," the old man chuckled, "but I ain't that good. We followed your trail down to the river before it got full dark and was going to bed down and pick it up in the morning. But then the boy saw a little of the glow of your fire up here in the trees. You shoulda gone farther in. Lucky for you it was us that spotted you, and not somebody else."

As they talked, the Indian woman, Morning Fawn, stepped out of the darkness of the woods and stopped a few paces behind the man. With her was a lean, sturdy young Indian of about sixteen, already as tall as most grown men, but still thin and not yet fully muscled out.

"Fawn said she planned to kill you with a rock during the night," the man said. "But then you were kind to her, and she changed her mind."

Parkman looked up at the Indian woman, and their eyes met for a moment. "I guess she liked my cornbread," he said dryly. He had considered tying her up again before he went to sleep but decided there was no need.

"She said you shared your food and gave her a blanket to sleep under."

"Glad the gentleman in me leaked out at the right time."

There was enough coffee left for the old man to have a cup, which pleased him enormously. Parkman broke out the leftovers from their evening meal, and the man and boy stuffed their mouths ravenously.

"Where are you from, mister?" the man asked. "Seems like you don't know enough about the wild country up here to keep your scalp for long."

"I'm a U.S. marshal up from Colorado," Parkman said. "I'm on the trail of some bad men that stole some army supplies and headed up this way." He decided not to mention that those supplies were rifles and ammunition until he learned a little more about where these people's loyalties stood.

"Do you think it might be some of them that attacked the camp over yonder?"

"Could be. They passed through here a day or two ago. You might of seen the wagon tracks. And I can't imagine there's that many white men who ride through this valley on a regular basis."

"Not and live to talk about it." The man turned to explain the conversation to the woman and the boy in their own language. He seemed to know it well, and Parkman took him to be another squaw man, like Sam Lyons.

When they were finished talking, Parkman asked, "What language is that?"

"It's Cheyenne."

"You speak it well. You must have been with them for a while."

"Eight years, maybe nine or ten. I lose track. I married me a Cheyenne woman, and for her sake I stayed on with the tribe. We had a baby, but she died delivering him, and my tiny little son wouldn't take to no other woman's bosom, so he passed on, too."

"I'm Ridge," Parkman said. The two men shook hands.

"They named me Bone Eater 'cause when they captured me, I was near to starving, and I'd pounded some elk bones to get at the marrow. Now I go mostly by Bone."

When they prepared to leave the next morning, they all seemed to be heading in the same direction by unspoken agreement. Parkman saw a lot of advantages to traveling with this group, at least for a while. Bone seemed to know this territory as well as old Sam had, but in the daylight, it was clear that he was younger and more fit than Sam and wouldn't be likely to slow Parkman's progress. The woman, Fawn, automatically took over the chores of cooking and clean-up in camp. And as for the boy, who Bone referred to simply as Boy, he had gone out before dawn with his bow and arrows and returned before the coffee was made with a possum for breakfast.

And then there was the other advantage to taking up with this party, perhaps more important than anything else. He would be traveling with people who lived in this wilderness and were familiar to the Indians they were likely to meet along the way. Parkman knew that would greatly increase his chance of survival.

"When we cut their trail, if they're still headed east, then they've got only two ways to go," Bone explained to Parkman as Fawn finished packing up the mule. He was drawing a rough map on the ground with a stick as he spoke. "If they veer southeast, they'll be headed toward easier traveling for their wagons, but they're also more likely to run into army patrols and suchlike. And since they've got four wagons of army goods, it don't seem the smartest choice to make."

"What's their other choice?" Parkman asked.

"They can turn up northeast and keep to the mountains."

"Could they get through there with the wagons?"

"Maybe, if they've got good scouts who know that territory, and have plenty of luck. I could probably lead wagons through there if they were made strong and if they've got four-up teams of stout, healthy mules."

"I guess we'll find out soon enough."

Their first stop was the Indian camp where Parkman had saved Fawn's life. A pack of wolves, then a grizzly bear, and lastly the buzzards had already visited the scene of massacre across the valley, and there was little Parkman's companions could do now for the mutilated corpses. Fawn spent a few

minutes by the damaged remains of an old man, singing chants
once again while Parkman and Bone waited stoically nearby.
Meanwhile, Boy foraged. He picked up the knife Fawn had
used to kill her attacker and stowed it in his pack, and he found
a few extra arrows for his quiver.

"The men of this camp had left a couple of weeks ago, heading east to hunt, and to see what other kinds of trouble they
could stir up," Bone explained. "Their leader, Gray Eagle, left
me behind because he thought they might tangle with some
soldiers, and he wasn't sure which side I would take in a fight
like that. I didn't argue 'cause I wasn't so sure about it myself. I
guess the time's coming when they'll run me off for good, but I
sure hate the notion of going back to live amongst the whites.
Maybe instead, I'll head for the high country and be an old
hermit 'till my time comes."

"Like Sam Lyons, the man I started into these mountains
with," Parkman said.

"Do you know Sam?" Bone asked. "So he's still hung onto
his hair after all these years?"

"He kept his own," Parkman said, "but when I buried him a
couple of days back, he was still hanging onto the scalp of the
man who shot him."

"That'd be like old Sam," Bone laughed, hardly seeming to
take note of the fact that his friend was dead.

"What should we do about these bodies here?" Parkman
dreaded the hard work of digging graves for them, as well as the
delay it would cause. If all he did was dig graves, he never would
catch up to Duff Joseph.

"They'll return to the earth, like all of us will one time or
another. I don't 'spose it makes much difference whether it's
under the soil or on top of it."

"That must be Fawn's daddy that she's sitting by over there.
What will she think of leaving him like that?"

"She's an Indian," Bone said quietly. "She understands the way of things like this."

Bone swapped out horses with Fawn because the one she had was healthier and better fed. Throughout the day, he spent at least half the time scouting ahead, and Boy was usually out on one flank or another. He rode a compact little pinto that he seemed enormously proud of, and Parkman thought that might be because it was his first horse. From time to time he slapped his heels against the horse's sides and tore out across the valley at a hard run, just for the fun of it. The horse seemed to enjoy it as much as Boy did.

During the times when Bone came back to ride with Parkman and the others for a while, he kept a steady conversation going. But it wasn't the kind of exaggerated yarns that old Sam had spun, like taking on a war party of a dozen angry Blackfeet and killing every last one of them, or eating the bark off a willow tree when he was close to starvation.

Bone's conversation was more of the reminiscent kind. He told Parkman what it was like to live with the Cheyenne Indians, especially back in the times when they lived proud, free, and unchallenged on the open plains to the east, and their worst enemies were some of the tribes whose hunting ground bordered theirs. He talked with great tenderness about living with his Indian wife, White Moccasin, and the overwhelming grief he had endured when he lost both her and his newborn son so close together.

"I grew up in the hills on the western side of Virginia. It was a hardscrabble life for a big family like ours, and I figured out early that I wasn't cut from farmer's cloth. When I was fourteen, I crossed the Smokies with a supply train that was willing to take me on, fighting the Cherokees all the way over, and later the Shawnee and the Chickasaw when we got on over into Kentucky. Already people there were clearing land and building cabins, and it still wasn't wild and wooly enough for me. I crossed over into Arkansas with a company of trappers, then made my way up through the Ozark Mountains to Independence, where the three main westbound trails started out.

"By then I'd got my hands on a decent Hawken and was a pretty good shot, so I hired on as a hunter with a band of Mormons heading west. But along the way I fell in with an old trapper who commenced to telling me what it was like away up north in Yellowstone country. I knew right away that that was the thing for me. I cut loose from those Mormons and never looked back."

"Funny thing, I grew up in Virginia myself," Parkman said. "Later on, before the war started, my whole family transplanted up to northwest Missouri, even my granddaddy and my mother. But I'd joined up with the U.S. marshals by then and was moving all over the place."

"Nice to partner up with a Virginia boy that knows how pretty it can be when the sun sets over the Blue Ridge Mountains."

"Yep. It sure can make you want to see what's on the other side."

They continued to follow the long valley all that day, and there was still more valley left for tomorrow. But it was narrowing and growing steeper now, and the water in the river churned and rolled with more energy. The wagon tracks they were following crossed the river a couple of times at available fords, seeking the most passable landscape on the other side. The looming mountains ahead grew closer, seeming impenetrable to Parkman, but Bone assured him that there was a difficult but navigable pass ahead.

Parkman was still uncomfortable riding out in the open like this, but Bone spent most of his time scouting out up ahead, checking out the trail and looking for any sign of danger. At least, he thought, they wouldn't be caught completely unaware, as he and old Sam had been. And they were closing the distance between themselves and Duff Joseph.

As nighttime neared, Bone came riding back on the trail and announced that he had found a spot that would do for tonight's camp. A short time later when they reached the spot, Parkman realized it was the same spot that Joseph's band had used, probably two nights before. He was a little discouraged that they were still so far behind.

The camp site was in a sharp curve where, after previous spring deluges, the river had chewed away at the bank, leaving a flat, sandy shoal after the waters went down. Fawn immediately dismounted and began to loosen the bundle of sticks they had brought along on Lucky's back. There was a spot where the water had eaten in under the ground above, and that's where she chose to make the evening fire. Parkman and Bone unsaddled their horses and hobbled them up on the bank where they could graze.

"Only one drawback to a camp like this," Bone said. "If it starts to rain, or even if we think it might be raining up in the high country, we got to get our gear and our own tails up out of this cut in a big hurry. Those flash floods will carry you away in the wink of an eye."

"Yep, I seen it happen down in Colorado," Parkman agreed, "back in Weatherby's Lode where I started out, and other places, too." His thoughts drifted back to the long, lazy days he had spent in that little town while his leg healed, and he wondered how long it would take for that kind of life to get old.

After dark, Boy came in with two lanky jackrabbits strung across the neck of his horse. Fawn took them from him, as well as his knife, and immediately began to skin and gut them for supper.

"That kid's a marvel," Parkman said. "To hit one of those long-legged critters with an arrow would be impressive enough.

But two? I guess the only thing left is for him is to tell us he brought down both of them with the same arrow."

"Wouldn't surprise me," Bone grinned. "They start young, and I've seen grown Indian men make shots that you'd swear I was lying about."

"Did you ever pick it up?"

"I tried, and I might be able to knock a squirrel off a tree if he was ten feet away and sitting still. But a ten-year-old boy would laugh at my misses. And besides, a gun's the thing out here. It shoots farther and kills deader."

"That reminds me, Bone," Parkman said. "I've got Sam Lyon's old muzzle loader and horn tied behind my saddle. I didn't want to leave it back with Sam, but I don't see myself ever needing it, with two long guns of my own already. I was wondering if Boy might want it."

"Are you joshing?" Bone said. "That boy would crawl across hot coals to get himself a gun, any gun. But are you sure you want to do this?"

"I think Sam would approve."

The Indian youth was apprehensive when Bone called him over, unused to be included in the talk of the men. But when Parkman picked up Sam Lyon's rifle and held it out, his eyes filled with wonder. He looked at Bone for reassurance, then took the weapon and held it up like some kind of trophy. His shrill howl of absolute elation could have stirred the dead.

Then he lowered the rifle and looked Parkman straight in the eye, something he had not done up until then. He said something in his own language, and Bone translated.

"He says you have made a man of him today. He will be your brother for life, and says he will gladly die for you if the day ever comes when he has to."

Hell, it's just a rifle, Parkman thought. But he saw that this was a significant event in the young Indian's life, and he didn't want to make light of it.

"Since he's a man now," Parkman said, "we can't go around still calling him Boy. Ask him if I can give him a new name." The boy nodded solemnly. "All right, then you're Little Brother from now on."

Bone told him his new name in Sioux, then pronounced it again in English. "Lid-dle Bro-her," the young man mumbled, then he smiled broadly.

"You're going to have to teach him how to use it, though," Parkman told Bone. "And you might want to warn him that it'll prob'ly knock him down on his rear end the first couple of times he tries to shoot it."

Chapter Fifteen

The next morning when Bone rode out to scout the trail ahead, he took Little Brother with him. The young man carried his rifle proudly across the front of his light, Indian saddle. Bone had taught him how to load it the night before, and Parkman hoped that he didn't shoot himself, or Bone, before he learned how to handle it properly.

Fawn had the camp broken down and the mule loaded by the time Parkman finished his second cup of coffee and his morning smoke. She hardly ever spoke, even when Bone and the young Cheyenne were around, and when it was only her and Parkman riding together, she was as silent as a turtle. He figured she might still be in mourning for her dead daddy, but it was hard to tell anything about what she was thinking or feeling from her expressionless features. But now, at least, Parkman felt a little more confident that she wouldn't be smashing his head with a rock the first chance she had.

Bone said Fawn's husband went off with the other men of the band. When, or if, they returned, Fawn would become her husband's first wife, because his previous first wife was killed in the raid on their camp. Fawn would waste no grief on that other woman, Bone said, because the two of them despised each other, and the first, younger wife, had always relegated most of the hard work in camp to Fawn.

Storm clouds were blowing in behind them by midday, and soon after, they were riding along in a downpour. Parkman broke out his oiled slicker, and Fawn draped her blanket over her head and shoulders. After a while the river began to rise, and the rain obliterated the tracks left by Joseph's train of wagons. But that was all right for now because Bone was confident about the route they must take to get past the looming mountains ahead. All Parkman and Fawn had to do for now was follow the river, and the only problem they would face is if they had to cross it for one reason or another.

Parkman was starting to think that the rain would never stop, and that they would have to build a cold, wet camp that night, completely exposed in the open valley. There was hardly anything worse than trying to get even a little rest when you were soaked to the skin and cold down to your bones.

But the rain had stopped by the time it got too dark to press on. They had no wood left, and the buffalo chips near about were too wet to burn, so it was a fireless camp, with only jerky to chew on for supper. By the time they were ready to bed down, Bone and Little Brother had not yet returned, which began to nag at Parkman. Anything might have happened to them in a place like this.

Parkman slept fitfully, waking and grabbing for his Colt with every little noise. By the time the moon began to rise he was lying there wide awake, wondering if it might provide enough light for them to saddle up and push on. A few feet away Fawn was snoring lightly, seeming perfectly at rest in these uncomfortable circumstances. This was a way of life to her.

Somewhere not too far away, Parkman heard the quiet plod of horses' hooves, and then someone talking Indian. He raised the revolver once again and sat up, waiting for any indication of who might be approaching. He looked over at Fawn. She was sitting up and looking around, too. In a moment she spoke up in a quiet guarded voice, and Parkman felt a rush of relief, knowing she must have recognized Bone talking to Little

Brother somewhere nearby.

"Lawdamercy, I thought we never was going to find you," Bone said, riding up close to the camp and stepping down. "We rode down two or three miles on the other side, looking for your camp, then swam the horses across the river and started back up this side. I thought we was going to have to stop for the night and then commence to looking for you again in the daylight."

Little Brother busied himself untying bundles of sticks from his and Bone's horses, and remarkably, Fawn had a small blaze started in a short time.

"Some storm, wasn't it?" Parkman said. "We'd have been as lost as a blind man if we didn't have the river to follow. And I was worried for you, too."

"Well, we had good reason to take so long." Bone turned to the side and said something to Fawn, and she went over to retrieve the coffee pot from one of the packs. Nobody would be getting any more sleep tonight, Parkman saw.

"We came across four men riding a few miles behind those wagons," Bone said. "We followed them until they stopped for the night, into the edge of the woods a few miles ahead, and then we lit out this-away to give you the word."

"Joseph's men, I expect," Parkman said.

"Yep, and if you ran into them in open country tomorrow morning, you'd have a fight on your hands."

"So, what now?"

"I figure the best thing is to ride north for a while 'til we've crossed some hills and are out of sight of the river. Then we can turn east and circle back around 'til we come across the wagon tracks again."

Another delay, Parkman thought. And the feeling that they might be running out of time was beginning to weigh heavily on him.

"Somewhere in those woods, we could set up an ambush and probably take out all four of them when they turn back the other way," Bone suggested. "I'm sure Fawn and the boy wouldn't mind doing some knife work on some of the bunch that wiped out their camp. And I got to say, I'm not against claiming a couple of coup myself. I was sort of a guardian for those people back there, and I let them get massacred."

"But doesn't it make more sense to stay after the main band, and the devil that leads them?" Parkman said. "You can cut away and set up any kind of ambush you want, but I've got orders, and I'm going after Duff Joseph and those guns, even if I go alone."

"Guns, is it?" Bone said. "I figured as much."

Parkman realized that he had revealed more than he meant to, and he wondered what kind of mixed loyalties that might again stir up in the heart of the old mountain man. On the one hand, he lived with the Indians and certainly wanted them to be able to defend themselves. But on the other hand, he was a white man, and he must have some feelings about seeing the Indians get their hands on those rifles, and seeing his own people shot with them.

"Does that change anything for you, Bone?"

"I guess it leaves me as confused as I already was. Times is changing, whether I want them to or not, and sometimes I feel like I don't belong on either side no more." Fawn poured coffee for them, and Bone took a sip, then poked the fire with a stick, staring thoughtfully into the flames. "It sets me to thinking again about heading out into the wild country and maybe letting some grizzly take me down for his dinner after I've got too old to hobble around anymore." He stirred the fire again, sending a cloud of small glowing cinders up into the sky. "But I ain't even sure there is any truly wild country left out there anymore."

By the time the sun was up, Parkman, Bone, and Little

Brother were laying on the ground at the crest of a hill, watching four mounted men in the distance riding west down the valley. The riders were on the opposite side of the river from last night's camp and seemed to be following the tracks that Bone and the young man had left while they were searching for Parkman the night before.

With any luck, they might ride right on by the spot where Bone had crossed the river and then lose the trail entirely. Parkman certainly hoped so, because he disliked the idea of getting into a situation of having Duff Joseph's main band ahead of him and four armed riders coming too close behind.

"All right, it's time to get moving again," Parkman said.

Topping the crest of a hill to the north, they discovered a vast herd of buffalo in the valley beyond. Along the way Parkman had seen clusters of these huge beasts here and there at a distance, but he had never witnessed a sight like this before. There were hundreds of them, probably thousands, grazing calmly on the grass and brush below.

"I expect that the scouts for the Cheyenne I was with will find this herd soon," Bone said. "And a herd this big might even draw some Sioux over from the east. That could mean trouble. The Sioux and the Cheyenne get along most times, but when it comes to a tribe's hunting grounds, you never can be sure."

"It seems like there's enough buffalo in this one valley to feed thousands of Indians," Parkman said.

"Maybe," Bone said. "But they can't kill them all. They've got to have food this time, and the next time, and the time after that. They've got to have meat to jerk for the winter, and hides for tipis and their winter robes. You're looking at the difference between life and death for the tribes down there, and it's why they fight so hard to keep the hunting grounds they claim. They never kill more than they need, and they don't cotton to other tribes, even friendly ones, roaming into their territory to hunt."

The herd was grazing slowly north and hardly seemed to pay any notice to the small party riding calmly in a wide circle ahead of them. Bone kept them at least a quarter mile away, but still, at some points, a large bull would separate from the herd and take a few defiant steps toward them, snorting and pawing the ground in challenge. But Bone kept their party at a safe distance. Soon they had completed their loop and were on the other side of the herd.

"That oughter do it," Bone declared, glancing back at the sprawling, meandering throng of animals. Parkman might not be an Indian, but he knew enough about tracking to understand that Bone had also used the buffalo herd to cover their trail. He pulled his reins to the right, heading them back east toward the forest ahead.

The campfire had burned low. Fawn had finished her chores and was stretched out on her pine needle bed, her blanket pulled up against the evening chill, humming quietly to herself as if singing an evening prayer. Little Brother had wandered out into the darkness earlier, carrying only his bow this time, doing whatever Indians do in the woods at night. Parkman figured he was probably circling the camp, ensuring that nobody was sneaking up on them unaware.

Parkman and Bone were both stretched out on the ground near the fire, elbows leaning on their saddles, sipping the last dregs of coffee in their cups before turning in. It had been a long day, with little to no rest the night before, and they were both ready to turn in.

The marshal was satisfied by the progress they had made. They had located the tracks of Duff Joseph's wagons in mid-afternoon and were pleased to find that now they were less than a day's ride behind them. The mountain pass they were headed for was steeper and narrower than the one they had encountered a few days before, and it appeared to be rough going for the wagons. At one point they had discovered a spot where Joseph's men were forced to build a ford of sorts with rocks gathered up for that purpose. That alone must have taken hours, Parkman speculated, and they weren't even close to the crest of the pass, where the going must become even more challenging.

Earlier in the evening Bone had been talking about his travels through this northwest territory, and the odd and often dangerous characters, white and red, that he had sometimes encountered along the way. But eventually he went quiet, puffing on his pipe and staring into the darkness, as if his own yarns had triggered other ancient memories that he chose not to share. Parkman tapped his tin cup on a log to empty the last of the grounds from it and set it aside. He took a last draw on the nub of his smoke, nearly burning his fingers in the process.

"Our talk about Virginia the other night set me to wondering about something that's been a puzzle to me for most of my growed-up life," Bone said at last. He was quiet for a moment, and Parkman waited patiently as his companion sorted through his thoughts.

"Many's the time on a stormy winter night," Bone said at last, "I've found myself hunkered down under a ledge, or huddled under a lean-to made of sticks and skins, wondering if the puny little fire I'd made would keep me warm enough to still be alive the next morning. And about then, I'd remember sleeping on a pallet by the stove in our home back in Virginia, comfortable and warm as a swaddled baby even on the coldest nights.

"Or maybe I'd be riding like the devil someplace, doing my best to get away from some hostiles or other that was after me. And I'd have to question my own sanity for deliberately putting myself in the middle of this wild country where men go about slaughtering one another as a matter of course.

"I could've packed my kit and gone on home any day I wanted, and still could even now. Back there, a lot of men live happy lives plowing their fields, or being carpenters or masons or cobblers or store clerks. They take wives and make babies, and when it's all over, they get buried in cemeteries alongside their kinfolks. Then once in a while somebody comes along to lay flowers on their graves. It ain't like out here where a man's bound to die in some ugly way, and his bones end up scattered in some forgotten place.

"It don't make a bit of sense to me how I've lived my life," Bone said, "but here I am still, and no plans to head back to Virginia any time soon."

"I s'pose I don't spend much time pondering why folks do the things they do," Parkman admitted. "And if I did come up with some answers, they'd probably be the wrong ones. It seems like some men are born to follow a plow, and there's others made to follow that damn sunset over the next mountain."

"You're right, I guess. I can't think of much I'd have done different if I had another chance at it."

"Maybe there's some things I'd have done differently, but what good does it do now? It's done, and nothing can be changed."

"Yep, it's done, the good and the bad." Bone fell silent, spreading his bedding on the ground and preparing to go to sleep.

Parkman did the same. The days were long now for both of them, and neither was in his prime. They needed to rest.

"It occurs to me, Bone," Parkman said as he pulled off his boots and stretched out. "Men like you and me spend too much time alone and have too much time to think. But the things we think don't matter so much as the things we do."

A few feet away on the other side of the fire, Fawn's rhythmic pattern of snores began to grow louder. It wasn't likely that anybody would ever know what regrets that woman had, Parkman thought. Or maybe she was one of the lucky ones and didn't have any.

The next day Bone again rode ahead following their noontime meal, and because there was now danger from behind as well as ahead, Bone sent Brother to ride their backtrail and sound the alarm if there was any approaching danger from the rear. For an isolated mountain trail buried deep in the wild, wide-open wilderness, it struck Parkman that things sure seemed to be getting crowded.

The marshal himself, and the nearly mute Indian woman who rode along behind him, leading the pack mule, stayed off the trail that climbed up the pass as often as they could. There were times when that wasn't possible, though, when the tumbling little stream wound through sections with sheer rock walls and steep mountainsides that would make a wild goat think twice. Parkman wasn't so much worried about the tracks of their animals, because their hoofprints would easily blend in with those made by Joseph's caravan. But he was worried about rounding a pile of boulders or a rocky outcrop and coming up face to face with a gaggle of hard cases that had only ill intentions on their mind.

Fawn seemed to know this pass well. Occasionally Parkman would hear her grunt, and when he turned, she would wave her arm off to one side or another, pointing out a narrow little rocky trail that they could veer away on and follow for a while. He appreciated the moments of safety that these periods in the deep woods provided, even if they did have to dismount frequently and lead their mounts along the most questionable stretches. Occasionally, his bad leg complained to him, when a boot sole twisted sideways or the trail ahead was too steep for too long. But the painful wound didn't come to mind nearly as often now, even in these trying circumstances.

Parkman heard a single shot from back down along the trail behind them, followed by a barrage of gunfire a few seconds later. When that died down, a single savage howl echoed up the mountainside. He recognized it. It was the same devilish commotion that Little Brother had cut loose with the night Parkman presented Sam Lyons's ancient rifle to him. Everything sounded startlingly close, but these mountain slopes played tricks with noises.

He and Fawn were off the main trail, so Parkman merely drew the Winchester from its scabbard and hunkered down behind an outcropping of rock to wait and see what happened next. Fawn simply vanished into the trees.

Within a short time, he heard horses passing by on the main trail below, moving fast from the sound of it. He figured that they must be the four-man rear guard that Duff Joseph had sent out to scout his backtrail in case they were being tracked. Dusk was approaching, and the last thing they would want was to be stranded out on a mountain trail when darkness fell. By the time they got back, there was no telling what sort of report they would deliver to their boss, Parkman thought with a chuckle. By then one young Indian lad with a fifty-year-old smooth-bore rifle might have turned into a dozen braves howling for their scalps.

Parkman's concern for Little Brother ended when the boy appeared a short time later, riding his sure-footed pony up the narrow trail to where they were. When he spotted them, he grinned broadly and waved the rifle above him in a sign of victory. For safety's sake he didn't whoop and holler, but he sure looked like he wanted to.

"Did you get you one of them?" Parkman asked. He pointed a finger at his chest and made as if he was tumbling out of the saddle. No, the boy indicated, shaking his head. He ran a pointed finger close by his skull and made a frightened face, indicating that he had scared the hell out of them. But he was still as proud as if he'd finished off the whole lot.

They pushed on as long as the light allowed, then stopped at a spot no more than twenty feet off the main trail to wait out the night. They were near the crest of the pass now, and there was no place flat and straight enough even for a person to lie down and sleep. Parkman sat with his back against a tree, hat pulled down over his face, to await the dawn. Fawn and Brother found similar roosts, and they all kept their horses nearby. There was little or nothing for their mounts to graze on, and the animals would be hungry and surly in the morning.

He slept fitfully, dreaming in bits and snippets, jolting awake at every random forest noise. Once he heard a cougar cry somewhere in the rocky heights above them, its call somehow sounding both mournful and fearsome. The smaller night creatures scuttled along the forest floor, curious about these intruders into their domain, but not so nosy as to come up close. The horses and mule, as uncomfortable as the humans, slept hardly at all. Occasionally one of them would snort out their displeasure, but none seemed to signal approaching danger.

In one dream, Parkman saw glowing, merciless eyes surrounding them, wolves he thought, inching patiently forward for the kill. But he had no weapons, and his arms and hands were heavy as lead as he tried to raise them to defend himself. He startled himself awake with a short quick yelp. Close by, Fawn turned her head sideways and looked at him, then tilted her head down and went back to sleep.

When Parkman woke again, he realized that he had actually managed to sleep undisturbed for a while. The moon was up, lighting the sky and speckling down through the trees to paint the forest floor with alternating patches of light and dark. There was movement in the trees nearby, and in a moment, Brother came back from answering nature's call. He loosened the rawhide reins of his horse and turned his head to Parkman. He patted his chest, then pointed away in the direction they had been traveling. "Yu' Tah Huhu," he said quietly.

Parkman had heard this phrase before. It was what both Fawn and Brother called Bone. He assumed it must mean "Bone Eater" or something similar.

Instinct told Parkman that he shouldn't let the boy ride out alone in the dark to look for Bone in these broad, endless wilderness spaces. But who was he to try and stop this young Indian brave from going out in his own home territory and trying to find his friend and protector?

Parkman pointed to the rifle and made a motion like shoving a ramrod down into a barrel. Brother nodded. He was loaded up.

"Be careful out there," Parkman muttered quietly.

After the young man was gone, Fawn plundered into one of the packs and pulled out a leather bag of jerky. She gave Parkman some, then handed a canteen to him. It wasn't likely that either of them would get any more sleep tonight, he thought.

Shortly after dawn, more horsemen rode by along the trail below, grumbling and cursing at the bad luck of being assigned rear guard duty. They weren't even attempting to be quiet, and Parkman ruminated over the fact that Duff Joseph probably didn't have the luxury of picking from the best when he put together his crew for a job like this one. More likely he just gathered up whatever frontier trash that were willing to go along.

In his experience, the marshal thought, scum was drawn to the company of other scum for dirty work like this. That was why he had not felt even a minute's regret at leaving the pieces of Homer Bradberry scattered around the forest floor after Sam Lyons sliced him up and then gave up the ghost himself. The idea that the lives of some men didn't matter was one of the ways he had dealt with the violent life he led. Somebody had to stop men like these from doing their worst.

Fawn walked down the hill to the stream below to fill their canteens and water skins. Remarkably, she came back with an eighteen-inch trout, which she apparently grappled from the water. Her dress was wet to the waist as she held up the fish for Parkman's approval. Something that might have slightly resembled a hint of a smile played across her face and then was quickly gone.

Fawn skillfully gutted and skinned the fish, then slipped it under the ropes on the mule's packs. Hopefully they would be somewhere that was safe to start a fire before it went bad.

They continued along the narrow game trail they had been following, but as they neared the crest, it played out, and they were forced to go back down to the main trail by the stream. The tracks left by Joseph's wagon train were fresh and clear now. They had probably passed through here as recently as yesterday evening, Parkman thought, and they would have had to stop overnight, as he, Fawn, and Brother did.

At one point they found a broken wagon wheel cast off on the side of the trail. They must have brought extra wheels along, in anticipation of this, but the time it took to make the switch only meant that he was closer than ever to them. Parkman drew out the Winchester, checked the load, and began riding with it perched across the saddle in front of him. Joseph was a clever old coyote, and it was possible that he might dispatch more than one gaggle of men to cover his backtrail. One farther back, and the other closer, made good sense.

He and Fawn had crossed the stream yet again to the left side, when he heard a call from the nearby woods, barely audible above the noise of the churning water.

"Ridge Parkman. Over here." Bone rode his horse outside the line of trees, while Brother remained back in the shadows.

"We been waiting for you nigh onto half a day," Bone complained. Parkman saw that the sun was just up into full view to the east but didn't argue. "Decide to sleep in, did you?"

"Naw, I had to wait while the woman went fishing." Parkman nodded his head back over his shoulder so Bone could admire the trout. "I guess you'll quit galivanting and show up for supper tonight. Else I'll have to eat your share."

"No more need for galivanting," Bone reported. "The wagons passed by this spot late yesterday and stopped for the night a ways down the other side. That's why we waited here for you, so you wouldn't ride right on top of them without knowing."

"How many rear guards are strung out behind?" Parkman asked.

"Four went out about daybreak, like the ones that was trying to track us before. And then he left a man here and there in the rocks to kind of hopscotch along behind. He's a careful man. That's why we'd better get off this trail and stay off, now that we're close."

"And I assume you know how to do that?"

"Shouldn't be a problem." Bone grinned as he turned his horse away. "Just follow along."

Parkman fell in behind Bone's horse, with Fawn and the mule next in line, and Brother bringing up the rear. At first Parkman thought they must be about to ride straight up the side of the mountain, but then the trail meandered off to the right, and they rode into a high, grass covered plateau. They released the animals to graze for a while, and the four of them walked to the edge of the plateau.

To the east, the view spread for miles and miles across yet another broad valley, and on to a hazy range of mountains in the distance. But, more importantly, they had an excellent view of the east side of the pass below them.

"Don't get too near the edge," Bone warned. "If you commence to falling, you might not hit bottom 'til sometime next week."

It was indeed an impressive distance down, and near the bottom in the canyon that spilled out into the valley, Parkman spotted a tiny, faraway line of wagons and riders on horseback, creeping along like a row of ants. They hardly seemed to be moving at all.

"I've been following this outfit for I-don't-know-how-many hundreds of miles," Parkman said. "But this is the first time I actually laid eyes on them."

"They don't look like so much from way up here, do they?" Bone said. "Seems like we could go ahead and mash them with one hand and then head on home."

Parkman didn't answer. He was counting heads. Four wagon drivers, with another man sitting on the seat beside each of them. Four on horseback maybe a hundred yards ahead of the wagons, and two outriders on either side. Two more bringing up the rear. Add to that the four riders who had passed down their back trail this morning, and probably a couple of scouts far ahead. Twenty-four at least, maybe more. That was going to take a lot of mashing.

"Plus, there's five riders shadowing them about a mile to the south," Bone added. "I don't see them now, but I got a look at them yesterday. Indians I'd say, from the way they ride."

"Braves from your camp?"

"Could be. When we're down out of the mountains again an' I've got some elbow room, I figgered I'd ride over that way and find out. Cheyenne, or Sioux maybe. If they're Cheyenne I'd probably know them and feel safe enough. But if they're Sioux, I'd need to be cautious."

"If they're your people, it would be good to have some allies," Parkman said.

Bone chuckled at that. "If word gets out what's in them

wagons down there, and that you come along to stop them, you wouldn't find a friend for a hundred miles in any direction. Except me. Maybe."

"That's not the best news I've heard lately. Even the part about you, maybe."

They walked back toward where the horses were grazing. Fawn had built a small fire with old, dry sticks that hardly sent any smoke rising, and she had the coffee pot boiling. She also had the large trout skewered on a stick above the flames.

"That there's a good woman," Bone said. "Never have to tell her to do nothing. She just does it. Maybe, if it happens her man's dead, you can take up with her, Marshal."

Parkman glanced over at Bone and saw that he was joshing. "I got a woman waiting for me down in Colorado, an' one's plenty."

They saw Little Brother a short distance away, nosing around a jumble of rocks at the base of a small cliff that rose above the plateau. He was stirring around on the ground with a stick, and when they drew nearer, they realized what he was investigating. Half a dozen decaying bodies lay scattered about, mostly rotted to the bone now, but with a few tatters of buckskin clothes and patches of dried brown flesh still visible.

As Parkman watched, Brother pulled an arrow out of an exposed ribcage, examined it, and tucked it into the quiver hanging across his back. Then he moved on.

Bone knelt beside one of the corpses and lifted a patch of buckskin that still bore some remnants of beadwork. As he did that, the skull moved slightly atop the exposed spine, seeming to stare at this living man from its sunken empty sockets. What little skin remained on the face gave it some remaining human characteristics, and the thick, sun-bleached hair lay in a tangle beneath.

"Crow, I'd guess," Bone said. "But I don't know that much

about them other tribes." He said something to Brother, and the young man replied, holding up another arrow that he had taken out of a flattened quiver. "Blackfoot, he says. I wonder what in the devil they were doing this far south? That first arrow the boy took from between them bones, that was Cheyenne."

Soon Fawn came over from the fire, and, like Brother, she began to poke around for anything of value. She picked up the patch of beadwork Bone had looked at and kept it.

"This was Indians fighting Indians, then?" Parkman said.

"Don't make a lot of sense to the likes of us, does it?" Bone said. "With all the whites pouring in here like water from a broken dam, it seems like all the tribes would band together to drive them off. But some of these tribes have been hating each other since the start of time. They don't know any other way."

Soon losing interest in the scavenging, Parkman went back to the fire. He turned the fish roasting over the flames, then poured himself a cup of coffee. The first sip scalded the end of his tongue. Now that he had gotten a glimpse of his quarry, he was eager to go. But people and animals had to eat and rest occasionally, didn't they, no matter how it raked on his nerves to waste the time?

CHAPTER SIXTEEN

Parkman lay stretched out on the ground at the crest of a hill, no more than two hundred yards from where Duff Joseph's wagon train had stopped for the night. Confident in their numbers and their fire power, it seemed, they took no precautions to conceal their presence here.

Four fires burned in the camp, and their herd of horses and mules was grazing in a gully nearby. Some of the crew had already spread their blankets on the ground under the wagons, and a few others were lazing around the fires. Parkman had seen no sign that guards were posted out in the dark, away from the camp, and he was surprised by Joseph's seeming disregard for safety so deep into Indian country. Maybe he already had some sort of deal set up with them, the marshal thought, and a meeting place already chosen. That would be bad news.

Bone had left them two days ago after their small band descended from the mountain pass, and they hadn't seen him since. He had instructed Brother to stay with Parkman and Fawn this time, which clearly disappointed the young brave. Bone told him it was because he might be useful, like before, if any danger came near to Parkman and Fawn. But Parkman knew there was another reason as well. He was going out to locate the small band of Indians they had seen from the mesa high up the mountainside and didn't want a young man to look after if there was trouble. Brother now seemed to consider himself a full-grown warrior, but he needed some seasoning yet.

Now that Parkman's small band was down in the open country again and knew what direction Joseph was headed, they had no need to track him so closely, and they were easily able to avoid the riders that Joseph sent back to watch the trail behind. It seemed to Parkman that the old Texas desert rat might be letting down his guard a little, which suited the marshal fine. But it also might mean that Joseph was nearing his destination, and his confidence was growing.

The moon was full and high in the western sky, bathing the rolling landscape with its pale-blue light. It would set again in a few short hours, and another bank of clouds threatened from the northwest. Parkman knew he needed to return to their own small, hidden camp before the moonlight vanished and the rains started. But it was no more than a two-mile ride to the north, and there was time.

For now, he wanted to learn more about the routine of these men, so that when the right time came, he'd be better prepared for what he might encounter.

He swung the Sharps rifle around and rested it on the ground in front of him, drawing a bead on one of the men standing by the fire, wishing he could pull the trigger. He shifted his aim a couple more times, taking out others in his imagination, grinning in the dark. But he knew it wouldn't be as easy as that. He could never hope to kill even a fraction of their numbers before they swarmed over him.

Besides, it wasn't the men he was after. It was the cargo in those damned wagons, cases of rifles and ammunition that, in Indian hands, could take the lives of countless soldiers, settlers, prospectors, and heaven only knew who else. But a barrage of gunfire into the sides of those wagons stood little chance of setting off the kind of conflagration required to destroy them all. Any way you looked at it, that was close-up work.

He crawled back down the hill, then walked the quarter mile

back to where he had left General Grant. He needed rest and food, and he knew he should get back to their own camp before the moon dipped behind the mountains and the rain started. Fawn had cobbled together some sort of lean-to with a buffalo skin she had salvaged from the camp of her people, and he looked forward to sleeping under the scant shelter it would provide. The only problem would be resting so close beside the Indian woman, and trying to sleep despite her snoring.

In a moment of private mirth, he had considered renaming the woman, as he had the boy. She Rumbles at Night would fit. But he figured she might not take to her new moniker, and there could be consequences. She slept every night with a long, sharp knife held tightly in her grip.

Brother came back from his early morning hunt with a fat rattlesnake draped across his saddle. It was a big fellow, as long as Brother was tall, and the youth had left his arrow in its head, just to show off. Fawn muttered a few words under her breath that wiped the proud grin off his face as she took the snake and went to work on it. Most people better respected a rattler even when they thought it was dead, and they usually cut the head off straightaway.

The storm had blown by last night without finding their camp, and Parkman felt well rested this morning after a good night's sleep. The horses and mule were fresh as well, ready for their day's work.

Bone found them about noon, having ridden through the night, and through the storm, in a broad arc in front of Joseph's outfit. He had a lot to report as he fell in line alongside Parkman.

"I met up with those Injuns we saw. They were Cheyenne, and things went well because I knew a couple of them, and they vouched for me with the others. I've got a decent reputation with those people, and one of them was some kind of distant relative of my dead wife. They all got a good laugh when he told the others the story about how I come to be called Bone Eater. I grinned along like a fool, even though there's a dozen versions of it by now, and none of them close to the truth."

Parkman let him ramble for a while, knowing he would get around to making his report eventually, and they had time enough on their hands now.

"The way he told it, an old chief called Many Feathers had walloped me in the head with his war club, and I'd gone plumb crazy for a while, so they didn't kill me right off. Instead he kept me around camp, and I lived with the dogs, fighting them for scraps of food and catching chewed-on bones in my mouth when the chief tossed them at me. That was the bone-eating part, and they enjoyed it considerable, so I grinned and went along like it was God's own truth.

"And then he got into the part about how I slowly got my good sense back, commenced to standing up on my hind legs, and saved the life of Many Feathers's favorite wife during a raid by the Crows. The chief made me his son and married me off to the prettiest girl in camp, which ain't any more true than the rest. My little White Moccasin was a fine, faithful wife, and I cherished her dearly, but she was a long ways from a looker. Near as homely as Morning Fawn over there, but of a far better disposition."

To make it up to Brother for leaving him behind on the last trip, Bone had assigned him the job of lead scout. Brother took the job very seriously, roving far ahead, and only reporting back every hour or so about the way ahead. They were traveling in the same direction as Joseph's wagon train, a couple of miles to the south, and were pulling well ahead.

As soon as Bone completed the report on his meeting with the Cheyenne, if he ever made it that far, Parkman wanted to discuss the plan he had been turning over in his mind all the previous day.

"Turns out those braves were advance scouts for a much larger village that is working its way north, looking out for better hunting grounds. Seems like the main village has several hundred people in it, and a large herd of horses. There was ten scouts to start with, but when they got wind of the white man's wagon train, they decided to split up. Two went back south to tell the chiefs, and four more cut away, still looking for good hunting. The rest are keeping track of Joseph's bunch.

"It was good news when I told them about that big herd we come across on the back side of them mountains," Bone added.

"They don't know what's in them wagons, then?" Parkman asked.

"Not yet. But it won't take long once a couple of hundred Cheyenne warriors rain their fire and brimstone down on those white men."

"I don't care if they string Joseph's gang up and slice them into rawhide," Parkman said coldly. "It would be proper revenge for a thousand sins that old man's never been made to account for. But I don't aim to see them get their hands on all that armament."

"Looks to me like you're chewing off a pretty big bite there, Mister Lawman. Talking big and doing big don't always come together the way you want 'em to."

They saw Brother galloping his horse over a hilltop ahead. The boy seemed to be working that pinto of his pretty hard, Parkman thought, but the sturdy little horse was up to the challenge.

Bone probably already knew the lay of the land ahead, but he still held back and let the young Indian make his report, translating it for Parkman along the way.

"He said the hills begin to break apart a few miles up ahead,"

Bone said. "Lots of cracks and splits and gullies, and rows of rock sticking up out of the ground."

He turned his head back to Brother to let him say more.

"The earth is red and hard, all sand and rock. There is no grass, nothing for the horses to graze on. Only some brush and bushes. And there's no water to speak of. There are a few pools from the rain last night, but no creeks or streams. Rough going, it sounds like."

"Can the wagons get through it, or will they have to go around?" Parkman asked.

Bone asked Brother, then nodded in agreement with his answer. "They can get through if their mules are strong and their wagons are sturdy. But it will be slow going." Then Bone added more from his own storehouse of knowledge. "There's a river on the other side. If they can make it across, then they'll have to turn north for a couple of dozen miles to find a pass to the other side of that next range." Bone paused a moment, adding emphasis to what he said next. "And that would put them into Sioux territory."

Bone, Parkman, and Brother took turns watching over their small herd of four horses and a mule the next night. They had ridden hard and long to get ahead of their prey. With a growing number of Cheyenne in the area, it only made sense to watch their animals, even though they had two honest-to-goodness Cheyenne citizens in their camp, and one friend of the tribe. It had been Bone's idea, and Parkman figured that there must be no hard and fast rule about stealing horses from one another. He had no knowledge about the details of the code of honor for any of these plains tribes, but he did understand that they lived by a set of rules that few white men would understand.

It was pitch dark now, and at the start of his turn on watch, Parkman had stumbled down the hillside, talking quietly to the animals until General Grant let out a huff to let him know where they were. Both Bone's and Parkman's horses seemed to have been sleeping standing up, and Brother's pinto was down on the ground a few feet away. Fawn's horse and the mule had wandered away a little farther and were still grazing.

He couldn't imagine how any man, red or white, could locate this small herd in such darkness, but he had heard enough cautionary tales to believe that it could be done. Maybe Indians had some kind of sight that allowed them to see in the dark better than any white man could. Or maybe they could smell a horse, or hear one, a long way off. It could possibly be all three, or even something more mysterious.

Parkman found a patch of grass amidst the horses and relaxed onto one elbow. General Grant moved a little closer, as if he too was assigned to guard duty. He and the horse were fond of each other, and after the years they had traveled this land together, Parkman sometimes wondered if the two of them could almost read each other's thoughts. At any rate, he did credit the horse's quick reflexes and dead-on-target instincts with getting him out of any number of tight scraps.

Bone had been telling Parkman over tonight's campfire about an Indian legend he'd heard of where the first horses had come from. The way he told it, back before time, the gods had passed by here on their way back to the next world. They stood tall as giants, and their bodies and heads shone in the light like fire. And because the People treated them with respect and generosity, the gods gave them the gift of horses, which made them more powerful than their enemies, and all the wild creatures around them.

"Must have been the Spaniards," Parkman had noted. "Down Mexico way, they claim the first Spanish to set foot on this new land wandered all over kingdom come, looking for gold and such."

"Did they find any?" Bone asked.

"I think so, but not the buckets full they thought they'd stumble across."

"Well, there's still gold enough in these mountains for many a fool to lose his life and his hair over."

Staring out into the dense darkness, Parkman imagined what life must have been like for those early people, back before time. How had they managed to find food, and protect themselves from wild animals, and fight off enemies, with only clubs and spears, and maybe not even bows and arrows yet? How had they protected themselves through the cold, hard winters in these upper regions?

How miserable life must have been back in the days before coffee and whiskey and tobacco, he thought, chuckling to himself.

Every place he'd ever been, life never sat still, and he could tell that it was no different out here on the frontier. No matter how broad and endless the mountains and forests and open plains might seem right now, change was still coming, as relentless and unstoppable as one of those sudden storms that raked the land from one horizon to another with hardly any warning.

The wild Indians were already resisting the encroachment of civilization around the fringes of their ancestral territories. But Parkman knew they couldn't have any real notion of what was yet to come their way. It was like a man watching a tornado sweep across his fields and pastures but not having any understanding of what it would be like to get swept up in it.

Somewhere away off, he heard a wolf howl. He sat up and cocked his head this way and that, getting a better feel for the direction. But General Grant wasn't getting jittery and didn't offer any of those warning noises he made when he sensed that danger was afoot. The wolves might pass this way, but with the scent of man in the air, as well as the smell of smoke from the campfire nearby, they weren't likely to come too close. It was late spring, a time of abundance, and there was plenty of easier prey out there.

As soon as the first hints of sunlight began to outline the mountains far to the east, Parkman gathered up the horses and led them back to camp. All three of his traveling companions were still wrapped in their blankets but stirred at the sound of the approaching horses.

"Gonna sleep all day?" Parkman asked with false bravado. As the first one awake, it was his right.

Bone laid his blanket aside and stretched out his legs. "When I get old and settle in someplace, I'm gonna have me a goose down tick, and a goose down pillow. Sometimes I might not get up for days, except only to eat a little and answer nature's calling."

"Well those times ain't here yet," Parkman said. "And we've got many a mile to cross before day's end."

They were now near the broad stretch of broken land and desert-dry soil that Brother had described to them. It was going to be a hard ride with bad visibility in all directions, and Bone had warned that one day might not be enough time to get across. But it would be even worse going for the four wagons and the teams of mules that drew them. That's why Parkman and Bone had decided that today was the day to take a try at stopping Duff Joseph for good.

A few yards away, Fawn had slipped her dress over her head and was pulling on her moccasins. Recently she had taken to sleeping naked. Bone said it was common for Indians, men and women, and it seemed to show that she felt more comfortable in their midst. Brother didn't bother to undress since he seldom wore much but a breechcloth, and maybe a beaded headband with a single eagle's feather sticking up in back.

Bone gave Fawn and Brother a few instructions in their

language. The boy grunted and nodded his understanding, but Fawn only gave him that same flat, expressionless look and made no utterances.

"I told them to fill up everything that would hold water," Bone explained. "Even the cook pot and the feed bucket. We might not see any water again until we get to the other side of this rough patch. Not even any little trickles for the horses, so we'll have to provide for them, too."

Parkman took a quick inventory in his head. Fawn carried three water skins on her horse, and Bone and Brother both had one. Parkman had four canteens of his own, as well as a small keg strapped to the mule. Nobody would be taking any baths, which they didn't anyway, but they should have an adequate supply to get them to the other side. Brother led the animals down to the nearby creek and let them drink their fill, which should get them by for a while.

They came to the badlands without any warning. As they topped a rise, there it lay, stretching out before them like a vast spiderweb of red sandstone gullies. Parkman had been through this kind of fractured terrain down in Texas. He remembered how hard it was to ride through, and how easy it was to get lost once you were down in it.

"I'll lead out," Bone said, "I been through here a couple of times before. But I don't want to hear no cussing from back in the line if I get myself discombobulated now and again."

"It hurts my brain to even look at it," Parkman said. "You're in charge now."

As soon as they headed down into the first ravine, the horses started choosing their steps more carefully and treading lightly on the mix of loose stones and sandy gravel beneath their hooves. Parkman didn't even try to steer his mount. It was better to let him pick his own way along as best he could.

"It's not so bad where Joseph will make his crossing," Bone

said. "We'll keep going this way until a little past midday, then hook off to the right so we're sure to end up ahead of him by nightfall. Then it's your turn, Marshal."

"Yep. I got it all planned out."

"Are you going to pin on that badge before you ramble in and take them on?" Bone teased.

"I dast not," Parkman said lightly.

Bone kept his bearings by keeping an eye on the line of peaks ahead, and they didn't stop until the sun was high above their heads. Occasionally they came to flat patches, which Parkman thought of as plateaus for want of a better term, and it was up on one of them where Bone chose to stop and rest for a while. Brother broke out the feed bucket and gave the horses and mule a drink. Bone and Parkman strolled to the southern side of the flats and took a good look around to the south and southwest.

At first they saw nothing, but then, in the shimmering heat rising up off the land, Parkman spotted a row of small dark shapes, seeming to glimmer and float against the lighter backdrop behind them. "That must be them," he said, pointing away toward the distant specter.

"I'd guess so. And about where I thought they'd be."

At first the tiny images seemed only to dance lightly in the distance, as if they were floating up above the ground, instead of moving on it. But after watching for a while, he understood that they were moving forward at what appeared to be a painfully slow pace.

"They'll be getting into this mess pretty soon, and when the sun goes down, they'll have to stop and camp however far they are in. It's what you wanted."

"I suppose it is," Parkman said. But catching up to them in the right place was only the first part, and it was the second part that he was most worried about.

CHAPTER SEVENTEEN

Bone picked up one of the small, eight-inch-long cylinders that Parkman had taken from his saddlebags and examined it with interest. "Shotgun barrel?" he asked. "Looks like Damascus steel to me."

"I cut up a couple of old ten-gauge scatterguns into eight-inch pieces," Parkman said. "Filled them full of black powder, made holes for the fuses, and sealed the ends with wood bungs. It was Hattie's idea to stow them in canning jars to keep them dry. Kind of crude, but it's the best I could come up with on short notice."

"Might do the job." Bone picked up another of the handmade explosives and turned it over in his hands. "They might not explode like a cannon ball, but they should throw out plenty of flames."

"I'm hoping they blow up, but I won't know until I try one."

They had left Fawn and the horses about a quarter mile away and had moved forward on foot to draw close to their objective. Now they were hunkered down in a small cleft, close enough to see the glow of the fires in Joseph's camp. Brother knelt beside Bone, holding his ancient smooth-bore in one hand, and curiously turning one of the little bombs with the other.

"So what's your plan?" Bone asked.

"I'm hoping to get a couple of them stuck in under the canvas on each of the wagons, then light the fuses and skedaddle," Parkman said. "Even if they don't explode, they should scatter enough flames around to start the canvas and the wood crates on fire. Maybe even the wagons, if I'm lucky. I should have about two minutes to get clear before the fireworks start."

"Sounds easy enough," Bone said, his voice oozing with sarcasm.

"Wal, if you've got a better idea, now's the time."

The three of them crept closer to the camp, and Bone and Brother found firing positions nearby to give Parkman some cover during his escape.

The campfires were burning down now, and most of the men in Duff Joseph's band seemed to have already bedded down for the night. Only three or four men remained awake, idling around the camp and talking quietly among themselves. This seemed to be the best they had in place as far as guards were concerned. Up here in Indian territory, where death could come visiting unexpectedly out of any shadow, it was unlikely that any of Joseph's men were willing to range very far out into the darkness alone.

Parkman rose to his feet and started walking toward the camp, scuffling his boots on the ground and making plenty of noise so none of the men would get the idea that he was sneaking up. The two men at the closest fire turned their heads toward him suspiciously, their hands dropping down to rest on the hilts of their sidearms.

"I don't know what I ate," Parkman said, fumbling with his britches as if he were closing them up. "But it sure didn't agree with me."

"I told cookie that elk meat was going bad," one of the men complained. Both the men seemed to relax, accepting Parkman as one of their bunch. "But he said it would do for one more day."

The camp cook seemed not to be fully asleep and grumbled out from his bedroll somewhere nearby. "If you want some fresh meat, then why don't you ride out and shoot something? Maybe some of them redskins we seen this morning might even share a kill with you."

Parkman turned away before he got too close to the men at the fire, as if returning to his own blankets. It was a tight camp, he noticed, probably because of the nearness of the Indians the cook had mentioned. He figured they must have caught a glimpse of the scouting party that was keeping an eye on them.

The four wagons had been positioned one behind another in two rows about thirty feet apart. At either end, ropes had been stretched between the wagons, and the horses and mules were tied off to those. It was a clear, moonlit night, and as near as Parkman could tell, all the sleeping men were stretched out in the open ground within this makeshift fortification.

It was an ideal layout for his purpose. With all the men on the inside, he could do his work on the outside, place the explosives, and light the fuses without any sleeping men underfoot to see what he was doing. He went to one of the wagons and scuttled beneath it, as if that were his chosen sleeping place for the night. Then he eased on out the other side and stood up again on the outside of the camp.

Cutting one of the rope tie-downs on the side of the wagon, he slid two of the bombs inside, leaving only a few inches of fuse hanging out from under the canvas that covered the wagon's cargo. Then he moved on to the next wagon and did the same there.

The line of horses began to jitter and huff as he passed along behind them on his way to the other two wagons. Parkman paused and muttered low, soothing reassurances to the animals, but they had already caught the attention of the men standing around the fire, and a few of the sleeping men were also beginning to sit up in their bedrolls. It didn't pay to sleep too soundly at times like this, when Indians might be slipping up on them.

"What are you up to there, fella?" a voice asked from the darkness behind him.

Parkman froze for a moment, then said, "The boss has sent me out to take a look around the backtrail. He's worried them Indians might be coming along too close behind."

"Wasn't that what the bunch he sent out an hour ago was supposed to do?"

Parkman heard the unmistakable metal click of a hammer being thumbed back, and he froze.

"What's the beef?" one of the men at the fireside barked. He and another man started for them, drawing their revolvers as they came. The whole camp was getting stirred up now.

"I was coming back from doin' my bidness, and I saw this one fooling around the horses. Sneaking around in the dark like a thief, he was." Parkman heard him coming up closer and knew it was already too late to make a break for it.

The whole camp was astir now, and they roughhoused Parkman over near one of the fires. They all began to confirm that nobody there knew who he was.

"Make a way, boys," a gruff voice ordered from the back of the bunch. "What's the ruckus?" They parted as instructed, and a man stepped forward to stand right in front of their prisoner. He was a little shorter than Parkman, and a good bit older. He wore a filthy, coarsely woven Mexican serape over his shoulders and walked with a pronounced limp, seeming to favor his right hip joint. But the thing that convinced Parkman that this must be Duff Joseph, the man he had pursued for so many years but had never actually laid eyes on, was the dusty black bowler that sat askance on his head. Legend had it that Joseph had a strange affinity for head gear, usually the more curious the better. Down in Texas it had been rumored that he would wear the stovepipes of the businessmen he murdered, and sometimes sported around in the bonnets of the women he kidnapped. Parkman had never bought into the talk that Joseph even enjoyed trying on a woman's dress now and again, but with a man as warped and insane as this one, who could know for sure?

"Who the hell are you?" Joseph said, drawing his revolver and shoving it up under Parkman's chin until his head tilted back. "You the weasel that's been trailing us?"

"Not trailing. I been trying to catch up to you. I come across a fellow a few days back who said you might take me on."

"An' so to thank him, you chopped him up into dog meat and left the pieces out in the woods."

"I didn't have any part in whatever happened to him after we talked," Parkman said.

Duff Joseph stepped a little closer to Parkman, his head askance, and his cold, dark eyes probing. His breath smelled like an outhouse in hell, and his wiry, graying beard and hair needed serious grooming.

"Who the hell are you really?" Joseph asked again. This time it sounded more like he was pondering a puzzle than expecting a truthful answer. When he received no reply, he raised his pistol and gave his prisoner a solid rap to the side of his head. It didn't quite knock Parkman out, but it sent his head spinning and turned his legs to jelly. He would have folded and gone down if men weren't holding him up on both sides.

"Tie him to a wagon wheel and gag him good," Joseph said, turning away. "I'm used up, and I need some sleep. I'll get the truth out of him in the morning." After a few steps he stopped and looked back. "And you men that's on guard, you get your tails outside the wagons and keep a lookout like I told you. With the lot of you standing around spitting in the fire all night, we could wake up with our throats slit, and you'd be none the wiser."

Parkman's captors sat him down in front of a wagon wheel and trussed him tight, with his arms splayed out and his ankles bound together. His head was still swimming, and falling stars seemed to be flashing inside his eyeballs. His head felt like a horse had stepped on it, and he could feel the trickle of blood running down his neck and into his shirt. He hardly knew who he was, let alone where he was or what these men were doing to him.

After a while he closed his eyes and let his head sag back against the wooden spokes of the wheel. So much for the plan.

He was brought back around later by a few hard slaps from a gloved hand. He shook his head, tasting the blood inside his mouth, and opened his eyes, once more aware of the bad situation he was in. The man delivering the blows knelt in front of him, and close by stood Duff Joseph, leaning on a staff for support.

The man abusing Parkman looked familiar. He wore a dusty, tall-crowned hat with a wide, beaded band, and his small eyes seemed to glow like hot coals below the wide brim. His thick moustache dipped down below his chin. The whiskers were tightly braided and decorated with the quill of a feather on each end.

"If you were my prisoner, Marshal Ridge Parkman," the man said, his voice gravelly, "you would be dead already. Or wishing you were." His cheekbones were high and pronounced, and deep furrows of age were etched into his coarse, dark skin.

"Same here," Parkman mumbled. "Joe something, ain't it? Comanche Joe? No, that ain't right. Bloody Joe, ain't it? Bloody Joe Menendez."

"You've died many times in my dreams, after Fort Dodge," Menendez said. Parkman could remember the fight, but not much about who he might or might not have shot. "You wounded my father there, and after that he was crazy with pain until the minute he died."

"Wal, somebody had to put a stop to your Comanchero raids

before you murdered every settler within a hundred miles. You and your daddy and the rest of that bunch was getting plumb out of hand."

Standing nearby, Joseph had a slight smile on his face, as if he were enjoying the show. Turning his head toward his boss, Menendez said, "I'll give you half my pay at the end if you let me have one hour alone with this man."

"Nope, can't do it, Joe. I got other plans for him." Joseph chuckled. He hadn't changed a whit, Parkman thought. He still seemed to thrive on the hate and chaos and raw brutality. "Now you get your greedy tail going and make sure them wagons are ready for the trail. Then scout on ahead, like I told you, and make sure we can get across that river up ahead."

Menendez gave Parkman one final backhand slap before standing up and walking away to carry out his leader's orders.

The eastern sky was beginning to glow with predawn light, and most of the other men were busily engaged in starting their breakfast, gathering up their belongings, and saddling their horses. On both sides of the camp, others were hitching the double teams of mules to the wagons.

"I had a notion to whale the truth out of you this morning, about who you are and why you're tracking us," Joseph said. "An' then I was going to leave what was left of you here for the buzzards and coyotes to clean up." He stepped closer, grinning down at Parkman and waving a piece of paper in the air. "But that was before I found out we got a famous man amongst us."

"Famous?" Parkman muttered.

"Wal, it might not be so up here in the northern Rockies. But where I hail from down in the west Texas badlands and parts beyond, most men in my line of work know enough about the famous Marshal Ridge Parkman to fear and despise him."

"How'd you figure that one out?"

Joseph waved the piece of paper in his face. "One of my men

found this in your pocket and read it to me. A telegram from your boss saying what a murderous man I was and setting you loose on my trail. He must think highly of you, and not so well of us, to send you out by your own self to stop us."

"The odds seem about right to me," Parkman said.

"And you was going to stop us with these?" Joseph held up one of the shotgun barrel explosives that Parkman had brought along. Joseph mocked the whole idea of it, and a few men who were beginning to gather around joined in their leader's laughter.

"It might have worked. Under different circumstances."

"I've got half a mind to try one out, just to see," Joseph said. He dropped one of the small bombs between Parkman's bound legs. "But something like that, or staking you out for a buzzard feast, would be a waste of a valuable catch like you. I've got another plan for you entirely, Mister Marshal Ridge Parkman, sir."

Bending down with some effort, Duff Joseph retrieved the bomb, then turned away to supervise the breaking of camp.

Parkman wouldn't have let his thoughts show, but the idea of being staked out on the ground and left behind did have a certain appeal. Bone and Brother would be lurking somewhere nearby, perhaps watching them even now, and they would be able to free him before the buzzards went to work. But now, if Duff Joseph had something else in mind, it probably wasn't something Parkman should look forward to.

Although they could have easily tied him atop one of the loaded wagons, Joseph ordered instead that he be bound across the bare back of a horse like fresh game. Before they had finished the first mile, Parkman was already beginning to get an idea about what parts of his body would be the most miserable after this long day's ride on the trail.

They seemed to have brought along enough water in the large wooden barrels in the wagons, but nobody thought to offer any to Parkman. Nor was he given any food. His hat had been lost someplace, and as the sun rose higher throughout the morning, his back and head began to bake.

At one point, four riders caught up to the wagon train from behind and made their report to Duff Joseph. They had spotted a dozen or so Indians off in the distance and had dropped down into a ravine until they were gone. They didn't even seem to know what tribe the Indians belonged to, and Parkman wondered if they had a notion about the much larger bands of Cheyenne on the move nearby.

Joseph dispatched another group to scout their rear, and when Menendez and the scouts out front returned, he sent new men out in that direction as well. He was trying to be cautious, but Parkman had to wonder whether the old outlaw had any true idea about the enormous danger that actually surrounded him.

Joseph's bunch was a mixed band of misfits. By their clothes and outfits—wide sombreros, tooled boots, Mexican saddles, and suchlike—it appeared that some of his cronies had traveled north with him from the southwestern badlands. Most of the rest were the kind of frontier trash that might be cheap and available almost any place, men with guns for hire and no particular scruples about who they used them on. Besides Menendez, there were two other half-breeds, and one man that appeared to be a full-blooded Indian, but not from one of the local tribes. Ute, maybe, or Crow, Parkman speculated. These were the men Joseph conferred with most often about the terrain ahead and what dangers they might face.

By midday, Parkman's thoughts focused on little else besides the jolts of pain that shot through his midsection, and the parching thirst that turned his throat to sandpaper and swirled his brain into a despondent stupor. He wanted to ask for water, maybe only a swallow, but he knew it was no use. They would only be entertained by his misery, and his pride wouldn't tolerate that. He'd rather suffer.

During their midday break, Duff Joseph hobbled over to where Parkman was, still folded across the horse and only half conscious. After making sure that his prisoner had raised his head, the outlaw took a drink of water from the tin cup he held, then peeled off his derby hat and poured the rest over his head.

"A mite warm today," Joseph noted. "How are you faring, Marshal?"

"I been better," Parkman said. He was surprised by the raspy sound of his voice, and the reluctance of his tongue to shape the words. "But I got no complaints in particular."

"I bet you never knew that you're the one that give me this gimpy leg here," Joseph said, almost conversationally.

"No, I didn't. But if you recall, we never did face off close up." Parkman thought about adding that he was pleased to hear about the leg, but held his tongue. Even as bad as things were, he understood that this man had it in his power to make it a whole lot worse if he chose to do so.

"It happened when you and that posse come after me and my gang up northwest of El Paso. The bullet busted up my hipbone, and those good-for-nothings I was with scattered and left me there bleeding. You'd have had me that time if you'd rode a half mile further."

"We had wounded and dying to take care of ourselves," Parkman said. "And we were out of water. I was worse off than I am now and nearly perished myself before we got to Butler Springs."

But Duff Joseph was clearly not interested in Parkman's hardships. He had his own story to tell. "Took me nearly a year to get healed up and be able to gimp around as much as I can now. I holed up in Mexico, tended to by a woman who thought she was my wife. I nearly had to kill her when she tried to make off with my pouch of gold, but she dropped it on her way out

Greg Hunt

the door before I could get a shot off. She was mad at me about something, I forget what."

"Well at least you're walking," Parkman said. "That's more than I can say right now."

"I always wondered what you nailed me with. That was a fine, long shot. Better than I could've made at the same distance."

"A Sharps fifty-two."

"Still got it?"

"I did until recently." Parkman's neck was getting a crick in it from trying to raise his head and look at Joseph, so he lowered it again. There was an aching pain across his midsection from the long ride across the horse's back.

"I cursed you for a long time after that. Same as Menendez did about his daddy," Joseph confessed. "Swearing I'd get even with you someday. Then it came to me that with so much gold to be had out here in the wild country, only a fool lives for vengeance. But since you walked right into my camp and gave yourself up to me, I don't see no harm in settling the score."

The afternoon ride was a shorter one. They passed out of the barren and broken landscape into another span of grassy rolling hills. Tied face-down across a horse's back, it wasn't easy to get much of an overview of the terrain, but Parkman did catch glimpses of rising foothills, and the next range of mountains that rose beyond. Somewhere there was another river to cross, according to Bone, a swift, rolling waterway that would test the skills of Joseph and his crew.

When they stopped in mid-afternoon, one of the men came over and untied Parkman from across the horse's back. He slid to the ground in a disorganized heap, and the man walked away. His legs had gone numb, feeling for a while as if they would no longer be any use to him. But after stretching and massaging them for a while, he was able to struggle to his feet and hobble to the side of one of the wagons. There was activity all around him, and he stayed close to the wagon bed to avoid getting trampled by any of the passing livestock.

At one point two of the men paused to mock him as he stood leaning on a wheel, stiff-legged and still in considerable pain.

"Reminds me of a scarecrow," one said.

"Yep, he does for a fact," his companion agreed. "Another day like today, and he'll be crawling around like a lizard."

There's something to look forward to, Parkman thought.

A tall water barrel sat in the bed of the wagon behind the driver's seat. The lid was off, and a dipper hung by a string on the outside. Parkman raised a foot in the step-up, then caught hold of the back of the seat and pulled himself up where he could reach the dipper. The tepid water in the barrel tasted about as good as anything he'd ever put in his mouth. He drank two dippers full, then poured a third over his feverish head. It sure would have been good to have a hat right about then, along with his Colt. But both had disappeared in the ruckus the day before.

He sat down in the shade of the wagon and watched the activity around him. Nobody was paying him any attention or seemed to be in any hurry to tie him up again. He wasn't going anyplace anyway, not yet at least. He scanned the ridges of the hills surrounding them, looking for any sign that someone might be watching them. Either Bone or the boy, or both, were probably out there someplace, keeping track of what was going on. But even if they spotted him, still in one piece, there was little they could do for him right now. Maybe tonight, Parkman thought. But probably not. Joseph's men were likely to take their guard duty a little more seriously from here on.

When the camp chores were tended to, the men began to pile down and relax. Eventually Duff Joseph walked over to where Parkman was sitting, wincing at the pain as he lowered himself carefully to the ground. He pulled out the makings and rolled himself a smoke, then, remarkably, handed the tobacco over to Parkman.

"After this is over, I'll have enough gold to do me for a spell, or maybe right on out," Joseph said. "Then I'm bound for Mexico. I want to find me some sassy young señorita who'll rub my feet, an' cook my tortillas, an' bring me tequila when I want it." He seemed relaxed around Parkman now, as if they were two old acquaintances who met by chance on a faraway trail. Yet Parkman felt nothing but contempt for the old man after all the evil deeds Joseph had committed, and all the times they had done their best to kill one another. If he had a gun in his hand right now, Parkman would not hesitate to pull the trigger, despite the consequences. But he played along for now.

"Where you going to get your hands on that much gold?" Parkman asked.

"The Sioux got plenty. From the mining parties they been raiding," Joseph said. "I heard tell that they used to dump the little bags of yellow rocks out onto the ground, or give them to their children to play with, until they learned how the white men crave for it. When I first hijacked this shipment of rifles, I figured I'd have to trade them catch-as-catch-can all along the way for buffalo hides an' horses an' whatever else the redskins had to offer. But then these two breeds I hired on started telling me about the gold that the Sioux was stockpiling so they could buy guns and ammunition to make war against the white men."

"And you believe them," Parkman said. It all seemed to be settled facts in the mind of this crippled old man, he thought. The pile of gold, the señorita, the tequila, and all the rest.

"My men rode ahead and set the whole thing up with the Sioux. We aim to rendezvous with them in a few days and make the swap. They even sent me back a little taste, kinda like bait." Joseph reached under his serape and produced a small leather pouch, which he waved in the air between them. "An' plenty more like this yet to come," he said with a grin.

Parkman drew on his cigarette, studying Duff Joseph with an expressionless stare. In years past, back in Texas, he had been known as a bold thief and a heartless murderer, willing to kill anybody—man, woman, or child—if it served his purpose. Legend had it that he sometimes killed just for the sport of it, or if he was in a sour mood and somebody crossed him at the wrong time.

Joseph was an old man now. With his aged, wrinkled, buckskin flesh and the untamed weed patch of long, white hair, he looked like some kind of wild, dangerous madman that had wandered in from the wilderness. His dark, expressionless eyes revealed the soulless brute that still lived in this aging, broken body.

"I been on the trail for seven weeks now," Joseph said. "And that's not counting the three-week trip from Texas up into Utah. The whole journey damn near had me done for, and I'm ready to have it over with so I can head back south."

"And how many men did you kill to get this far, Joseph?"

"I quit counting the corpses I left behind a long time ago," Joseph admitted. "What's the use in it? And what's a life worth anyway? Yours, mine, or anybody else's? Just the price of a lead ball, most times."

"Some lives are worth more than others," Parkman said, his voice suddenly turned cold. "Somewhere down there in Utah you killed Ray Goode, a fine marshal and a fine friend to me. And if you were still man enough to do it, I'd be pleased to take you on any way you chose to settle that score."

Parkman expected some sort of painful retribution for that statement, but his challenge didn't ruffle the outlaw. "I never fought fair and don't aim to take up the habit at this ripe age," Joseph said. "Riding the trail today, I figured out what I want to do with you." He paused, clearly waiting for Parkman to ask what that decision was, but Parkman wouldn't give him the satisfaction.

"After my business is done with those bloody Sioux bastards, I'm going to hand you over to them, kind of like a present. And all the while that they're peeling the hide off your bones one strip at a time, I'll be somewhere close by enjoying the show."

CHAPTER EIGHTEEN

Parkman woke the next morning, once again tied to a wagon wheel. He was feeling better, having been allowed access to the water barrel, but his empty stomach was grumbling. Nobody had offered him any food, and his own stubborn pride prevented him from asking for anything.

He saw that the scouts had come in during the night and had described the chosen route ahead to their leader. Parkman thought they should be coming up on the next river, which Bone had described as a "rip-snorter." Beyond that the forest began again, and the foothill of the next mountain range came after that.

A man came by and untied Parkman from the wagon wheel. The man allowed him to climb up on the wagon for another drink of water, and then he was led to the horse that would be his transportation for the day. It was a lanky sorrel, definitely not the best animal in their remuda, and Parkman groaned at the thought of another long day splayed across its back.

"Duff says you can ride astraddle this time," the man said. "Said he didn't want you busted in half before he got his use out of you." Parkman was glad of the news, even if he would have to ride barebacked. "I'll be tying your feet together underneath," the man said. "And if you're dumb enough to try anything, you'll end up back on your belly like you was yesterday."

That didn't completely discourage Parkman from considering how he might try to escape. But at any rate, he'd have to wait until they got into the forest.

The sun was equally as relentless as it had been the day before, but with water in his belly and being allowed to ride upright, like a man, Parkman fared better. As they moved along, he scoured the landscape ahead and on both sides, hoping to catch some glimpse of Bone and Brother. But if they were out there, which was likely, they were smart enough to keep out of sight. Parkman wasn't the only one along on this ride with a sharp pair of eyes.

They topped a slight rise, then rode down into the flood plain of the river, passing into a wide band of cottonwoods and aspen. The shade and faint breeze were welcome after the morning ride in the blazing sun. They began to hear the churning rush of the river up ahead even before they came in sight of it. Parkman knew that meant rapids at least, and possibly even a waterfall.

As they approached the water at last, Duff Joseph waved the wagons to a halt some distance back from the river. Then he and a few of his men rode forward to consider the situation.

To the north, the river came into view around a tight, narrow bend. After that was a long run of roaring, tumbling rapids, absolutely impassable to anyone except perhaps a man in a canoe. Directly above that long string of rapids a tall stone promontory rose nearly a hundred feet into the air, sharp, jagged, and forbidding.

Below that first set of rapids, there was a long stretch of perhaps fifty yards where the river bed leveled and the flowing water lost some of its ferocity. Past that, the rapids began again, even wilder and more forbidding, heading into another sharp twist below that steered the river on out of sight.

After a few minutes of discussion, two of Joseph's men separated themselves from the others and waded their horses out into the river's eddy, staring hard to try and get a fix on what lay ahead. Then they encouraged their mounts forward, keeping about fifty feet between each other, and riding carefully. The man on the upper end, closest to the base of the first rapids, got the worst of the deal. Midway, in the river's strongest current, the man and horse disappeared suddenly, as if the river had simply swallowed them up.

A moment later the horse's head surfaced, its eyes bulging in terror as it writhed and lurched, struggling to swim. Then the man came up, gagging and helpless in the current, trying desperately to keep his tenuous grip on his horse's reins. His squall for help was quickly truncated as the river snatched him back under again. Struggling to save its own life, the horse flung his head sharply to the side, easily snatching the last lifeline from its rider's hand.

After that the man was swept away, the property now of the merciless current.

Downstream the second rider was struggling to keep his own mount under control but still managed to pull out his lariat and make an effort to lasso his companion as he rolled and tumbled past. But it was no use, and the loop of rope fell limply across the water. The unfortunate rider was swept over the falls. From time to time after that, his corpse appeared briefly in the frothy current, face down now, then face up the next time, no longer fighting to save his own life.

In the distance, Parkman heard Duff Joseph curse the dead man gruffly. "I can't spare no more men to such carelessness," the old outlaw complained. "What was his name anyway?" Nobody seemed to know, or at least nobody cared enough to answer.

The riderless horse managed to toss and flail himself into calmer water, and when his hooves found the river bed below him, he struggled up the bank onto dry land. There he stopped, exhausted and breathless, huffing and snorting the river water out of his twitching nostrils. The second rider also managed to make it to the other side, never having to pass through water much above the stirrups of his horse. He rode over and gathered up the other horse's reins, then looked back toward Joseph, as if some orders might be shouted over.

"All right, boys," Joseph called out at last. "There's nothing we can do for that poor bastard now, so let's get this river behind us." The men were still jittery from the catastrophe they had witnessed, and probably the horses and mule teams, too. But they were undoubtedly more afraid of their boss's wrath and began to line out to make the crossing.

Parkman lagged back, waiting until all four wagons were out into the current before following along. There were two men riding their horses on either side of each wagon, for what purpose he wasn't sure. And at least half a dozen more riders brought up the rear. After what they had all seen moments before, he abandoned his illusions of tumbling off the horse and trying for an escape. And besides, his ankles were still connected with a rope under his mount's belly, dooming any hopes of taking unexpectedly to the water.

When the last two wagons were about halfway across, a shot sounded out from somewhere to the north. Parkman thought at first it had come from atop the tall stone edifice, a dramatic spot to pull off an ambush for sure. But it would also be a good place to get trapped without any easy way to get back down to the ground again.

Then he spotted a man far upstream, kneeling on the bank alongside the higher end of the rapids. And he also recognized the distant sound of his own Sharps rifle being fired. He couldn't make out the face of the man from so far away, but he knew it had to be Bone.

The first shot easily passed through the front pair of mules hitched to the next to last wagon, and both animals went down like lead weights. The two mules behind bleated out their surprise and terror, fighting the harnesses around their necks and shoulder, trying to rear in their traces. Bone's next shot took out the driver of that wagon, which meant there would be nobody trying to bring the rebellious animals back under control. The press of the current tilted the wagon, then shoved against the underside with its full force. The wagon toppled sideways, taking out the two riders on the downstream side before tumbling into the rapids below.

Meanwhile Bone squeezed off his third and final shot, knocking the driver of the last wagon off his seat and into the current. By then a couple of Joseph's men, more alert than the others, had spotted Bone upstream and were finding their range. Without ceremony, Bone rose to his feet and disappeared into the underbrush at his side.

Parkman was caught up in watching the last wagon topple and tumble over the edge into the rapids, carrying its dead driver and unfortunate team of mules along with it. Then he felt an odd tug on his pants leg and looked down at his horse's side. He was startled to see a face under the surface of the water, with a sleek, dark form attached to it. Brother. There was another tug on the rope that bound his ankles, and suddenly his legs were free. Then a brown arm rose up from the water and the hand latched onto his forearm, snatching him off the horse and into the water.

In the chaos of the moment, none of the outlaws seemed to notice Parkman and the Indian youth tumbling into the rapids. Most of the men behind had dismounted by then to make smaller targets of themselves and were pointing their rifles upstream, looking for something to shoot at. Up ahead, the rest of the crew were scrambling to get the remaining two wagons out of the river and into some kind of cover.

With their hands locked on each other's forearm, Parkman and Brother seemed doomed to die together in the raging current. But despite the danger, Parkman felt a quick pang of satisfaction that Duff Joseph would never watch him die in some agonizing manner in a Sioux camp up ahead. It was almost as if he would die on his own terms, which is all any man could hope for at the end.

Then he felt a sudden jolt, and his and Brother's sound grips on each other nearly parted. The youth had somehow managed to grab ahold of a fallen tree jammed among the tangle of rocks amid the current. The rolling, insistent water seemed determined to keep control of them, as it had with the men and mules that it had claimed before. But slowly, with an enormous effort of straining muscles and iron will, Brother managed to pull Parkman forward until he too was able to grab a waterlogged limb of the fallen tree.

For an instant, Parkman recalled the young man's vow to die for him if necessary during the solemn moment when he had passed over Sam Lyon's well-used rifle to him. They had not been empty words.

With great effort, the two of them inched along the length of the log until they had reached a spot where a flat slab of stone overhung the raging waters of the river. Once under the rock, the force of the water abated, and they were able to pause and give their aching muscles a moment of rest.

Sitting cross-legged, with his head tilted forward beneath the flat rock above, Parkman had time to survey the wreckage and chaos below. Broken pieces of the wagons were caught up here and there in the rocky channel of the rapids downstream, as were the carcasses of several battered and dead mules. He saw only one dead man, splayed and broken across a boulder, half in the water and half out. As he watched, the current claimed the man again, hauling him on downstream a few dozen yards before slamming him into yet another obstacle.

The only part of the scene that gave the marshal any satisfaction was the scattered crates of rifles and ammunition, and the small kegs of gunpowder. Some were shattered, their contents already dispatched to the bottom of the river, and others bobbed and twisted along in the current, ready to sink in their own good time.

It wasn't likely that Duff Joseph would be able to salvage anything from this devastation, even if he were able to cajole any of his men to wade out into the raging water. The hours and days and weeks that the old outlaw would be able to laze around some crude adobe cantina south of the border, chewing on his tortillas and swilling his tequila, had, within the span of only a few minutes, been cut in half. And that didn't even take into consideration that his little caravan had been reduced by several men, and eight sturdy mules. Joseph would have little remorse for the lost lives, but he would mourn for his lost cargo.

Parkman tried to stick his head out from under the stone slab to see what was going on up above, but the water rushing over the edge prevented that. They would have to content themselves with sitting here in their little refuge for a while, until they felt confident that the wagon train had moved on.

Parkman turned his head to the young Indian, crammed tight against him under the rock slab. His long hair was plastered to his head and shoulders, and, dressed only in a breechclout, he must have been freezing. Blood oozed from a series of long scrapes down across his ribs, but he paid no mind to it. His grin was broad and proud as Parkman once again locked their forearms in the Indian fashion.

"Thank you, Brother," Parkman said solemnly.

"Lid-dle Bro-her," the young man replied.

It was a mystery to Parkman how Brother seemed capable of

finding his way at night through the thick, trackless forest on the east side of the river. The landscape grew more rigorous as they progressed deeper into the foothills. To one side lay the next range of mountains, vaguely outlined in the moonlight. On the other side the river continued to rush and roar someplace close by, as it had since the beginning of time.

Brother let Parkman ride on his pony for most of the trip, and Parkman didn't protest, knowing that they would make better time than if he was afoot, trying to force his starved and abused body to keep stumbling along.

They had come out from under the rock in late afternoon and found the area on both sides of the river abandoned of horsemen and wagons, returned to its wild, solitary state. They crossed to the east side of the river, with the aid of sturdy staffs to help them keep their balance in the stiff current. Once on the other side, they walked south for a few hundred yards to where Brother had left his horse to graze. The river was wide and flat there, but steep banks on the western side prohibited it from being a passable ford for wagons. As they gazed out over the water, the carcass of a dead mule floated lazily by, its round belly already seeming to bloat.

As they were about to leave, Brother stopped and looked across the river at a tangle of brush. Something had caught his eye over there that Parkman had yet to spot. With a whoop of excitement, Brother leaped into the water and started swimming across. By the time he got there, Parkman had figured out what the keen-eyed youth saw. A twisted, broken body was caught up in the brush, bobbing on the river surface.

Parkman watched as the young man drew his knife, peeled off the dead man's hat, and took his scalp, howling victoriously as he raised his prize in the air. When he swam back across, Parkman saw that he had brought both the scalp and the hat back with him. The marshal realized that a few hours before, that same gray, tall-crowned hat had set atop the head of Bloody Joe Menendez, Joseph's Comanchero scout and second in command. After showing off his spoils to his companion, Brother tied the scalp to one end of his bow with a leather strap and crammed the hat into the leather possibles bag on the back of his horse.

Brother had some strips of meat that he gave to Parkman, seeming to understand that his strength and resilience were waning. Then he pointed to the horse's back and motioned for Parkman to mount up. As he swung up onto the horse, the marshal was glad for even the light Indian saddle as cushioning under his rear end.

Parkman had no real fix on how long they had been traveling. He dozed in the saddle from time to time, always awaking suddenly as his body tilted to one side or the other and he risked falling. The moon had drifted halfway across the nighttime sky by the time he began to catch an occasional whiff of wood smoke drifting through the pines. A short time later, Brother paused and held up his hand to indicate that Parkman should be quiet. Parkman saw a dim glow up ahead and knew that somebody had made their camp there.

Brother raised both hands to his cheeks and mimicked the hoot of an owl. He still needed a little practice, Parkman thought, but he wasn't far off the mark. A similar sound came echoing back, and Brother turned to Parkman to give him an approving nod.

The camp was situated a short way into the trees beside a sandy bar along the river, close to water and an abundance of driftwood for the fire. Bone had been there long enough to already get settled in, and Fawn had moved to the fire to lay a pile of sticks across the dying flames. Not far away Parkman spotted General Grant among the other animals, grazing lazily in a patch of grass at the edge of the trees.

It felt almost like a homecoming, Parkman thought. He certainly would enjoy bedding down in this camp among friends, rather than spending another night trussed to a wagon wheel.

But there was something different now, Parkman realized. Instead of four horses and a mule grazing nearby, as there should be, there were six horses. A few yards from the fire he spotted two additional bedrolls spread out on the ground. They were made up of buffalo hides, with colorfully woven Indian blankets on top. He paused the horse at the edge of the woods, uncertain of the situation, but Bone rose to his feet and called him on in.

"Turns out we had company for supper," the old squaw man announced. "Friends of mine." He motioned for Parkman and Brother to come on up, then turned to the side and made some kind of announcement in Cheyenne. A moment later, two braves came out of the trees, both carrying rifles. Parkman dismounted, and Brother took the reins of the horse.

"Glad to see you made it okay," Bone said. "After I got my shots off, I was too busy saving my own hide to pay much mind to how the two of you fared."

"The boy saved my life," Parkman declared with certainty. "I can't even start to tell you how surprised I was to look down and see him swimming around under my horse like a man-sized trout. I don't know how he done it."

"Once we seen which way them wagons was headed," Bone said, "we rode on ahead and worked up our plan. I wasn't sure he could pull it off either, but we were dead set on giving it a try. Especially the boy."

"Were these two with you?" Parkman asked, pointing to the two Indians. They were holding back, waiting for Bone and Parkman to finish their conversation.

"Naw, they was already here in camp when I got back," Bone

11

said. "The one with the two feathers is called Little Teeth, and the other one is called Furious. One look at him and right off you can figure out why. They been trailing us for a day or so, wanting to find out who we were. And when they caught up and found Fawn here alone, they stayed around to see if we'd make it back. They brought fresh deer meat with them, which we didn't refuse." Over by the fire Fawn was threading strips of meat onto long, sharp sticks to roast for Parkman and Brother.

After turning his horse loose with the others, Little Brother went to the two braves, who had taken seats on a blanket by the fire. He held up his bow, with Bloody Joe's scalp attached, and immediately began talking to them in their language.

"He's telling them about how he and I went on the warpath against many bad white men," Bone told Parkman quietly. They had taken seats on Bone's blanket on the other side of the fire. "He says the spirits turned him into a fish so he could save your life. He said you're a great and generous man, and that your medicine is strong. He says he's proud that you made him your brother."

"Wait 'til they see the rifle," Parkman said.

"The boy left it back here at the camp, and Little Teeth already claimed it," Bone said. "Furious decided he'd rather have your horse and outfit."

"That's not such good news," Parkman said.

"Maybe they'll change their minds once the boy gets through. He's laying it on pretty thick, telling them how an eagle guided us to the right place for the ambush, and how a talking fish swam alongside of him for good luck."

"I don't remember things exactly that way, but if it gets me my horse back . . ."

The two Indians were nodding their heads in approval, and over where she was cooking, Fawn had started to dance and chant a song under her breath. Soon the men joined in, as did the boy, pausing in the telling of his saga for the time being. Finally, Bone joined in as well, chanting the words of the victory song as his proud eyes remained on Brother. After a few minutes Bone stopped dancing and rejoined Parkman.

"He told them the man he scalped woke from the dead and fought with him," Bone said, "but he crushed the man's head with a stone and counted coup with his foot on his enemy's chest while he cut his hair off."

"Yep, that's about how I remember it." Parkman smiled.

The victory ceremony seemed to draw to a close as Fawn began to distribute the food she had cooked. In honor of his bravery, she delivered the first skewer of deer meat to Brother, and the next two went to the two Cheyenne braves. Then she brought food over to Bone and Parkman.

"See how cheerful she is?" Bone said. Parkman looked up at the squaw and thought he might have detected a hint of a smile pass briefly across her deadpan features. "Furious is her brother-in-law, and he delivered the news that her husband is still alive."

CHAPTER NINETEEN

When they were breaking camp the next morning, Parkman began to saddle General Grant as if the whole debate about who owned this horse was settled by his return. Both rifle scabbards were empty, and he knew that even if the ownership of the horse might be determined, there were still other important matters to be settled. Earlier Parkman had strapped on the spare Colt and holster that he always carried in his saddlebags. But a handgun, even the best available, which was what he carried, wasn't always enough to handle every situation in a place like this.

He didn't intend to let these two Indians ride off without even trying to get his weapons back.

When he heard footsteps approaching from behind, he waited a moment before turning around. Furious stopped a few feet away, holding Parkman's rifles in either hand. At first, they locked eyes and stared at one another, as if this might be a war of wills. Seeing the two of them standing face to face, Bone hurried over to intercede.

Furious spoke up. "You killed the men who attacked our village," Bone translated. "You saved my sister-in-law from rape and death, and she said you have taken care of her well on the trail. Because of that, I have decided not to count coup on you and take your scalp."

Looking over at Bone in puzzlement, Parkman said, "How in hell do I answer something like that? If I'm supposed to thank him for not killing me, I'm not sure I'm in the mood." The whole situation was downright annoying.

Bone said something to Furious, then told Parkman, "I told him you said he is a wise and courageous man, and you honor him for letting you live."

"I guess that's better than anything I might of thought up," Parkman conceded.

"It seems fitting for the situation."

The Indian's eyes moved off Parkman to General Grant, eying his size, powerful frame, and fine lines with a clearly envious expression. Then he raised both hands and held out Parkman's weapons to him. Maybe he was an honorable man in his own way. Parkman accepted the guns, gazing eye to eye with Furious and nodding his thanks. He had already stuck the Sharps down into its scabbard, when Bone piped up again.

"You might want to think of giving him somethin' in return," the squaw man said, "if you want this whole thing to turn out well. Somethin' that is clearly valuable to you."

Parkman turned back to Furious. The Indian was gazing back at him, expectant and waiting. Parkman handed him the Winchester, then went to his saddlebag and brought out two boxes of ammunition, which he also handed over. The Indian's hard, steady gaze seemed to soften slightly, and it was his turn to nod his acceptance.

That Winchester was definitely of value to him, Parkman thought, and he might miss it sorely during the rest of this business with Duff Joseph. He had carried it for three years now, and it would take a month's salary to replace it. But this was Cheyenne territory, home ground to Furious and his people, and the game had to be played by their rules.

When the camp was packed up and they were ready to leave, the four Indians gathered to the side to talk. Fawn did not take part in the discussion but nodded her head in acceptance as

Furious, who was obviously in charge, gave her instructions.

"He told her that they would be riding hard and didn't want a woman on a weaker horse coming along," Bone said. "He said they'll be back this way soon with many warriors, and she could join back up with the tribe then. She seems all right with that, but with her it's sort of hard to tell sometimes. On down the trail someplace, she might cut the both of us into little pieces, just out of pique."

But when it came to their younger companion, Brother had something to say when Furious apparently told him that he should go with them. Parkman was glad to see that by now, Little Teeth had also returned the young man's rifle to him.

"The boy says there is more war left to make here, and he needs to stay and watch over us."

"He might be right about that. Could be we need watching."

Little Brother's words must have been honored, because when the two braves mounted their horses and started away, he stayed behind. Shortly, they passed out of sight into the trees, neither looking back at the party they left behind.

"And where are they headed?" Parkman asked.

"Like I said, for more braves. I told them the men what wiped out that Cheyenne camp was part of Joseph's bunch," Bone explained. "They're going back for enough braves to make war on Joseph."

"How long will that take?"

"Wal, they don't exactly know where the main Cheyenne camp is, but I'd say anywhere from a few days to a week. If the tribe took up after that big herd of buffalo we saw and trailed north after them, it could take some time."

"Do they know yet what's in those wagons?"

"I didn't say nothing about it, and I never heard the boy say anything either. I don't think he's even figured it out yet. Chances are, they think the wagons are carrying trade goods and suchlike."

They rode on for a while, and the subject of the rifles and ammunition kept nagging at Parkman's thoughts. They had destroyed half of Duff Joseph's cargo, but there could still be hundreds of rifles in the two remaining wagons. The Indians wouldn't ride out and kill buffaloes with those firearms. They'd make war with them.

"When he thought I was practically a dead man already," Parkman said, "Joseph told me he had a rendezvous set up with the Sioux. Said they had gold to pay him off for the rifles."

"They might or might not," Bone speculated. "If their chiefs brought along enough warriors to the meet, I don't s'pose it would matter much if they had gold or not."

"How far is it to Sioux territory?"

"A man on a strong horse might make it in two or three days. But for Joseph, with those wagons and another range of mountains to cross, I'd say maybe a week. But it ain't like these Indians sink posts in the ground to mark off their hunting grounds. Most often, whatever lands they can take from another tribe and hold, that's theirs for the time being."

"I heard when the Cheyenne and Sioux lived south and east of these mountains, they were allies against the other tribes, and the whites. Does that still hold?"

"That's generally so when they need to join up and fight an enemy to both tribes," Bone said. "But it ain't unheard of for the two tribes to have at it amongst themselves if their blood gets stirred up. None of the red men I ever run across out here ever needed us white men to teach them that every alliance and treaty was made to be broken. These western tribes are proud and fearsome people, and absolutely loyal to their own. They don't never take no guff from anybody if they can do something about it."

That day they made decent progress through the steep,

broken foothills. It was encouraging to Parkman to realize that Joseph would have a much harder time of it trying to get through these thick woods and steep ups and downs. They needed to get ahead of the wagons again and set up another surprise for the outlaw band. If they could pull off one more ambush as successful as the one back at the river, their job would be finished, and they could all set a course for safer, more accommodating places.

But there would be no more broad, tumbling rivers to aid them until they got to the other side of the mountains, and that might be too late. They had to cook up something different for the next attack.

The next morning Bone rode ahead to scout, as was his custom. Brother was left behind to guide their small group on a series of game trails so they would leave no tracks on the main trail Joseph would be following. It was a cat and mouse game from here on, with death awaiting the losers. And after his painful loss of men and cargo at the last river they crossed, Duff Joseph would have his men on high alert.

They kept a cold, fireless camp that night. The temperature dropped as they rose into the higher elevations, and a quick heavy rain drenched them during the deep darkness. Parkman and Brother took turns trying to stand guard, relying more on their ears than eyes until the clouds blew past and the half moon rose in the sky. The horses were kept close by, munching on the bushes nearby and whatever scattered bunch grass they could find.

They were stiff, cold, and grumpy in the first light of dawn, starting out on the ride with their wet blankets wrapped around their wet clothes. Bone hadn't showed up overnight, nor did he appear through the long day as the sun rose in the sky and their misery waned. From time to time, Brother pointed out a marker on the trail which only he seemed to recognize, proving at least that Bone was all right, and somewhere up ahead.

At midday Fawn passed around a few pieces of jerky, holding the bag open in front of Parkman to show him how little was left in it. They saw a mountain goat on the treacherous rocks above them and Parkman knew he could have made the shot. But he dared not, unsure of how far the noise might travel. And even if he had killed the animal, they could not risk the smoke of a fire to roast it over. Joseph might be too far back to hear a shot or spot the rise of smoke, but his scouts would likely be closer.

They came to a place where the trail they were on merged with the main trail below, and they had no choice but to ride along it for a while. A fast stream flowed down the middle of the mountain pass, and while Brother took the horses and the mule down to water, Fawn waded out up to her thighs in the frigid water and began to gather water plants into a flour sack. Supper, Parkman thought with distaste.

He took his hatchet and chopped off a tree branch back in the woods, then tied it to the pack on Fawn's horse. She rode last in line and could pull the branch along to cover their tracks. Parkman knew it wasn't likely to fool a skilled scout paying close attention to the ground ahead, but it was better than leaving behind a clear trail of hoofprints. And Bloody Joe Menendez, who had probably been the best tracker in the outfit, was out of that line of work for good.

Brother shot a squirrel off a tree limb with his bow and handed it off to Fawn as they mounted up. She began to skin it even as they started up again. Their menu had come down to raw meat and water weeds. The Indians might not mind it, but Parkman sure did. He tried not to think about the inch-thick steak, fried potatoes, and apple cobbler Hattie had cooked for him on his last night in Weatherby's Lode.

Hattie. He realized that he had hardly thought of her at all for the past few days and wondered what that meant. What was she doing right about now? Probably delivering platters of food to hungry customers. And what was she thinking about him? He couldn't quite draw a mental picture of her pining away at night, longing for the return of the man she aimed to marry. It was hard enough to tell what was going on in a woman's mind when you were right there with her, and not worth even trying when you were hundreds of miles and several weeks apart from her.

Before long, Brother spotted a few small stones, stacked in a particular way by Bone, and led them off the main trail again. Fawn untied the tree branch she had been dragging along and stashed the rope under the pack behind her. Parkman heard his stomach growling and took a long drink of water to deal with his hunger. One of the differences between him and the Indians, he realized, was that they ate to survive, while he still liked to put something tasty in his mouth once in a while.

In late afternoon they came across Bone at last, sitting with his back against a tree, enjoying a smoke. Both he and his horse looked worn down, and Parkman figured he had probably ridden most of the night to get back here. But he delivered good news.

"I found a place where I think we can give that bunch some more hard treatment," Bone said. He was smiling when he said it, but his eyelids seemed about to sag shut. He drew a last time on his pipe, then tapped the ashes out on a rock and put the pipe away.

"There's a spot a few miles ahead where the trail passes between two walls of solid rock for a couple of hundred yards. That seems like the best place for us to have at 'em again."

Fawn came up with a canteen and a cloth bag and squatted beside Bone. While he drank, she took some food for him out of the bag. Watching, Parkman realized that during their ride the woman had cut the squirrel meat into thin strips and put them down into the bag with some salt. She had even broken the skeleton into pieces and dropped the bones in the bag to cure. Nothing useful went to waste. Bone tried a bite of the meat and nodded his approval to Fawn, as if it might actually matter to her whether he liked it or not.

"The place don't look wide enough for a butter knife to pass through," Bone went on. "But I know for a fact that the army took a wagon through there a couple of years back. They was looking for an outfit of prospectors that disappeared up here someplace, but they never did find 'em."

"Are you thinking we could lie in wait up on those cliffs and ambush them?" Parkman asked. "Even after the ones you killed back yonder, he's still got fifteen or twenty men with him. I can't imagine that we could kill them all before they got to us, or got away."

"There's fifteen or twenty men, but only two wagons. And after all, it's the wagons we're after, ain't they? If we can rain some fire and fury down on them wagons, then the men won't hardly matter."

Parkman thought of the remaining explosive bundles still stashed away in his saddlebags. Placed in the right spots on the wagons, he thought that they might do the job, but he had less confidence in the idea of throwing them off the top of a cliff. "I'm listening," he said.

"There's plenty of deadfall up atop those cliffs, and we got a bit of time, maybe a day or so, to gather some up at the edge. All we have to do is get those wagons stopped for a few minutes in the right spot, then light the wood and push the whole shebang down on them."

Parkman liked the plan, although he realized that the whole thing would depend on a heavy dose of good luck. But had he come up with anything better?

"All right, Bone. Let's make for the cliffs and have a look."

The next morning, they woke in another fireless camp atop the cliff on the north side of the canyon where Duff Joseph's outfit would hopefully pass through no more than a day or two from now. As soon as he stirred out of his blankets in the early morning light, Parkman pulled on his boots and walked over to the sheer drop-off. Below him was a straight wall of stone, stretching down fifty or sixty feet to the trail below. Bone was right that it didn't look wide enough for a wagon to pass through, but Bone still swore the army had done it. Parkman hadn't asked him how he had come across that information, deciding that it might be better if he didn't know.

He heard footsteps from behind and turned to see Bone approaching. Farther away, back in the camp, Fawn had gotten up from her blankets and walked over into the edge of the woods. Brother, who had returned to camp after his morning hunt, watched the naked woman dress with guilty, adolescent interest. In one hand he held a dead raccoon by the tail, and in his other was his bow.

"We can use the horses to drag some logs and brush over here and pile it up along the edge," Bone started up right away. He was proud of the details he had thought through. "Back a little ways, we'll have a fire ready to light and some dry branches across it to use for torches. Once we get the fire going all along the top, we'll push the logs over with branches, and the rest should go with it."

"And we'll blow rocks down into the pass so the wagons can't go no place until we push the fire down on them," Parkman said.

"I figure we only got to blow the upper end. Once them wagons are in the pass, there ain't no possibility they can turn them around and go back the way they came."

"Have you figgered out how we stay alive long enough to do all this blowing and burning?"

"Sort of," Bone said without conviction. "The rock face is too sheer to climb, so any of them that come for us, after they see where we are, will have to ride back down the trail and find the way up here. It'll take a little while, maybe long enough for us to do what we have to."

"Maybe," Parkman repeated. Bone paid him for his skepticism with a sour look.

It was a long morning of hard work for Bone, Parkman, and Fawn. The Indian woman was as sturdy and strong as most men and did her share of the axe work and heavy lifting. They had stationed Brother down the trail to signal if any of Joseph's scouts were approaching so they could stop making noise.

They started by dragging several logs up, positioning them along a fifty-foot stretch at the top of the cliff. Next, they covered the logs with armloads of smaller sticks and dead brush and topped it all off with larger sticks and tree branches. Then they loaded their blankets up with armloads of dry pine needles and scattered them across the top.

By early afternoon the three of them were exhausted and well ready to quit when they heard the signal from Brother indicating that someone was approaching up the trail. While Parkman and Bone crawled up to the edge of the cliff to have a look, Fawn wandered back down into the woods on a mission of her own.

A few minutes later, three riders cautiously entered the western end of the pass, holding their firearms in their hands and scanning the cliffs on both sides as they proceeded forward. Both Parkman and Bone drew back, and Parkman found a crack in the rock where he could watch the riders without being seen.

Two of the scouts were the half-breeds Parkman had seen

while he was a condemned man in Duff Joseph's custody. They were careful and alert, riding with their rifles lying ready across the front of their saddles, accustomed to this line of work and clearly on their guard during this risky passage. The third man was some piece of saddle trash that Joseph must have hired along the way, and he was a tangle of nerves. He held a revolver in his right hand, his head constantly jerking from side to side as if the whole mountainside must be loaded with dozens of Indians ready to attack. At one point, when a hawk soared into sight to check them out, the man's gun whipped around, and it seemed for an instant that he might snap off a round.

It was a wonder, Parkman thought, that the other two hadn't already left him dead along the trail someplace. He was like a keg of powder ready to explode, and his unpredictability put them all at risk.

In time, the three riders passed on out of the canyon and out of sight along the trail, but Parkman and Bone stayed in place, knowing that they would soon return. Half an hour later they came riding back, still cautiously on guard as they passed through the canyon in the other direction.

When they were gone again, the two men rose and started walking back toward their camp.

"I think I'll trail after them for a while," Bone said. "I'd like to get an idea where Joseph stops for the night so we'll know about when to expect them at the party."

As he walked away to get his horse, Parkman went over to see what Fawn was up to. She was pounding some sort of concoction into mush on a flat rock, then dumping the mess into a pot of water to soak. It consisted of acorns and mushrooms, and she was soaking it to drain away some of the bitterness. He didn't recognize the kind of mushrooms she had gathered, but he had eaten acorns before and recalled that they weren't his favorite. And that was even after they had been cooked up into little cakes that looked something like potato patties. To one side she had already laid out strips of raccoon meat on another flat rock to cure in the sun.

As he sat down nearby to keep Fawn company, even if they never spoke a word, his stomach began to grumble about the meal that was on the way. He wondered if raw, salted raccoon would taste any better than raw, salted squirrel had. He didn't get his hopes up.

Bone came riding back about sunset, which told Parkman that Joseph's camp couldn't be that far down the mountainside. He looked weary and trail worn and seemed to be in a retrospective mood as the two of them walked over to the edge of the cliff and sat down with their legs hanging over the side.

As the sun dipped below the horizon and the sky to the west lit up with blended shades of pink and gray and orange, they sat quietly for a while, tossing pebbles over the side and thinking their own thoughts.

It was a strange thing, Parkman considered, that out in the remote reaches of such a vast, beautiful, and wild place as this, there could still be so much hatred, bloodshed, and greed. He didn't remember much about the history he had been taught so long ago in the schoolhouse back in Virginia, but he did recall thinking even way back then that anywhere men went, they seemed to feel the need to fight, and kill, and take. The red men wanted to defend and expand their hunting grounds, and he was willing to bet that when they went up against other tribes who were their ancestral enemies, not one in a hundred of the soldier braves could have explained why the tribal hatreds had started in the first place.

And then there were the white men, pouring westward so quickly, and in such endless numbers, across the prairies and mountains, taking what they wanted, fighting and killing and dying to own what the Indians believed could never truly be owned by anyone. It was a strange thing to Parkman to realize that he was caught up right in the middle of such enormous change and still understood so very little of it.

Yet here they all were, each side with their own conflicting needs and desires, and everybody willing to kill or die for what they wanted. The Sioux wanted weapons to match those of their enemies so they could fight on. Duff Joseph wanted the gold he thought the Sioux had, and the lifestyle it would provide for him in his dotage. The Cheyenne, approaching in great numbers across the plains, wanted vengeance.

And what about him? Parkman wondered. What did he want out of all this that was worth risking his life for? To do the right thing as he saw it, or to enforce the law of the land? Those things seemed altogether too high and righteous when you looked at them from the right slant, and maybe not worth dying for in the end. He didn't know.

But he did know that any man who wanted to hold his shoulders straight and be satisfied with who he was had to keep pushing to do the right thing, even when he didn't understand much of what was going on around him or why he believed what he did.

If he had to live his life like Duff Joseph had lived his, Parkman thought, he'd rather put a bullet through his skull right here and now.

Beside him, Bone sent a long stream of brown spittle spiraling down into the canyon, then wiped his mouth on the sleeve of his shirt. He had taken to chewing pinches of the smoking tobacco Parkman provided to him, which Parkman thought was a waste. Over this entire trip, the marshal thought it interesting to realize that the only basic supplies he had not run out of were smoking tobacco and coffee.

"This might sound like a damned fool question," Bone said,

"but what's it like in a town?"

"Why? You thinking about visiting one?"

"Maybe not just visit," Bone admitted.

Parkman pondered the question a moment before answering. It was hard for him to imagine that such a possibility had ever crossed the mind of the raggedy old mountain man.

"Well, on the up side, there's usually somebody around to talk to, and you can most always find a drink of whisky if you get thirsty. An' there's places to get inside to stay dry and warm when it rains and snows."

"All that would be nice," Bone said. "It sure would beat waking up under a lean-to in the wintertime an' wondering if your toes were going to break off when you stood up. But what about the other, the down side of things?"

"You've got to have money to pay for about anything you want. Every shot of rotgut will cost you something, and you'll have to pay for your food. You'd have to find work someplace."

"Work for money?" Bone said, as if the whole notion was foreign to his ears. It had probably been decades since he had put in a day's work for cash payment. "Funny thing, I ain't even seen no money for years. But I could work with horses, maybe, or hunt, and then sell the meat."

"If you go down to Colorado, there's always work in the mines. But I've got a feeling being down in a hole in the ground for twelve hours a day wouldn't suit you."

"I expect not."

"Or you could scout for the army. But that would put you square up against the same people you've been living with for all these years."

"Nope, I don't think that would suit me either," Bone said.

They both fell silent for a moment. It was nearly dark now, and they knew they should eat something and hit the blankets.

"I'm not one to tell a man what to do," Parkman said. "But it seems to me you made your choice a long time ago, and now you've got to see it through to the end. I don't think you'd like a town."

"Maybe not," Bone said.

Parkman had already been awake for a while, staring up at the stars, when he saw Fawn stirring on the other side of the camp.

It would happen today. He wondered if he would live long enough to ever see the stars again after the fight they had ahead of them.

Fawn pulled her dress on over her head, then rose from her blankets and walked out toward the woods. Brother's blankets were empty. He had either gone out hunting, or was scouting back down the trail to see who might be coming in their direction. Bone was still asleep, growling and snorting as he usually did. That was probably what woke him early, Parkman thought.

He pulled on his boots and strapped on his sidearm, then walked a short distance away from camp to relieve himself. On his way back, he glanced at the empty space in the midst of the camp and yearned for a fire. It still seemed like a day shouldn't be allowed to get started without a cup of coffee and a smoke.

He and Bone talked very little as Fawn served up last night's leftovers onto metal plates and passed them to the men. Everything was ready now, and all they could do was wait. That, and hope to hell it didn't rain.

Parkman saw that ants had gotten into the food overnight, but he ate it anyway, busy little crawly critters and all. Even if their ambush was successful, they couldn't possibly kill all of Joseph's men, and if they had to flee for their lives, there was no telling when their next meal might be. For now, he ate for strength and survival, like the Indians.

The sun was up and the sky was bright by the time Brother returned. He hadn't brought any game with him this time, but he did have news to deliver as he scooped the leavings out of the pan with his fingers and stuck them in his mouth. Fawn gave him the few remaining strips of raccoon, and he shoved one of them in his mouth with the acorn mush.

"He said they broke camp and started out," Bone said. "Time to get ready."

Parkman got the remaining shotgun barrel explosives out and carried them over to where they were to be used. For a while, both he and Bone kept an eye on a tall, dark tower of clouds rolling in from the northwest. But they blew on past to the north of them, and soon the sky was clear and bright again. That must be a sign, Parkman thought, and then felt silly for the notion. A sign of what? Fawn and Brother packed up camp and tied their horses in the edge of the woods.

Then they all waited some more.

The first noise they heard from Duff Joseph's caravan was the high-pitched squeal of a dry wagon wheel. He'd lose the wheel if he didn't take care of that, Parkman thought. But then he realized that Joseph was about to lose a whole lot more than a wheel. Next came the rattle of the straining wagons, the vile curses of the teamsters, and the occasional crack of their whips over the behinds of their straining mules.

The first men to come into sight in the tight space below were the same two half-breed scouts who had come through here yesterday. They were riding even slower now, their rifles ready and their eyes scanning every crack and bush up the steep canyon walls and along the ridgeline on both sides. Parkman waved his hand for the others to stay down and watched the men's progress through the same crack in the rock he had peered through yesterday.

The two scouts rode the length of the canyon and a little beyond, then turned their horses and rode back through as cautiously as before.

Moments later, the full cavalcade began to come into view. The scouts started through first, followed by six mounted men about fifty feet back. They were heavily armed, and as jittery and cautious as the scouts. When the first team of mules came up to the entrance to the canyon, they seemed to balk at the tight spaces, but a few well-placed kisses on their rumps with the whip encouraged them on. The second wagon followed along about twenty feet behind. Before, the wagons had outriders on either side, but this space was too narrow for that. Instead, armed men rode on the tops of the cargo, hunkering down as best they could. A stretched-out line of several mounted men brought up the rear, herding along several riderless horses ahead of them. Duff Joseph himself drove one of the wagons, snapping the whip and pouring out an encouraging stream of curses.

When both the wagons were deep within the confines of the canyon, Parkman crawled over and lit the fuses to the explosives. He had wedged the six little bombs, all he had left, down behind a tilted slab of stone that leaned precariously away over the canyon. If the bombs did their job as planned, the slab of rock would fall away, and the rubble it took down with it should be enough to block the passage of the mules and the wagons they pulled.

With the fuses hissing, Parkman and the others began to light a string of fires along the line of wood they had gathered at the edge of the cliff. At first the flames seemed pathetic and slow, but as they spread into the kindling and piles of pine needles, they began to lap hungrily upward into the thick piles of dry wood.

The explosion was not as loud as he expected, crammed down into such a closed space, but a thick cloud of smoke and dust shot up into the air in its wake. Parkman moved over in that direction to see what damage the bombs had done, and his heart sank to see that the slab of rock had shifted perilously out over the canyon, but had yet to fall away.

"Bone, come over here and give me a hand!" Parkman called out urgently. By now their presence on the cliff was all too obvious to the men below, and he made no effort to be quiet. "Tell the woman and the boy to keep at the fires." He lay down on his back at the edge of the cliff and began to kick frantically against the dislodged slab of stone. In a moment Bone dropped down beside him and began kicking, too. They couldn't see down into the canyon, but they could hear men shouting and mules braying, and soon the shooting started. Parkman wasn't sure if they were the targets until he heard a bullet sing off a rock only inches from his leg. But he and Bone couldn't stop what they were doing. In a short time, the outlaws would have the wagons driven out of the canyon, and all they would have left up here would be a long, useless bonfire.

When the slab of rock finally broke free and fell, Bone almost went over the edge with it, but Parkman grabbed him by the neck of his shirt and pulled him back. He could hear the panicked squall of men and animals below in the canyon but didn't risk looking over the edge to see what sort of chaos they had caused.

Waiting for the long pile of wood to catch thoroughly afire now became the hardest part. The wood was dry and willing to submit to the rising flames, but it took time. Down below Parkman could hear the pounding of hooves and the random, urgent shouts of men. Above all the rest, it seemed as if he could hear the shrill shouts of Duff Joseph desperately slinging orders in all directions.

What he didn't hear, the marshal realized with satisfaction, was the squeal of that one wagon wheel that was in want of greasing. The wagons weren't moving.

Parkman and Bone soon agreed that the fire was sufficiently

ablaze to do its work below. Using long poles that they had kept aside for that purpose, they began to shove the burning logs and branches over the side. Their hair singed and their bare skin seared as they shoved against the flames, but neither of them seemed aware of it at that moment. As the burning wood tumbled over the side, clouds of tiny cinders rose in the canyon updraft, standing out against the blue sky like glowing red stars.

"It's workin'! We did it after all!" Bone declared victoriously. His face was as red as raw beef, and the tips of his scraggly whiskers were singed, but he had a wide grin on his roasted features. Parkman was sure he must look much the same, grin and all. Fawn had walked down to the horses and was pouring water over her singed and smoky head. Brother was standing at the edge of the cliff to survey the scene below, but Bone shouted for him to step back. Soon enough the men below would gather their wits and resume shooting at anything that moved above them.

The explosions down below sounded one after the other, several seconds apart, and even from where he stood, Parkman could hear the satisfying roar and crackle of the burning wagons. He thought he might crawl over in a minute to look down on the destruction they had caused, but before he could do that, Brother shouted out in alarm and began running for the trees where the horses were tied. He paused once to turn and snap off a shot with his rifle at the riders who had appeared in the trees to the west, but it didn't seem to come anywhere close to whatever he shot at.

There were several men in the pack, half a dozen or more, back into the edge of the trees on one side of the cliff, snapping off ill-aimed shots from atop their jittery, prancing horses. They didn't seem sure about how many opponents they might be going up against and didn't want to break out into the open until they found out.

"Time to go!" Bone said, breaking into a run toward where Fawn and Brother were moving their horses deep into the trees. Parkman was right behind, pausing once to fire a few rounds to make them thoughtful.

They leaped astride their horses and charged into the virgin forest, following no trail and risking the lives of themselves and their mounts in this rugged terrain. After riding for a couple of miles they stopped to survey their backtrail and to listen. Then they realized that nobody was chasing them.

"If it was me, I don't think I'd come after us either," Parkman noted. "I'd be heading out of here instead. Revenge ain't that important if you're too dead to take pleasure in it."

"With Cheyenne behind an' Sioux ahead," Bone said, "they've got an interesting trip out of here, whichever way they choose."

CHAPTER TWENTY

They stopped early along the edge of a small, tumbling creek and relaxed for the rest of the day. Fawn built a friendly, crackling fire, too big for their actual needs, and boiled a pot of coffee. Parkman rolled smokes for all of them, and for a while they sat around, enjoying the finer things. Brother choked back coughs a couple of times as he drew the smoke into his virgin lungs, but he puffed along with the rest of them, feeling oh so manly. Both the coffee and the tobacco were probably unfamiliar to Fawn as well, but she drank and smoked without revealing any hint of pleasure in their celebration.

Eventually, Brother could hold back his joy and pride no longer and rose up to dance around the fire and chant a victory song. Soon Fawn joined him, arms hanging at her sides, shuffling her feet in the pine needles and chanting out the song with Brother.

After a few minutes of this, Bone set his tin cup on the ground, swallowed the nub of his smoke, and muttered, "What the hell," as he rose to join them. He knew the song, and he knew the dance, and soon he was caught up in the sacred excitement of their victory. For a while, he was as much a Cheyenne as the others.

And you want to go live in a town because your feet get cold, Parkman thought.

Later Fawn sent Brother out to forage for food, and not long after they heard the roar of the old muzzle-loader roll through the woods. Soon the young man returned, carrying the long gun in one hand and his bow in the other. The half-grown deer slung across his shoulders had an arrow buried deep in its throat.

"I'll be teaching the boy some things about Old Sam's Hawken as soon as we get back," Bone said.

That night Parkman slept more deeply than he had since he left his cot in the back room of Hattie's café. He dreamed about riding fast and free, with no worries on his mind, across the open rolling hills. General Grant was galloping along at a comfortable pace, and there were no Indians behind, ready to claim his scalp, nor any filthy outlaws ahead to track down and kill. He was somehow vaguely aware that there was whiskey up ahead, the good kind brought in from the east. And a hot meal awaited him, with Hattie sitting across the table, telling him what his life was going to be like after they married. She had plenty of plans.

He slept late, not folding back his blanket until the sun was already casting its first rays through the pine forest. The air was sweet and fresh, and it was still chilly enough for that first cup of coffee to be a comfort.

Bone had gone out scouting early, back down the way that they had come the day before, and he delivered the welcome reassurance that nobody was back there looking for them.

"I'd like to go back to that canyon," Parkman said. He scalded his tongue with his first sip of coffee, then took another. "I'd like to see whether Duff Joseph's body is somewhere there, or if he got away from me again. I need to make a report back to my captain."

"Me an' Brother was hoping we could get a look, too," Bone said. "It ain't too many times in a man's life that he helps pull off a thing like that, and it seems a shame to ride on off and not get a gander at the hellfire and perdition we served up. This'll give us big stories to tell when we get back with the People."

It was a steep and broken pathway up out of the ravine where they camped, and across to the scene of yesterday's fight. Going on instinct, Bone led them on a roundabout route that brought them to the entrance of the canyon on the western side. As the tall rock walls began to close in on them on either side, almost like the jaws of a vise, Parkman got a little taste of the tension that Joseph's band must have felt as they entered into this death trap.

Riding in the lead, Bone paused his horse and fired a couple of shots down the length of the canyon. In response, several wolves slunk away, and a scattering of buzzards took to flight. But none of them went any farther than they had to. They weren't done here yet.

The smell of burning wood still lingered in the air, and up ahead a few thin trails of smoke drifted up from some of the smoldering logs they had rolled down from up above. Parkman glanced up, and from this angle the rims of the rock walls appeared far higher than he knew them to be. Out of habit and instinct, his eyes scanned the ledges above for any sign of movement, but there was none.

Fawn and Brother were clearly terrified to be in this place, as if vengeful spirits might leap out at any moment to steal their souls.

The corpses of dead men and animals lay strewn about in all sorts of grisly postures. All eight mules that had been pulling the wagons were dead. The enormous slab of rock that rained down from above had smashed the first team of four, and the second four, still in their traces, had perished more gruesomely from the fire and the explosion. The wagons themselves were reduced to little more than ash and charcoal, set ablaze by the rain of fire, and scattered all about by the exploding kegs of gunpowder and crates of cartridges.

There were remnants of many rifles all over, but they would

never be of use to anyone. The stocks were burnt off or splintered, and the metal actions and barrels were charred and mutilated by the heat of the fire.

The corpses of a few dead horses lay about, and the wild animals had already gone to work on them. Dismounting because of the narrowness of the canyon and General Grant's growing jitters, Parkman walked on farther up, past the piles of rubble. He found the bodies of three dead men and a dead horse, examining the remains of each man carefully. Then he turned and started back, counting dead men as he went and looking closely at each one.

"I count nine dead," Bone said. "How about you?"

"The same," Parkman said. "And none of them Duff Joseph."

"Not unless he's the one with his legs sticking out from under them mules."

"Naw, that's not him either. The boots are wrong. Joseph wore pointed toe riding boots. I remember, because he kicked me with them while I was in his camp."

"He could have burnt clean up," Bone suggested. "Or maybe was blasted into little pieces when that powder went up."

"I can't count on that," Parkman said. "To my way of thinking, he's still alive."

He looked back down toward the direction they rode in, and saw that Brother and Fawn had overcome their fear of this place. He watched as Fawn placed her foot in the middle of a dead man's back, skillfully sliced around his skull, and pulled the thatch of hair free. Nearby, Brother was busy at the same business.

It disgusted Parkman, but he didn't try to stop them. Their land, their rules, he thought.

"The Cheyenne never trusted me all the way because I didn't like taking scalps," Bone said. "I won't say I never done it, but only a couple of times when my blood was up during a fight."

Parkman turned and walked back to where General Grant was waiting. As he raised one leg to mount up, something up ahead caught his eye. It was wedged in behind a stone at the base of the rock wall and waved slightly as a gust of wind blew past. Curious, he dropped the reins again and walked over.

"Hey, Bone. Have a look," he called out. "I found my hat."

CHAPTER TWENTY-ONE

It was unnerving the way the Cheyenne braves appeared out of nowhere. First there were only three, riding along about a hundred feet back as the trail descended from the last of the foothills and the forest played out.

"Don't worry; just ride," Bone said, slowing his horse a bit until he was riding close alongside Parkman. "If they was going to start a ruckus, they'd already be howling by now."

Soon Parkman realized they were being flanked on either side by several more horsemen, who seemed to appear mysteriously, and the bunch behind had grown to a dozen or more.

This was their third day on the trail after the brush-up with Duff Joseph, and in all that time they had not caught sight of another human being, red, white, or any other color. They had come across a campsite on the way down from the canyon, which Bone had judged to be an Indian camp two days old. Nor had they, in any place, come across the hoof prints of the shod horses that Joseph and his survivors were riding. It was clear enough that the wily old bandit intended to stay off the main trail until he had gone far enough west and south to make a run for it out of Indian country.

Without his wagons full of rifles and the small, well-armed army he had put together to defend himself, he would have realized that he and his men were no more than another small party of intruders, unwelcome here, and fair game for any band of warriors that discovered them.

Parkman had decided not to try to track Joseph any further. Not only were they at least a day behind, but he knew that if he did, he would most likely have to go it alone, which was a fool's errand in the shape he was in now. He was out of supplies, nearly out of ammunition, and way too close to being out of luck. He could tell that Fawn and Brother were ready to rejoin their people. And although Bone didn't mention it, he thought the old man probably was as well.

He figured that if his dead friend Ray Goode came back to life long enough to give him some advice, he would say it was time for Parkman to haul his freight back to safer territory.

"It's a good sign that they ain't got their faces painted for war," Bone said. "I think I recognize some of them, but it's hard to tell. An' some of them probably recognize me. Also, it's good we got two Indians riding along with us. But . . . ."

That *but* twanged Parkman's nerves, and he decided he might not want to know what it meant.

As they topped a small rise, they saw one lone Indian sitting aside his horse in the middle of the trail. Pretty doggoned dramatic, Parkman thought. They rode along for a short while longer, as their Indian escorts closed in around them. Bone stopped a few dozen yards away from the lone Indian ahead, and Parkman stopped beside him.

He was older than the other Cheyenne braves that now surrounded them, with long, gray hair that spilled down across his shoulders. He wore an impressive, feathered headdress with elaborate bead work around the band, and revealed beneath his open, decorated leather vest were the scars of past battles.

"I know him," Bone said. "He's called Between the Clouds. He's the chief of a band that lives north of here. I never stayed with them, but I followed him into battle against the Pawnee a couple of times in years past. Always out front, and always taunting his enemies, no matter how many, to ride forward and try him out. I never seen a man more fearless."

Parkman studied the man, wondering if this was a moment in which his fate would be decided. He gazed at the Indian's face, which might have been carved from a block of granite, and saw no mercy there. But if he was fated to die right now, right here, he vowed to take this man with him.

Eventually, Between the Clouds made a small nod with his head, which seemed to be the sign for them to ride forward. Brother and Fawn held back, seeming awed to be in this legendary man's presence. The Indian chief waited, sitting straight and rigid atop his horse, as if he had a steel rod tied to his spine.

"He's the keeper of the four sacred arrows for the tribe," Bone explained quietly to Parkman, "and that makes him big medicine. The arrows have to be honored before they go into battle, and if they don't do the ritual, they'll lose the fight. They're in that leather pouch tied behind his saddle."

The chief ignored Bone as they stopped their horses in front of him, instead studying Parkman's face intently. He didn't seem particularly impressed by what he saw. In his filthy, trail-worn outfit, scraggly and exhausted after so many weeks of travel, Parkman could imagine what a sad case he must look like to this stern, rigid chief dressed in all his finery. But the Colt hanging at Parkman's side still made them equals.

"Reckon why he came clear out here to meet us?" Parkman said quietly.

"No idea."

Bone said something to Between the Clouds in Cheyenne, and the chief cut his eyes to him briefly before returning them to Parkman.

"I told him that whether he decides to treat you as a guest, or take your life, you are honored to be here with him."

"I don't figure I would have put it quite like that," Parkman grumbled.

Never looking back at Bone, the chief said something in his language.

"He's asking if you're the man who counted so many coups against the women killers," Bone answered. Then with a chuckle he added, "He says you don't look like you would be such a great warrior as that."

"Tell him I didn't do it to earn his praise," Parkman said with annoyance.

"That might not be such a good idea. It's said about Between the Clouds that he thinks pretty highly of himself."

"Well then tell him that it was all of us that done it, even the woman. An' you might as well let him know that I'd be dead now but for you an' the boy risking your necks to save me. An' I wouldn't have made it this far without that Fawn woman neither."

Parkman was seldom able to tell what was going on inside any Indian's head, or even how Bone would twist and change his words into something acceptable. But he took the chief's nod to mean that he might be thinking more highly of him than he had before.

Between the Clouds spoke a single word, then turned his horse and started away.

"He says 'come,' " Bone said.

The Cheyenne camp of Between the Clouds's band stretched out for half a mile or more up a wide, winding gulley. Parkman was surprised to see so many Indians gathered together into one place, and asked Bone if he knew why.

"Don't know for sure," Bone said. "It could be because they're fixing to make war on somebody, or maybe a celebration of some kind. Or it might be because of that big buffalo herd we seen a while back."

A spirited little stream gurgled down the middle of the gulley, with plenty of wide sandy flats on either side. Parkman figured that they must have chosen this spot because the cut was deep enough to conceal their tipis. Countless horses grazed free on the grassy flats above the camp, with some of the younger men scattered about to keep an eye on them. He wondered how they were able to remember which horses belonged to who, but they seemed to know. He disliked the idea of letting General Grant and Lucky loose in such a way, imagining them lost within the vast Indian herds, or deliberately stolen and hidden someplace. But he knew he'd have to. Horses and mules had to eat, too.

The mood was casual and festive in the camp. The smaller children ran and laughed among the tipis, playing stick games that Parkman didn't recognize or understand. Probably something to do with war, he thought. The women and the older girls were gathered in small clusters, sewing and cooking and slicing raw meat into long, thin strips to prepare it for drying. The men sat in groups, telling tales among themselves and talking to the attentive young men, as Furious had done with Brother, no doubt sharing legends, customs, and tribal history with them.

A few looked up curiously as Between the Clouds and his entourage rode by, but none of them seemed to give the two white men among the party any hateful or hostile looks. Most of the braves who had surrounded them earlier cut away here and there, no doubt to rejoin their families, friends, and sects. At one point, Fawn also turned away, sliding to the ground in front of a cluster of women who were pounding meat, grain, and berries into pemmican. In the first minute with her own people, she probably said more than she had during all those weeks on the trail. As Parkman and the others moved on, she never even turned her head or offered a grunt of farewell to the three men she shared so many camps with.

"She'll be wanting to know where her husband is," Bone

said. "I expect she'll have no more truck with us now that she's the queen bee in his camp."

The sun hung in the middle of the western sky by the time Bone found a cluster of tipis belonging to the people he knew and lived with, his own family in a way. As he, Brother, and Parkman slowed their horses and turned aside, he called out something to Between the Clouds. Never pausing, the gray-haired chief turned his head to the side and gave a nod, then rode on, now followed by only three young braves.

Bone and Parkman dismounted and handed their reins off to a couple of willing boys nearby who would take the animals up to the flats to graze. Bone led Parkman up to the entrance to one of the tipis where an old man sat alone, staring off into the distance as if recalling times and people now long gone.

"This is Rides in Thunder," Bone said by way of introduction. "He's my wife's granddaddy, but he took her in after her own daddy was killed in a dust-up with the Crows."

The old man sat cross legged on the ground, smiling a toothless smile at nobody in particular. He wore a simple buckskin shirt and pants over his withered frame. A beaded headband with a feathered decoration dangling down on one side held back his long, gray hair.

"He don't have any notion about how old he is and don't care," Bone said. "But he said once he was a grown young man away back when them explorers passed through here. Lewis and Clark. That'd put him at eighty-five, maybe ninety."

From the hazy look in his eyes, Parkman figured Rides in Thunder must be blind, or nearly so, and as Bone yelled out a greeting, he realized that the old man was almost deaf as well. Bone spent a moment chatting with his grandfather-in-law, both of them nearly shouting at the other.

"He wanted to know if you've got any whiskey," Bone told Parkman with a chuckle. "When I told him you didn't, he asked for tobacco. I told him we'd fill his pipe after we get settled in."

Two other younger men sat a dozen feet away, eyeing Parkman curiously, and Brother had joined them. The youth seemed to have launched directly into his tales of battle and slaughter. The men listened half-interestedly, clearly believing only part of it. But there was no denying the trophy scalps that Brother had tied to his bow and belt.

Bone and Parkman sat down cross legged by the old man, and the women brought them food. Parkman gave it high praise and showed with signs how good it was, although he wasn't completely sure what he was eating. Some kind of animal organs, he thought, and probably the best they had.

As Bone gave Rides in Thunder his own version of their travels, Parkman began to see that the old man understood only a part of it, even though Bone was nearly shouting out his words. Occasionally the grandfather would nod his head and grunt out his approval, and once he raised a frail arm and made a chopping motion, as if he were delivering a deadly blow to some hated enemy. Parkman wondered how many ancient battles were probably running through the old man's head as Bone told his tales.

They rested there through the afternoon, and Parkman was directed to a comfortable pile of buffalo skins inside the tipi, where he fell into a deep sleep. His dreams were mundane for the first time in a while. He didn't even jolt awake in alarm when later Bone crawled into the tent and shook his boot to wake him.

Through the triangle opening in the side of the tipi, Parkman saw that it was dark outside, and a fire was burning several feet away. He heard some women nearby talking to one another, and a few horses occasionally clomped by the camp. He barely made out the dim shape of Rides in Thunder sleeping peacefully on the other side of the tipi.

"You're gonna want to see this, Marshal," Bone told him. "Brother was out roaming the camp, passing some time with the boys his age, and he come back here with news."

"What is it, Bone?"

"Better you see it for yourself," Bone said, grinning like he had a surprise gift waiting. "Come on; we'll both have a look together."

In the pale moonlight, they followed a path that wound along beside the curves of the stream. Brother had come along to lead the way. On both sides, most of the Indians seemed to be settling in for the night, the women finishing their last chores and letting their cooking fires die down. Parkman thought he had a pretty good idea what they were going to see, but he was content to let his two companions keep their secret.

After a few minutes, Brother led them aside into a jumbled, rocky area that was too rough for anyone to erect their tipis in. Up ahead he spotted half a dozen men squatting around a fire, all armed, talking quietly among themselves. Some of them rose as they saw the visitors approaching. Among them, Parkman recognized the two half-breeds who, days before, had served as the advance scouts for Duff Joseph's wagon train. They scowled fiercely at him, and for good cause, he thought. He must have come pretty close to blasting the side of a cliff down on their heads.

Bone held a short conversation with one of the men in the group. The man picked up a burning faggot from the fire and led them back deeper in the jumble of rocks. Not far away, several bodies lay strewn about as if they had been carelessly tossed there, which indeed they probably had. They were battered, broken, and bleeding, and it took Parkman a moment to realize that at least some of them were still alive.

"This man said that they were already halfway up into the mountains, trailing the white man's wagons, when the spirits roared out up ahead in the clouds. After that, they were scared to go up any higher, but they scattered their war parties out all over the side of the mountain. Eventually they rounded up these men coming down."

"Didn't those scouts tell them that it was the sound of the wagons exploding?" Parkman asked.

"I expect them two said whatever it would take to keep themselves alive," Bone chuckled. "An' if it took angry gods to do it, then that's the tale they stuck with."

Some of the prisoners were asleep or unconscious, and the rest lay about fighting their bonds, or moaning in their pain and misery. One of them noticed the presence of Bone and Parkman in the flickering light, and a desperate glimmer of hope shone in his eyes. He had a bleeding wound low on his left side about where his leg joined his body, and the broken shaft of an arrow protruded from one leg. He lay on his side, with a leather rope tied around his wrists and stretching up behind to his neck.

"You're that marshal, ain't you?" His voice was raspy and desperate. "Can't you get us out of this fix?"

"I don't see how," Parkman said.

"I can't die like this, Marshal. I got a wife in Coffeeville that I planned to take up with again after Duff paid us off. I'm not like the rest of these bad hombres. I aimed to turn my whole life around when this was over." His eyes were large with fear, and the plaintive whine in his voice was almost embarrassing.

"Well that wife of yours is a widder now," Bone said, his voice filled with rebuke. "You boys shoulda taken that to mind before you started killing and defiling somebody else's wives."

"T'warn't me."

"Then tell the Injuns that."

"Maybe a drink of water, then," the man pleaded.

"Right down there," Bone taunted, nodding his head toward

the stream. "Go get you some."

The Indian with the burning faggot moved from man to man, letting the light dance across each battered body and damaged face in turn.

"What's going to happen to these men?" Parkman asked Bone.

"Nothing good."

The last crumpled form they came to was so abused that Parkman could only recognize him by his pointed Mexican boots. "You dead yet, Joseph?" he said.

Even the simple act of turning his head and opening his eyes seemed to cause Duff Joseph pain, and it took him a moment to gather his wits and recognize the law man.

"I got gold, Parkman," Joseph said. "Hid away over in Utah. You get me out of this fix, and it's yours. All of it."

"You haven't got squat," Parkman said.

"Honest to God," the outlaw pleaded.

"Don't bring His name into this. You hadn't had no truck with Him for all your life, and it's too late now."

"I don't mind the dying, but I ain't looking forward to the way they'll do it," Joseph admitted.

"Same as you had planned for me," Parkman reminded him. "I'm not a man for torture, but the idea of the squaws in this camp chopping you up into little pieces don't bother me even a little bit."

Joseph began to spill out a stream of bile and curses, but Bone stopped it short with a kick in the head.

Parkman turned from Joseph, and his eyes swept one last time over the bloody remains of his broken, defeated enemies. He had spent weeks trailing these men with only one goal in mind, but now that he stood amidst them, he felt no satisfaction in knowing that they were all condemned to horrible deaths at the hands of their Indian captors. He felt empty now that it was all over. "I've seen enough," he told Bone.

CHAPTER TWENTY-TWO

Parkman and Bone had made their camp up into the trees, with a fire only large enough to roast some meat and boil some coffee. Where they were now seemed quiet and empty enough after all the risky places they had been. But they were still in Indian country and still valued their lives and hair.

Parkman ruminated that he had plenty to be thankful for in all of this, and high on the list was that he hadn't run out of his two bare essentials, coffee and tobacco. He planned to give the remainder of both to Bone when they parted in the morning. He was also going to give the mule to his friend. He was tired of bothering with that contrary beast and wouldn't need a pack animal any longer. Not where he was headed.

Bone poked the waning fire with a stick and watched the small cloud of sparks rise from it. "I'm still thinking about that town," he admitted. "All that whiskey waitin' to be drank."

"Why don't you come along with me, then," Parkman said. "You could have yourself a rip-snorting binge for as many days as your gold held out. Then when your poke was empty, you could ride back up thisaway and go back with the Cheyenne."

"I ain't so sure they'd take me back," Bone said. "Me being a white man and all. Times is changing so fast, and they're learning the hard way that they can't hardly trust no white man no more. Not even the ones like me. So many of the old timers, the trappers and hunters and squaw men, are taking up with the army as scouts and even soldiers.

"One day a man's sitting around the fire with them, passing the pipe and cozying up to their women, and the next day they're leading a troop of soldiers to attack their camp."

"Men like Duff Joseph don't help matters much either," Parkman said.

"At least he's burning in hell by now, though."

"Yep. No man ever deserved it more."

The only thing that had kept Joseph and his men alive for as long as they did was that the tribal leaders decided to wait until the whole tribe was together before the ceremonial punishment began. After visiting the prisoners that night, Parkman told Bone that he wanted to leave the next morning, before the bloody rituals began. Bone offered to go along to guide Parkman out of Indian territory, but Brother stayed behind, not wanting to miss the gruesome executions.

"I got me another reason to stay now," Bone admitted. "I didn't want to tell you earlier 'cause I didn't want you riding me about it all the way down here."

"What's that?"

"It's about Fawn. It seems like her husband showed up, but he brought another wife with him, when Fawn had her hopes set on being number one wife for a while. So she rolled her blankets and got out of there that same night."

"Then she unrolled them in your tipi?" Parkman said, chuckling. "And you took to the notion of having a woman that don't talk your ears off?"

"She talked a'plenty that night," Bone admitted, somewhat embarrassed, "and I mostly kept my mouth shut, seeing how her blood was boiling. She said she'd stay with me long as I didn't beat on her, or bring some other younger woman into the tipi. Hell, I been a bachelor for a long time, Marshal, and I like the idea of having myself a woman to cook my food and warm my blankets, even if she's a rough piece of work like

Fawn. No young woman is going to cotton to an old strip of leather like me. So sometimes a man settles for what he can get."

"And what about Little Brother? Will he go to live with his relatives?"

"I asked him to stay with us, like a son. There's still some lessons I can teach him, about that Hawken, and other things. And with a hunter like him in the tipi, I'll never want for food roasting over the fire in my elderly years."

"So, it seems like some good came out of all this bad business after all," Parkman said.

They heard the faraway, prolonged hoot of a whistle and walked down to the edge of the trees to have a look. In the soft, bright moonlight, the broad valley spread before them as clean and lovely and wild as the day that God put it there. Only one thing was different now from the day of creation, Parkman thought. A couple of miles to the south, a dark scar sliced across the valley floor, running east to west as straight as an arrow's flight.

The whistle sounded again, and off to the west they saw the distant glimmer of the headlight on the front of the locomotive. In time, as it drew closer, they began to hear the chug of the churning pistons and the rattle of the metal wheels clacking along the tracks. A constant huff of steam and smoke rose from the smokestack and arced back to dissipate in the night air. Behind the coal car, rectangles of light glowed from the windows of the passenger cars behind.

"You figure you'll be able to flag one of them things down and stop to take you on?" Bone asked.

"If the engineer in the first one don't," Parkman said, "I'll convince the next one that he should."

CHAPTER TWENTY-THREE

The rough-hewn planks beside Parkman's head vibrated with the rowdy commotion and gay piano music in the Chuck-a-Luck saloon on the other side of the wall. Sleep would be impossible for a few more hours yet, but he really didn't mind. It was enough to be stretched out on the fresh straw tick, feeling the ache slowly drain out of his bad leg, and knowing that at least for a while he could sleep safe and dry indoors.

The piano player was pounding out a crude rendition of "Buffalo Gals," and Parkman's toe tapped the footboard of his cot in time to the music. It was a new song, at least to him, and he liked the lively tempo and carefree lyrics. On the other side of the wall he could picture drunk miners and lead-footed teamsters stomping around the dance floor with bawdy, painted women in their arms, or even by themselves, having a high old time. If he wasn't so tired, and if his leg felt a little better, he might be next door among them. But tonight, his first night back in Denver, all he really felt like doing was lazing around like a worthless bum.

As noisy and crude as these accommodations were, they were better than most in the young town of Denver and provided everything that Parkman needed at the moment—a roof, a bunk, and reasonable assurance that nobody would slip up on him while he was asleep and slide a knife into his innards.

When he arrived here this afternoon, after a tiresome journey back by train and stagecoach, Captain Mullins had taken him out for his first good meal since he left Weatherby's Lode. Parkman had stuffed himself with seared red beef, fried potatoes, fresh-baked bread, and apple dumplings, all washed down with fresh milk and coffee. After that, all he really wanted to do was sleep, but instead he and Mullins went back to the marshal's office. There, over a few glasses of bourbon, Parkman had given him a summary of his mission up north in the mountains.

The most important piece of news he delivered, of course, was the fact that he had caught up with Ray Goode's killer and had stopped Duff Joseph from delivering hundreds of stolen rifles to the rebellious Indian tribes up north. The captain said he'd wire the news south so the lawmen there could take Joseph's wanted poster off their walls.

Over the next few days, he'd still have to write a more complete account of his journey for the higher-ups back East. Parkman dreaded that part, knowing he'd have to lie about some of it and leave out other things that he wasn't particularly proud of.

Once Mullins had decided that the third glass of whiskey had sufficiently mellowed Parkman, he brought up the news he had to deliver.

"While you were up north, I got a couple of letters from that woman you were sweet on over in Weatherby's Lode," he announced.

"Hattie O'Shea."

"Yeah, that one. Seems like she grew tired of wondering if your bones was bleaching out in the mountains someplace. She asked me to tell you that she took up with another man, a drummer of some sort, and was on her way to California." Mullins went quiet for a moment to see how Parkman would take the news. But for the life of him, Parkman couldn't figure out how he felt about it himself.

"We talked about going over to Missouri and raising horses,"

Parkman said, more to fill the silence than for any other reason. "My mother has some land, and it seemed like a good idea at the time."

"I understand," Mullins said with a reminiscent grin. "Before she passed, Rosario used to convince me of all kinds of things and leave me thinking it was the best idea I ever had. Maybe this was how it was destined to work out from the start."

Parkman nodded his understanding. Hattie might have made a pretty good wife, even if the word "love" had never been spoken between them. And he might have enjoyed raising horses.

"Cap'n, if you don't mind," Parkman said, "I think I'd like to go back to the barracks and do nothing but sleep for a day or two." He rose and started for the door, then paused, remembering one more thing. He reached in his pocket and pulled out a small leather bag.

"Would you mind passing this along to Ray's daughter and her aunt?" he said. "It's a little gold that came my way along the trail. Not much, no more than two or three hundred dollars' worth, I figure. But it might come in handy."

"In case you're worried, Ridge, they don't carry a grudge against you for what happened."

Parkman gave his boss a steady gaze, then put the pouch back in his pocket. "Well, sir, then maybe I'll take it over myself."

Through the wall, the piano player had finished his rendition of "Buffalo Gals." Soon he was joined by a fiddle player, and they launched into another song that Parkman had never heard before. He couldn't make out most of the words because of the rollicking background noise, but it was something about a woman named Sally O'Malley who never would dally.

The outside door banged open, and a man clomped into the small barracks that Captain Mullins had set up for his men to use when they were in Denver. It was Brady Stark, another of the marshals, half drunk and wearing that stupid grin that Parkman could never stand to look at for long. The two of them had known each other for a couple of years, but Captain Mullins had never paired them up because he knew they didn't get along.

"So, you finally decided to sashay on back here to Denver and collect your back wages, huh, Parkman?" Stark unbuckled his gun belt and dropped it on a bunk across the room.

"Yeah, the captain wrote and told me that he needed somebody around who could set his whiskey glass down long enough to get a little work done."

"We all heard what kind of work you was up to out there in gold country," Stark taunted. "Sitting around in a rocking chair while some horse-faced hussy shoveled grub into your face and fluffed your pillow. And all the time swearing to the Cap'n as how you were nearly a goner from some little flesh wound."

Parkman sat up on the edge of the bunk, knowing that trouble was stirring up. "Step over here for a minute, Stark," he said. "I think I've got a boot that might fit into that stinking privy that you call a mouth."

Stark took down a half-full bottle from the shelf above his bunk and turned to face Parkman with a drunk, stupid grin on his face. "Wal, we could roughhouse if you take exception to my brand of humor," he said. "Or we could drink. Your call."

It wasn't a hard choice for Parkman to make.

ABOUT THE AUTHOR

Over the past forty years **Greg Hunt** has published over twenty Western, frontier, and historical novels. A lifelong writer, he has also worked as a newspaper reporter and editor, a technical and free-lance writer, and a marketing analyst. Greg served in Vietnam as an intelligence agent and Vietnamese linguist with the 101st Airborne Division and 23rd Infantry Division.

Greg is a native of Missouri, with strong roots in the Midwest and Deep South. He now lives in the Memphis area with his wife, Vernice.

The employees of Five Star Publishing hope you have enjoyed this book.

Our Five Star novels explore little-known chapters from America's history, stories told from unique perspectives that will entertain a broad range of readers.

Other Five Star books are available at your local library, bookstore, all major book distributors, and directly from Five Star/Gale.

Connect with Five Star Publishing

Visit us on Facebook:
  https://www.facebook.com/FiveStarCengage

Email:
  FiveStar@cengage.com

For information about titles and placing orders:
  (800) 223-1244
  gale.orders@cengage.com

To share your comments, write to us:
  Five Star Publishing
  Attn: Publisher
  10 Water St., Suite 310
  Waterville, ME 04901